FOUL PLAY AT SEAL BAY

JUDY LEIGH

Boldwood

First published in Great Britain in 2023 by Boldwood Books Ltd.

Cover Design by Rachel Lawston

Cover Illustration: Rachel Lawston

A CIP catalogue record for this book is available from the British Library.

Paperback ISBN 978-1-83751-460-1

Large Print ISBN 978-1-83751-456-4

Hardback ISBN 978-1-83751-455-7

Ebook ISBN 978-1-83751-453-3

Kindle ISBN 978-1-83751-454-0

Audio CD ISBN 978-1-83751-461-8

MP3 CD ISBN 978-1-83751-458-8

Digital audio download ISBN 978-1-83751-452-6

Boldwood Books Ltd
23 Bowerdean Street
London SW6 3TN
www.boldwoodbooks.com

To Kiran and Ken.
Thanks for the idea of a Cornish sleuth.
This is all down to you...

GLOSSARY

All right - Hello, how are you? I'm fine. It can be used as a greeting, question and answer all within the same conversation.

Ansom, ansum, ansome, handsum - Nice, handsome, good.

Bleddy - Local pronunciation of 'bloody' as an emphasising adjective.

Dreckly - At some point in the future; soon, but not immediately.

Emmet - A tourist. It actually means an ant.

Giss on! - Stop talking rubbish!

Heller - Lively, troublesome child.

Jumping - Angry.

Maid - Any girl or woman, often used as a form of address.

My bewty - My beauty, a term of affection. Bewty can also be substituted with ansom.

Oggy - Pasty (from Cornish language *hogen*)

Proper - Satisfactory, good.

Teasy, teazy - Bad-tempered.

Tuss - An obnoxious person.

1

Morwenna Mutton and her bicycle sped down the hill as one. Houses rushed past in a blur on either side as she plummeted towards the shining sapphire half-moon of the bay. She spun the pedals; it would be a harder ride uphill on the way home, but that was later, and this was now. The road plateaued out as she pushed her trainer-soled feet harder for extra speed, flashing past the pop-up shop where Susan and Barb Grundy raised their knitting needles in greeting. Morwenna waved back. She could imagine them talking right now, their voices a low cluck:

'There goes Morwenna on her way to the library. It must be almost nine o'clock.'

'Look at her, all that hair and stripey leggings, and at her age too.'

'They are all the same, those Mutton women, not one of them cares what anyone thinks.'

'I know, Barb – she's no spring chicken. And there's no man in the house now to calm her ways. Whatever does she think she's like?'

Morwenna grinned as she swerved around a car – the driver

hadn't noticed her – and took a left-hand bend into a paved street. Of course, she had no evidence that Susan and her sister Barb were talking about her but, bless them, they talked about everyone all the time, their gossip hiding warm hearts as they sat in their shop knitting to raise funds for the Lifeboats Institution.

She slowed down outside Seal Bay Library, a Victorian red-brick building, the wooden door already gaping wide to greet visitors. She cocked a rainbow-striped leg over the saddle and wheeled the old sit-up-and-beg, complete with basket, into the library. One day she'd get one of those modern electric bikes: it would certainly help with the steep hills that made her lungs heave each evening on the way back to Harbour Cottages. Years ago, she'd whizz everywhere with no effort, but now going uphill was slower and harder. Besides, it was the first day of September; the rains would come soon and it was always less fun checking in borrowed books when you were drenched from head to foot and steaming.

Morwenna shook her hair free from her collar, a fountain of silver. Now she was in her sixties – sixty one – people said she should cut it or wear it in a sensible bun. It would be more appropriate, apparently. Morwenna laughed: the word appropriate wasn't invented for her. She'd always had long hair. She wasn't going to change now. She leaned the bike against a wall in the corridor and sauntered into the library, smelling the welcoming dusty aroma of much-loved books. Louise Piper was efficiently arranging novels from the returns trolley onto the shelves. She turned, short flame hair, a flash of red lipstick, and smiled a greeting. 'Nine o'clock. Bang on time. Kettle's on. Cup of tea?'

'I'd love one.' Morwenna stowed her jacket and bag in her locker and watched Louise's brisk movements affectionately. Louise was absolutely reliable; she ran the Seal Bay library five days a week with military precision. Ten years younger than Morwenna, she was her complete opposite: sensible, inscrutable, married. They were the perfect partners. Louise handed Morwenna a mug with the scrawled slogan: *No one's perfect but being Cornish is near 'nuff.*

Morwenna took a sip. 'Are we on for a swim on Sunday, bright and early?'

'Wouldn't miss it.' Louise slurped milky brown liquid from her own mug. 'It's a shame we can't get more people to come. If only they knew how good it is for body and soul. Will your mum come along, or will it be just us two and a few random stragglers?'

'Mum keeps threatening to turn up, but it's too early for her. She sleeps in until lunchtime and then grumbles that her hips are sore.'

'She is in her eighties though.

'That's no excuse,' Morwenna protested. 'She's always telling me we're from strong female stock.'

'What about your daughter?'

Morwenna shook her head, her hair spilling over her face. 'No way. Tam's too busy with the tea shop and looking after Elowen, although I'd love to take the little one swimming with us. She's like a dolphin in the water; she's desperate to join in. Tam says she can come when she's ten, but I think now's as good a time as any. Five isn't too young. She'd be safe with us in shallow water.'

'She would,' Louise agreed. She put down her cup and reached for a pile of books. 'It's time to tidy up.'

'We seem to have a lot of stray books this morning.' Morwenna gazed at the pile on the counter. 'Has Lizzie been up to her tricks?'

Louise was serious. 'She has. She's been at the biscuits again too. The packet was open when I came in, crumbs all over the floor. And she's been rearranging the books under the counter. You probably ought to address her properly: Lady Elizabeth Pengellen – we should respect the dead.'

'You don't really believe she's haunting the library, do you?'

'I do – I find books every day where I know I haven't left them: by the door, beneath the shelves. And she loves snacks. She even had a bite of a cheese sandwich I left behind.' Louise's eyes were round. 'We definitely have a restless ghost at large.'

'It's probably my fault there are books left out. I didn't eat the cheese sandwich though.' Morwenna grinned. 'Being serious, it is a known fact that Lady Elizabeth died in terrible circumstances at Pengellen Manor and is said to haunt the town library because it was her sanctuary. Apparently, her husband treated her badly and the only way she could escape him was by coming here to read.'

'I believe it.' Louise was serious. 'Then her husband broke her heart, and she took poison. Lady Elizabeth's only solace was her books – she often hid away amongst the ordinary folk of Seal Bay. Now she's returns to us each night.'

Morwenna waved a copy of *Wind in the Willows* she'd just found beneath the counter. 'Well, I agree with her about being among books – a good read is the best companion.' She finished the last gulp from her mug and joined Louise, who was arranging novels on shelves. 'Who needs a man when you can read a good book?'

'But love is everything...' Louise touched a copy of *Sense and Sensibility*. 'Jane Austen said, "To love is to burn, to be on fire."' She sighed. 'I'm so lucky to have my Steve. We've been married thirty years this Christmas, you know.'

'She also said, "Friendship is certainly the finest balm for the pangs of disappointed love,"' Morwenna quipped quickly. 'I'm done with romance. It's too much like hard work.'

'You can't mean that.' Louise paused before she asked, 'Do you think you and Ruan might get back together one day?'

'After all those years, bringing up Tamsin through thick and thin, for richer and poorer? We became a habit – we were just going through the motions in the end. Ah, we're still friends, but no, things went wrong for us.' Morwenna was lost in thought for a moment. 'I still see him some mornings, heading off at dawn. Being a fisherman keeps him going. I don't think he'll ever retire from the boats – it's his first love, the sea.' She shrugged. 'His only love.'

'Isn't it difficult, having him living across the road?'

'It's great when I run out of teabags,' Morwenna joked. She indicated two books. 'Oh look – *Emma* and *Northanger Abbey* are in the wrong places – Lizzie was busy last night.'

Louise put a finger to her lips. 'She'll hear you.'

'If she does, I'll ask her to tidy up once she's finished reading...' Morwenna's eyes twinkled.

There were footsteps in the corridor and Louise jerked around nervously, startled as a rabbit. A young man walked in, slender in a smart jacket and jeans, a sweeping fringe over his eyes. Morwenna rushed across. 'Hello, Simon. How's it going?'

The young man leaned on the counter. 'I need something to read...'

'Then you're in the right place.' Morwenna smiled. 'What are you looking for? Something on business? Economics? More John Maynard Keynes?'

'I finished uni a year ago. I've just been bumming around since.' Simon shrugged. 'My dad says I need a job...'

'How is Alex?' Louise asked, strolling across to the counter.

'I never see him much – or my mum,' Simon grunted. 'They do their own thing.'

'Well, it's such a big house – I expect it's easy to lose them.' Louise leaned on her elbows. 'And you have such a lovely view of the sea. I always say to Steve, if we had pots of money, that's the house I'd like to buy. It's remote, beautiful, on the romantic cliff top, the best spot in Seal Bay.'

'I want to get a flat in Truro. Or London.' Simon gazed around the library. 'I was born in London – but we've been here for ten years now. I'd love to go back. Nothing ever happens in Cornwall.'

'Oh,' Morwenna said brightly. 'So you came in for a good book. Shall I recommend something escapist? A fantasy, perhaps?'

Simon shrugged. 'I don't know – I thought maybe a book about gambling – one that shows you how to win lots of money...'

'We have *The Logic of Gambling*.' Louise suggested.

'Yeh, that'll do for starters.' Simon fumbled in his pocket for a library card. 'I'd like to be rich and independent. It'd be better than working for Dad.'

Louise rushed over to a shelf and found the book almost immediately. Simon turned to Morwenna. 'I bet it's quiet in the tearoom now the holidaymakers have gone.'

'The emmets, as we call them in Cornwall? Yes – one more week and that'll be the last of them.' Morwenna said sadly. 'Trade always drops in September and it doesn't pick up again until March, although we usually manage. We expect a dip in trade, out of season. But it's good to have the visitors. I like meeting interesting characters from all over the country.'

'This time of year has its compensation, though,' Louise said, placing the book in front of Simon. 'I always think you and

Tamsin make such a good job of keeping the business going off-season.' She smiled. 'Do you remember the Proper Ansom Halloween Night? Proper Ansom is such a good name for your family's tearoom – a proper ansom Cornish welcome's always guaranteed. We had a great night, dressing up as vampires and ghosts!'

'And not a sign of Lizzie.' Morwenna raised an eyebrow.

'I like the calm atmosphere in the autumn,' Simon said quietly. 'I can sit with a coffee and read without anyone disturbing me.' He avoided Morwenna's eyes. 'Tamsin's really nice. She never hurries me up or asks me to buy more coffee – she just lets me look through the window for hours at the sea rolling in.'

'Sounds wonderful. Don't forget your book,' Louise reminded him.

Simon's dreamy expression left his face and his eyes narrowed as he gazed at the book. 'This is what I need; a lucrative hobby.'

'Don't we all?' Morwenna agreed, but Simon turned slowly, engrossed in the blurb on the back cover as he ambled out of the library.

'Bless him,' Morwenna said kindly. 'He's lonely, I think. He's never really settled here.'

'He's nothing like his dad. Alex is ambitious. And his mum has a high opinion of herself.'

'The Truscotts are all right,' Morwenna replied. 'It's hard being accepted in Seal Bay if you're not a local.'

'They've been here ten years, he said,' Louise protested.

'Imelda Parker, Elowen's teacher, has lived here for twenty years and there are still some people who think she's an outsider. And she was born in Penzance.' Morwenna winked.

'The Truscotts own so much of Seal Bay. I think that's why

people don't warm to them, because they are entrepreneurs.' Louise smiled. 'Simon's sweet on your Tamsin. It was written all over his face.'

Morwenna laughed. 'She'd eat him alive. Besides, she's a good deal older than Simon. And she's getting engaged. The party is on the ninth. Are you coming?'

'I wouldn't miss it.'

'We're holding it on the beach. Fancy dress, pirate theme. Bring a bottle – we're organising food.'

'I can't wait,' Louise replied. 'I love a good dance and fancy dress. Mind you, there will be some clearing up to do the following morning.'

'That's all sorted, the family and neighbours will pitch in. Unless we ask our resident ghost to do it,' Morwenna said. 'If you're listening, Lizzie, there's some litter- picking on the beach next weekend.'

Morwenna and Louise were quiet for a moment, all ears. Then, in response, a dull creak came from a distant corner of the library. Morwenna lifted an eyebrow meaningfully and whispered, 'I think she heard us...'

Louise's face was a picture of horror as she held her breath. Morwenna squeezed her shoulder and grinned. 'Only joking.'

'What are you like?' Louise tutted loudly.

Morwenna lifted her empty mug. 'Time for another cuppa – and a biscuit, I think, before our resident ghost steals them all!'

2

At half twelve, Donald Stewart, polite and formal behind a white goatee beard and metal-framed glasses, arrived for the afternoon shift in the library. Morwenna was on her way again. As she lifted a leg over her bicycle and crammed her bag in the front basket, she heard him talking quietly to Louise. 'I believe I can communicate with the dead. There is a definite presence here, a strange coldness to the air...'

Morwenna smiled at the thought of Louise and Donald trying to contact the ghost. She followed a bus around a road-island into town towards the front where the Proper Ansom Tearoom stood, painted white and blue with a panoramic window overlooking the sea. An old white van was parked outside, blue letters on the side that read Jack the Painter, a cartoon of a young man smiling with a brush in his hand. A ladder was leaning against the wall, under the topmost window of Tamsin's flat above the shop. Morwenna tugged her bike inside and rushed to the toilets, coming out moments later wearing an apron. She grinned in the direction of the young woman with the light brown ponytail, blue striped t-shirt and dungaree shorts who was collecting cups on a tray.

'Time for my afternoon shift.' Morwenna flapped her arms. 'I'm all sweet-smelling now. Nothing like a good wash and some strong deodorant, as my mum always said...'

'Tell the whole teashop, why don't you, Mum?' Tamsin Pascoe grinned, pulling a face.

Morwenna looked around. A couple in anoraks were inspecting the cutlery; a family of four in the corner nibbled a shared cake. A curly-haired man in paint-spattered overalls was slouched in a chair, eating a scone, pushing half of it into his mouth. Morwenna nodded to him. 'How are you doing, Jack?'

The young man tried his best to reply with his mouth full. 'Fine thanks, Morwenna.'

'Are you on your lunch break?' She took in his overalls. 'Or just here for a chat with your fiancée?'

Jack Greenwood looked momentarily awkward until Morwenna gave him a friendly wink. Tamsin took over. 'I've asked Jack to give the outside wall a lick of paint while the weather holds.'

Jack finished the scone. 'Tam wants the flat upstairs painted too.'

Tamsin grinned. 'Now we're both living here, I thought it was time for a smart new look. Jack's going to give the place a complete facelift and do Elowen's room. She wants sunshine yellow walls.'

'She's our little ray of sunshine.' Morwenna gazed towards Jack who was washing the scone down with tea.

Tamsin moved towards Morwenna, muttering, 'Mum, can you take over here? I need to get back behind the counter Table two want cream teas and table five have one piece of cake between them. See if you can get them to buy some drinks...'

'Right.' Morwenna glanced at Jack, who put his feet up on a chair, and she stifled a smile. Nine months ago, he'd arrived from somewhere up country, met Tamsin and began a painting and decorating business from a tiny bedsit. Then a month ago, he moved into the flat. Morwenna thought he seemed like a nice young man, but in her heart, she worried that they'd set up home too quickly. She believed in taking time over decisions, but she knew why they had moved so quickly: they were impetuous, in love. And they wanted to be a family, with Elowen at the heart. Morwenna wondered how her granddaughter would adapt – her family's happiness was everything.

Her own relationship to Ruan Pascoe, Tamsin's father, had been happy at first. It had lasted well, then it had become routine, then it was nothing. Finally, it was over, eighteen months ago. She wanted more than that for Tamsin. Besides, Jack would be a stepfather to Elowen, and Morwenna hoped that Tamsin had someone who'd care for her. Jack seemed to love the little five-year-old girl, swinging her high at every opportunity, making her laugh. After all, Elowen would never know her real dad. Morwenna wasn't even sure that Tamsin did, but that was another story and, as far as Morwenna was concerned, the less said about that the better. Elowen came first.

'Mum,' Tamsin hissed. Morwenna had been staring though the window towards the rushing sea, in dreamland.

'Sorry.' Morwenna blinked, then she scurried to the family on table five. 'Can I get you all some drinks?'

'A pot of tea for two and home-made lemonade for the children,' the mother replied, all rounded vowels. She smoothed her trousers.

'And another slice of that lovely lemon drizzle cake.' The father beamed, showing gleaming teeth. 'Do you make it on the premises?'

'My daughter makes it. She does most of the cooking here,' Morwenna said with a smile. She noticed Jack sit up straight from the corner of her eye, his face shining with pride.

'Mummy, can we have cake too?' one of the children asked. He was around Elowen's age, his hair parted smartly at the side.

'You can all share mine,' the father replied quickly and Morwenna wondered if the family was short of money, despite appearing so neat and tidy. So many people were less well off than you'd think nowadays. She imagined them on holiday on a budget, at a camp site or in a small caravan, trying to have fun without spending much. She resolved to come back with an extra piece of cake; she'd say it was the end slice, she didn't want it to go to waste – they could have it on the house.

As soon as she'd deposited the fresh tray and two slices of cake in front of the family, she rushed back in to collect the cream teas for the couple in matching anoraks. Then the door-bell chimed and Carole Taylor blustered in, a flustered woman with bright cheeks. Two small girls pushed through the narrow door in front of her. The smallest, dark plaits swinging, hurried to Morwenna and clutched her waist, almost butting the tray. 'Grandma!'

'Elowen...' Morwenna put the tray down and bent over to kiss her warm cheek. 'How are you, my bewty?'

'I'm all right. Can me and Britney and Carole have some lemonade?'

'I'll bring you some over.' Morwenna smiled. 'Take a seat, Carole – you must be worn out, looking after your own little one all morning and Elowen too.'

'I'm all in – I'll be glad when they're back at school next week. They're both in Miss Parker's class. I like her, even though she comes from Penzance.' Carole collapsed at a table and Britney, round-faced and blonde like her mother, copied her actions.

'The emmets are almost all gone now – it'll be quiet at the guest house until the spring.'

'I bet,' Morwenna called over. 'It must be nice to have a few months off from running the B&B.'

'Vic has me helping at the garage through the winter. He says I'm good at selling cars – he says I have a persuasive face.' She beamed. 'You should buy a car, Morwenna. We can do you a good deal at Taylor Made Motors.'

'I'm still doing all right with the bicycle.' Morwenna picked up the tray and delivered the cream teas. Then she returned with glasses of lemonade.

Elowen clambered on Jack's knee and was chattering happily. 'And I had to tell Oggy not to be such a naughty boy, but he kept running ahead of me on the sand and I told him his paws would be all messy when we got home and Mummy would be cross...'

'Where's Oggy now?' Jack asked, his arm affectionately around Elowen.

'He's on his lead, silly.'

'Oh, of course he is,' Jack said with a grin in Tamsin's direction. He had little experience with children but he was trying his hardest.

'Oggy?' Carole mouthed. 'She's been talking about him non-stop all morning. I haven't a clue what she was on about.'

'It's her dog – he's a golden Labrador.' Morwenna explained.

'What?' Carole frowned.

'He's invisible, you daft old bat.' Britney chimed. 'Only Elowen can see him.'

Carole's cheeks turned purple. 'Hey, less of the daft old bat, young lady.'

'But that's what Daddy calls you,' Britney retorted and reached for a glass of lemonade, oblivious to her mother's embarrassment.

Morwenna offered a complicit wink. 'We hear about Oggy and his antics all the time. We just go with the flow.'

'Talking of the flow,' Carole changed the subject. 'Do you still go wild swimming every Sunday morning?'

'Most weeks, yes,' Morwenna said. 'I've been swimming in the sea since I was Elowen's age. We used to just call it swimming then, although we were always fairly wild!'

'I might join you one of these days.' Carole's voice was full of enthusiasm. 'I need to get fit. Vic's always telling me that.'

'You'd be very welcome.' Morwenna grinned. She knew already that Carole wouldn't come. She said the same thing every week. The good intentions were there, but Carole lacked the willpower, or the time, or the energy. Morwenna wondered if she should offer to call round for her, to make sure she turned up.

'Can I come swimming, Grandma? Can Oggy come?' Elowen called, scrambling from Jack's knee and rushing to wriggle on a seat next to Britney. 'Oggy loves swimming and so do I, although I know the water is too bleddy cold because Great Grandma says it is.'

'Great Grandma doesn't come very often.' Morwenna took a breath. 'Drink your lemonade, my bewty, and we'll talk about it with your mum dreckly.'

'Great Grandma says 'dreckly' all the time.' Elowen pulled a face. 'It's supposed to mean soon, but when she says it, everything takes ages.'

The tearoom was quiet for a moment, people eating, drinking. Tamsin came out from the kitchen with a cup of tea and plonked herself down for a short break while things were less busy. She hugged Elowen, blowing a kiss to Jack who greeted her with a wink. Then the doorbell chimed and a man sauntered in, causing everyone to sit up in their seats. Alex Truscott had that effect on people, in his pristine suit, tie blown over his shoulder in the wind, hair just over his collar. A scent surrounded him, cedar, an expensive cologne. He raised two hands as if conducting an orchestra, encouraging everyone to remain seated, to carry on as normal. Then he turned to Morwenna. 'I popped in to see you – or your mother, if she's here – I'm not sure who I ought to talk to.' As his eyes fell on Tamsin, he smiled the easy grin of a man who liked women and was comfortable around them. 'Maybe it's you I need to talk to, Tam. Who is the actual owner of the tearoom?'

'All three of us are,' Morwenna retorted.

Tamsin stood up. 'Tea or coffee, Alex?'

'Strong coffee, black, no sugar.' Alex smiled, his eyes unchanging. He was oblivious to the fact that Jack was watching him as if he was an intruder. Carole folded her arms across her chest defensively, and Morwenna placed her hands on her hips, chin thrust out.

'What can we do for you, Alex?' Morwenna wanted to know.

'Can we talk... privately?'

Morwenna shook her head. 'Is it about buying the tearoom again? You asked me during the summer and I said no. The answer hasn't changed.'

Alex arranged his face in a politician's smile. 'Perhaps I should take you and Tamsin and Lamorna out to dinner and we can discuss it properly over a bottle of wine?'

Morwenna breathed in deeply. 'The answer will still be the same. Mum and I told you that last time you asked.'

'Morwenna,' Alex sighed as if bored. 'It's the end of the holiday season. The tourists will be leaving soon. The tearoom doesn't make as much money off season – Lamorna told me herself it was difficult to manage last winter and, according to the papers, this next one will hit Cornwall hard. So why not cut your losses and sell now?' He gazed up as Tamsin came back. She placed a cup of coffee in front of him and he touched her wrist fleetingly. 'Thank you, Tam.'

Morwenna examined his face. He was handsome, probably in his early fifties, an arrogant mouth set in the confident smile of someone who always got his way in the end. He leaned back in the seat, stretching long legs elegantly, sipping coffee as if he were already the proprietor. 'Lovely, Tam. You make the best coffee.'

'Thank you.' Tamsin smiled and Morwenna noticed how her expression was suddenly shy. Alex Truscott had power over women, a magnetism that he relied on.

Morwenna spoke up. 'We're definitely not selling.' She frowned. 'You own plenty of other places in Seal Bay – why would you want to buy the tearoom?'

'I need a business for my son. He's done nothing but bum around the beach since he finished his degree.' Alex tapped manicured nails on the table. 'This place would be ideal for Simon. Of course...' He gave Tamsin his most seductive stare. 'You'd stay in the flat above, you and little Elowen. The rent would be minimal, naturally.'

Morwenna noticed that he had ignored Jack completely. He spoke as if no one else was in the tearoom except himself and the person he was addressing. 'How about it? I'd give you a very good price.' He pressed Morwenna's hand, his thumb against her wrist. 'You could retire. I'm sure you'd like that.'

Morwenna didn't skip a beat. 'I'm sure I wouldn't. The tearoom is Tam's livelihood.'

'And how old are you now, Tam?' Alex swivelled round. He took his time, his eyes straying over the striped top, the dungaree shorts.

'Twenty eight.' Tamsin's face was suspicious. 'What's that got to do with anything?'

'You have responsibilities; you have Elowen to think about. I'd offer you a job behind the counter. You'd be perfect,' he told her.

'Behind the counter?' Tamsin frowned.

'I'd turn this place into a takeaway, pizzas and burgers. It would do extremely well.' He played his trump card. 'It's what the Seal Bay community needs all year round.'

'I don't think so...' Tamsin frowned, just as Britney chimed, 'I like pizza. Mummy, can we come here for pizza?'

'The answer is no, Alex,' Morwenna said quietly. 'Now you ought to finish your drink and leave my guests in peace.'

'Very well.' Alex sipped his coffee then stood up. 'My price is on the table throughout September. But if this is a hard winter in Cornwall financially as is predicted, then naturally my offer will reflect that when you decide to sell. We'll talk again.' He turned to Tamsin. 'Think about what we've discussed, Tam – after all, we're talking about your future and Elowen's.' He seemed to notice the other diners for the first time as he delved into his pocket and placed coins on the table. 'I bid you all good afternoon. Enjoy your tea...'

The doorbell clanged and he was gone. The couple in the matching anoraks turned back to their teapot and scones. The family of four shifted in their seats and the father asked for the bill.

Carole said, 'Well, I think he has a point. I mean, he might be from London, but he has plenty of money and swagger. Last year he gave a thousand pounds to the Lifeboats and everybody says what a good man he is. He and his wife do a lot for our little town. He bought the Range Rover from Vic and he always brings it in to us for a service. There's not much money in Seal Bay nowadays, so you should take your chance while the offer's on the table, Morwenna.'

'He makes my skin crawl, truth be known.' Tamsin shuffled away, round- shouldered, busy with the bill.

Jack scraped back his seat and muttered, 'I'd better get back up the ladder – it'll rain later.'

Elowen wrapped her arms around herself and muttered, 'Oggy and I don't like him, do we, Oggy?'

'But he's going to get everybody pizzas,' Britney insisted.

'He's got a point,' Carole said again. 'The Proper Ansom Tearoom used to be a thriving place. In winter, it's as quiet as The Blue Dolphin Guest House, but at least we have the garage to fall back on. I remember years ago you'd be able to buy twenty different flavours of ice cream and milkshakes here, and all those different teas, Lady Grey and Chamomile and that funny smelling Lapsang Shoe Pong. Now you only do a few cream teas and coffees. It'll be a long cold winter, you mark my words.'

There was silence for a moment, then Morwenna shook her head. 'The tearoom isn't for sale. That's our final decision.' Her hand clenched itself into a tight knot. 'The tearoom as a pizza takeaway, indeed. You wait until I tell Mum... she'll be furious.'

3

'Giss on! He never said that, did he?' Lamorna Mutton was standing on the beach early on Sunday morning in a red swimsuit, hugging a fluffy beach towel.

'He did, Mum. As I stand here.' Morwenna smoothed her rainbow swimsuit. She shivered, holding up a stretchy swim cap, bundling her hair beneath. 'Shall we go in?'

'Dreckly – hang on – I've got to get this hat on...' Lamorna made several attempts to tug on the vintage swimming cap, composed of dozens of brightly coloured petals. Each time it slid from the smooth dyed-blonde locks of which she was so proud. 'Bleddy thing won't stay on.'

'Here, Mum, hold your hair and I'll pull it on for you.' Morwenna tugged the cap on the top of her mother's head and it stayed there like a balloon. 'Keep still...'

'So, let me get this right, Morwenna. Alex Truscott wants to buy our tearoom so he can turn it into a pizza takeaway and he wants to charge our Tamsin for the privilege of staying in the flat?'

'That's about the size of it.' Morwenna wondered if the swimming hat was too small or if her mother had an unusually large head.

'This thing doesn't fit properly – I'll just go in without a cap.'

'It's important to keep your head warm, Mum, and the bright colour makes you visible.'

'Me, invisible? Never!' Lamorna stamped her red-toenailed foot in the sand. 'And we aren't selling our tearoom to anyone.'

'Exactly.'

'Over my dead body.' The foot stamped again. Lamorna breathed hard. 'Or his dead body. I'd swing for him.'

'Tam got the full-on Truscott charm offensive, you know, persuasion dressed up as flattery.'

'What did her fiancé say? Jake or John or Jim, or whatever his name is...'

'You know it's Jack, Mum.'

'He's an emmet. Why does she want to marry an emmet?'

'She thinks he's a nice emmet.'

'I'm not sure I like him, to be honest. There's something shifty about him.'

'Tam loves him, Mum,' Morwenna said. 'He's her choice.'

'I don't trust him.'

'Do you trust any man nowadays?'

'Morwenna, isn't that the truth – what are we like?' Lamorna cackled. 'A couple of hard-boiled old women without a man in the world. Who gives a monkey's about men anyway?' She laughed again. 'They grow on trees, ten a penny. I won't be without one for long. Your dad taught me a lesson, though – never depend on them, they'll let you down. Especially Freddie.'

'Mmm.' Morwenna was used to her mother's rants about her father. She'd last seen Freddie Quick when she was four years old.

'Quick by name, quick by nature, that man. Here today, all

the promises and the charm of an alley cat on heat, then gone tomorrow.' Lamorna trotted out an old worn phrase. 'I thought you and Ruan would stick together for the long haul, but no, you threw him out to live in the house across the road. Oh well.' Lamorna's face was suddenly sad. 'And Tam comes back from a holiday six years ago in the pudding club. What are we like, we Mutton maids?'

'Unlucky?' Morwenna offered.

'Not at all.' Lamorna thrust back her shoulders. 'We're strong and independent and we keep our wits about us. Men are just chaff on the winds of change. I brought you up to rely on yourself.'

'You did, Mum, and I'm glad of it.' Morwenna waved a greeting. 'Here are the others. We can get in the water now. I'm starting to get cold.'

'Me too.' Lamorna hugged the beach towel over her cleavage. 'Are you sure this wild swimming will help my arthritic hip? I might be in my eighties now, but I don't feel a day over twenty...'

'It's definitely beneficial.' Morwenna grinned. 'Good for your mental health, improves circulation. It's even supposed to help with your sex life.'

Lamorna narrowed her eyes and scrutinised the approaching group. Louise Piper was scuttling forward in a long tent-like towel; behind her were the Grundy sisters, Susan and Barb, in matching tight costumes and white caps. Straggling a few paces behind was Donald Stewart wearing a wetsuit and a pink rubber cap, hugging a basket of sandwiches. Lamorna noticed him wave in her direction and groaned. 'It's doing nothing for my sex life so far.'

'Hi,' Louise called happily. 'Steve's not coming. I don't think he enjoyed last time. He's got a bit of a cough... Besides, he has to get up early tomorrow. Driving that lorry full of fish halfway round the country takes it out of him.'

Morwenna grunted assent. 'I called at The Blue Dolphin for Carole Taylor but I couldn't raise her.'

'She's still slugging in her bed now the guest house is quiet,' Barb suggested. 'I don't think they've had anyone to stay all week.'

'She could do with the exercise,' Susan added and they gave each other a knowing look.

Louise smiled. 'Six of us then? I thought Elowen might come.'

'She wanted to. Tam says she's too young. She's very protective.' Morwenna recalled the discussion she'd had with Tamsin. 'Jack's taking them out for a picnic. He's cheering Tam up after the Alex Truscott episode. Elowen wanted Oggy to come sea swimming with her but...'

'Oggy?' Susan and Barb asked together.

Lamorna barked a laugh. 'I'll tell you. She isn't allowed to have a dog at home, so she just makes one up and gets everyone else to believe he's real.'

'Shall we get into the water?' Morwenna hopped from one foot to the other. 'It's cold.'

Barb and Susan threw their arms in the air. 'We were born ready.'

'I'm ready,' Donald added. 'But beware going in headfirst like Mr Darcy from *Pride and Prejudice*. That would be very dangerous.'

'I'd jump straight in with him, that handsome one in the film with the wet shirt. I'd leap in and drag him out,' Lamorna piped up, 'and then I'd give him mouth to mouth...'

'Come on,' Morwenna urged, throwing her towel on the sand. 'I'm off. Follow me in.'

'Right behind you!' Louise called from behind her shoulder.

'Dreckly...' Lamorna said, although she stayed where she was. She had no intention of moving.

Morwenna began to run towards the water, feeling her heart beat faster. As the waves splashed around her feet, she heard her mother call, 'I might just stop here and have a quick paddle instead,' then she was in up to her waist, shoulders, ears, and swimming.

The ice of the sea took her breath away as she moved her arms and legs in a steady rhythm. Morwenna loved the sensation, the air punched from her lungs, the cold water biting at her hands and feet. She felt as if a lobster had clamped itself to her buttocks. And she was suddenly calm and laughing out loud with the joy of it. Louise bobbed up next to her and they swam together for a while in a controlled, steady way, aware of their breathing rate, taking a few steady head-up breaststrokes. Morwenna looked around for Donald and the Grundy sisters – they had been coming to the swimming sessions since March, so she wasn't worried for their safety, but she liked to check on them nonetheless. She saw two white hats and a pink one bobbing closely together, buoyed on the waves. They were fine.

Louise grinned and called, 'I'm f-f-freezing – I just love it.'

Morwenna nodded just to keep herself warm. She leaned back and closed her eyes. Being held in the arms of the ocean made her feel calm, cleansed, and after a few seconds, her thoughts steadied. She felt peaceful, as if nothing mattered except to float in the moment, thrilled by the chill of the water. Worries seemed to dissolve on the tide as she watched the scudding clouds overhead. Thoughts about Tamsin came to her, the engagement party on the beach, the plans for a Christmas wedding. Morwenna hoped she and Jack would live happily ever after. Her mind moved to Elowen: she'd be a survivor like the rest of the Mutton women. The future was an uncharted territory; Morwenna would not always be around to help her daughter and granddaughter. She wondered if she should get Elowen a dog. Tamsin had said a strict no, not in the flat, but the child was desperate. Then Morwenna recalled Alex Truscott, his suggestion that business would be slacker than ever this winter. Tamsin said Jack would try to support them, but custom for his decorating business was unpredictable. Morwenna breathed out: she felt herself let go and the worries wafted away on the waves like flotsam.

Ruan's handsome face appeared in her mind, his affectionate smile, and the anxiety returned like billowing surf; she'd never loved anyone as she loved him. They'd been together for years; she'd believed he was a keeper. They'd brought Tamsin into the world, adored her, and in the busy routine of life they'd somehow lost each other, and love had been replaced by silence and empty space. It had been worse than that at the end. It had been a car crash, a crumpled wreck from which their relationship could never return.

Morwenna tried to let go of the images and realised she was cold. It was time to swim back. The others were already on their way; Louise was shouting and waving an arm. Morwenna returned the wave, a sign that all was well, and she pushed strongly towards the beach.

Lamorna's bare feet were in exactly the same sandy spot. She shivered beneath the towel. 'You look colder than I am. Glad I didn't come in. No wonder the lifeboats are always out there rescuing people, all you bleddy wild swimmers getting yourselves into trouble.' She gazed around at Donald, smiling as he attempted to open a Thermos flask of coffee, spilling it everywhere as he quivered violently. Louise was struggling to adjust the strap of her swimsuit, her teeth rattling like peas in a bladder.

The Grundy sisters were walking around hugging themselves, flapping their arms like strutting chickens, legs all gooseflesh, water trickling in a steady stream from their swimsuits as they tried to warm up. Morwenna gazed down at her skin, mottled blue and red, and grinned. 'That was absolutely great.'

Lamorna looked pleased with herself. 'I'm perfectly warm here. I enjoyed my little moment's reflection on the beach. The hip still hurts though. So, come on everyone, get changed, quick as you like. I need a strong drink after all this exposure to the cold.'

* * *

Later that night in number four Harbour Cottages, Morwenna sat in bed in pyjamas reading a book by the glow of a lamp. She clutched a mug of hot chocolate between her palms, sipping slowly. The curtains were open, lifting on the night breeze. She looked up from her book and gazed out across the harbour, staring at the inky water and the tiny glimmering lights of bobbing boats. Her thoughts moved to Ruan in the cottage across the road, number nine with the sea-green door. She hadn't seen him for a few days and she couldn't help the strange feeling that found its way to her heart and nestled there. She imagined him tomorrow morning in oilskins, making his way through wind and drizzle in the glimmer of dawn towards the waiting trawler. They had argued about the dangers of his life as a fisherman so many times. 'Fishing's in my blood,' he'd say, and Morwenna would say nothing and worry in silence.

She watched a little longer: the harbour was peaceful now, yellow lights shimmering, reflecting shot gold on the water. She hoped Ruan was happy. But it was too late to think about it now. Tomorrow would be busy. She'd be out first thing, cycling to work at the library as usual, then waitressing in the tearoom in the afternoon. There would be fewer customers now, but she and Tamsin would devise new ideas to bring in more punters. They'd all be fine. She was sure Alex Truscott would be back. Something about him disturbed her: he was cocksure, too determined to get his own way, and it could only bring trouble. Morwenna preferred a peaceful life nowadays. She'd concentrate instead on Tamsin's engagement party next Saturday. Friends would be there, family, Ruan too, and there would be dancing and pirate fancy dress. It was just what she needed.

4

As the evening of the party approached, one small area of Seal Bay beach looked like a fairy tale scene. Morwenna had put up strings of coloured lights around a gazebo; a trestle table had been covered with salads, pasties, pizza, flans, Yarg cheese, crusty bread, a Stargazy pies, Licky pies and piles of scones with jam and cream. Jack, handsome in his Captain Jack Sparrow costume, was finding it difficult to keep his fingers away from the buffet. Morwenna watched fondly as Tamsin grabbed his hands. 'There will be nothing left if you keep eating it all, Jack.' He kissed her and Morwenna noticed the easy affection between them. Then Lamorna was at her side.

'It's looking good. We'll turn the music up and let our hair down. We can show these young ones a thing or two.'

Morwenna flung a loose arm around her mum. 'Tam's happy.'

'It's what she wants, I suppose. One man, stability. But he wouldn't be my choice for her.' Lamorna raised an eyebrow. 'Have you seen the engagement ring, though? It's like a bleddy pebble.' She tugged Morwenna to face her. 'I'm loving the groovy pirate gear you've got on.'

Morwenna looked down at the glittery top she'd teamed with yellow leggings and boots, the pirate hat and plastic cutlass, and at her mother's costume, the green hoop earrings, the low-cut dress, painted-on beauty spots, hair in ringlets, bare feet. She hugged her again. 'We make a right pair.'

'We're bleddy 'ansom.' Lamorna laughed, then she elbowed Morwenna lightly. 'Have you seen who's here with the beer?'

Morwenna glanced across to where her mother was pointing. Two men dressed as pirates, in striped shirts and cut-off jeans, were carrying a barrel, hoisting it on to a trestle, and she felt a familiar lurch in her chest. Ruan Pascoe, still lean and muscled in his sixties, was with Damien Woon, who owned the boatyard. It had belonged to Woons as long as Morwenna could remember and Damien, hefty and powerful, with low brows and a huge beard, had been Ruan's friend for years. Ruan noticed Morwenna and a smile of recognition spread across his face, then he went back to the beer barrel. Morwenna moved her gaze across the beach. People were starting to arrive. The Grundy sisters, Susan and Barb, were posing in flouncy dresses and piled wigs, their heads together, pointing at people, probably rating the fancy dress. Louise and her husband Steve, both in eyepatches, breeches and boots, were talking to Donald Stewart whose pirate garb included a grey wig with a ponytail. Carole Taylor and little Britney had arrived, proclaiming themselves pirates' molls in shiny dresses, helping themselves to lemonade. Elowen, in a cabin-boy headscarf, waistcoat, jeans and drawn-on tattoos was playing in the sand, throwing an imaginary ball towards her imaginary dog, calling, 'Fetch, Oggy!' Damien Woon helped himself to Yarg cheese to go with his pint. He was hacking crusty bread with a huge knife.

Lamorna laughed. 'I told Tam not to bring cutlery down from the tearoom. It'll end up in someone's pockets – there'll be nothing left to wash up.'

Morwenna was watching her daughter again, hand in hand with her new fiancé, and she felt her mind drifting to her ex again. She pulled herself together, grabbing Lamorna's shoulder. 'Come on, Mum, let's get this party started.'

Seconds later, 'Paranoid' by Black Sabbath was blaring out across the beach. Morwenna and Lamorna launched themselves into wild moves, dancing on the sand for all they were worth, Morwenna shaking her fountain of hair, Lamorna waving her arms as if directing traffic. Various people joined them, Steve awkwardly dad-dancing and Louise shuffling her feet. Tamsin and Jack were smooching, despite the fast pace of the music, as more people began to arrive.

Time passed and darkness filled the beach, grainy shadows of people moving beyond the twinkling lights. Morwenna was feeling pleased with herself, with the success of the gathering, watching leaping dancers, the groups that hovered by the trestle tables, eating, laughing. She looked around for Elowen. There she was, dancing with Tamsin, Lamorna, Carole and Britney. Then she felt a hand on her shoulder. Morwenna turned to see Jack standing next to her, tall and handsome, his eyes shining. 'Morwenna – I wanted to say thanks for organising all this.'

Morwenna smiled. 'I'm glad to do it. It's important to celebrate.'

'I'm so happy.' Jack fidgeted as if he had something he needed to say. 'It's just that...'

'Jack?'

'You know my mum lives up in Gloucestershire? She isn't in good health, hasn't been for a while, or she'd have been here.'

'You must miss her.'

'I do, but it was her idea for me to move down to Seal Bay. I'd been here on holiday a few times. I love it here, and she said, "Go on, Jack, set up a new life. See what the wind blows in." She gave me her blessing,' Jack explained. 'She hasn't even met Tam yet – she'd love her. I sent a photo of us with Elowen. I keep saying we'll go up to see her before the wedding, but she's so ill.

'Can't you go up for a weekend?' Morwenna immediately felt sympathy for him. Jack was living so far away from all the things she valued in her own life.

Jack shifted his feet. 'I might visit her soon.'

'She'll come down for the wedding, surely?'

'She won't, I'm afraid. And I've got no other family.' Jack shook his head. 'Mum has type two diabetes. She can't get out or travel.'

'Oh, that must be so hard.'

'She has a nurse who helps.' Jack shrugged. 'Mum's glad I'm down here, starting a new life.'

'It must be difficult, though…' Morwenna imagined how much she'd hate missing Tamsin's party. Then an idea came to her. 'How about I take lots of photos and you can send them to your mum, so she gets the flavour of it all? Lots of you and Tam and Elowen.'

'Oh, would you?' Jack beamed. 'That'd be great.'

'I'll send them to you and you can pick your favourites,' Morwenna grinned. 'Right. I'm on a mission now.'

'Thanks, Morwenna.' Then Jack touched her arm. 'Oh – look who's here.'

Alex Truscott was strutting towards them in a suit and tie, an elegant woman on his arm, her face deeply tanned, her hair shining blonde. He called out a greeting. 'Morwenna. Good to see you.'

'Alex, Pam,' Morwenna said quietly as she felt Jack slip away.

She watched him head back towards Tamsin to join in the dancing. She didn't recall having invited the Truscotts but the party was on a beach where anyone might stroll by so, in truth, anyone from Seal Bay was welcome.

'Congratulations to Tamsin,' Pam said, her face exaggeratedly sweet. 'Let's hope at least one of the Mutton women can hang on to a man...'

'Ah, she's a good-looking girl, Tamsin,' Alex returned, watching his wife bridle. 'And weddings don't come cheap, Morwenna.' He smiled. 'My offer for the tearoom is still good.'

Pam fiddled with a gold necklace with a diamond heart. 'Do we have to talk business, Alex? Can we just go for dinner?'

Alex kissed her cheek lightly. 'You know I never take a break from work, Pammy.'

She looked around and pointed to the bar. 'There's Simon, getting himself drunk. I'll go and talk to him while you finish bartering.'

Morwenna watched her walk away. She turned to Alex, her chin raised. 'Pam seems full of joy tonight.'

'She's not really interested in business. Spas and sail boats and spending money are more her thing,' Alex commented drily. 'So, how about it, Morwenna? Can we do a deal on the tearoom with Tamsin? What do you think?'

'It's not going to happen.'

'This will be a tough winter, heating, overheads. Let me take the place off your hands.'

'Alex, look... I know you do a lot for the community.'

'I'm glad you can see that. I care about Seal Bay. I've made it my family home. And Simon would benefit from running a business of his own. You're a mother, Morwenna, you get it.' Alex took a step closer. 'We worry about our kids. Simon needs something to settle him. He's not grounded. It's the perfect solution for us both. Tam will get married, have more babies – she could use the money.'

'No, I'm sorry but—'

'There's no way you're getting your mucky fingers on the tearoom.' Lamorna pushed in front of Morwenna, her hands on her hips, shouting for all to hear. 'Go and sling your hook, Alex Truscott. You're not having my business. And if you hassle my family again, I'll bleddy kill you, do you hear me?'

Alex smiled, took a step back, raised his hands. 'Lamorna, I can see you're passionate about the tearoom. I only asked... but we'll just leave it here for tonight, shall we?' He acknowledged the crowd who had stopped dancing to watch the argument, then he turned back to Morwenna. 'We'll talk again. Enjoy the evening – great party. Tell Tamsin I send my best wishes – I'll have to pop by with a present for her and her fiancé. Now I'll just head to the bar and find my wife...'

Lamorna's face was red with rage as he walked away. 'I'll swing for that man.'

Morwenna wrapped her arms around her mother; she felt small and fragile. She was shaking uncontrollably now and Morwenna felt protective of her. 'It's all right, Mum. He's not important. Let's enjoy the party.'

Elowen was next to her great grandmother, taking her hand. 'Come on, let's do some pirate dancing, me, you and Oggy.'

Lamorna let herself be led away and Morwenna recalled her promise to Jack to take photos. She clutched her phone, pleased that it had an ultra-low light option, and began to snap away. She took several photos of dancers, Elowen's smiling face, Lamorna with her arms in the air, Jack and Tamsin kissing, Donald Stewart doing some kind of fling. Many of the men had gravitated to the bar. Simon Truscott was watching Tamsin, drinking beer, talking loudly to his mother. There was no sign of Alex, then she saw him talking animatedly to Damien Woon, who was scratching his beard and frowning. The Grundy sisters had their heads together discussing someone, and Louise was tapping her feet. A woman stood in the shadows, dark hair, dark clothes, watching. Morwenna wasn't sure who she was. There were plenty of people eating; a burly pirate held up a half-eaten pasty and as Morwenna took photos, he muttered, 'Proper job.' A Captain Pugwash lookalike was ripping the bread apart with his bare hands; a Long John Silver pushed a whole scone in his mouth and smiled for the camera.

Morwenna wandered back to the dancers, capturing twirling figures she hadn't already photographed, more of Elowen, dancing alone, pirouetting. The music changed from Blondie's 'Call Me' to Eric Clapton's 'Wonderful Tonight' and couples started to smooch and slow dance. Morwenna took three more photos, then she felt someone standing next to her, turned and gazed into Ruan's gentle eyes. She wondered if he was going to ask her to dance, but he simply said, 'Hello.'

Morwenna smiled. 'It's a good party. Thanks for bringing the beer.'

'Our little girl's engaged.' Ruan murmured and Morwenna felt an ache between her ribs.

'She is.'

Ruan said, 'I just saw the fuss with Alex Truscott. You don't want to sell the tearoom?'

'No.'

He nodded. 'Best to hang on to it, I think. We'll pull through any bad times. It's Tam's future. Her's and Jack's.'

'That's what I think.'

'He's a nice lad. We've been for a pint a couple of times.'

'Oh?' Morwenna had no idea. 'That's nice.' She looked down at her pirate boots.

Ruan was looking at his feet too. 'I might offer to get Elowen a dog.'

'Tam's not keen on the idea.'

'She's not.' He tried again. 'I saw Lamorna lose her rag. She's feisty as ever.'

'She's getting on, but she doesn't let it hold her back.'

Ruan hesitated. 'None of us is getting younger.'

'We're not.' Morwenna squeezed her eyes closed, embarrassed by her words; it was time she walked away. The small talk was excruciating. After all these years, they had nothing to say.

'You're taking photos then?'

'For Jack's mum... she can't travel.' She shifted her feet. She'd go soon.

'He told me. She has a weak heart.'

'Diabetes,' Morwenna corrected him.

The noise of an idling engine made Ruan glance towards the road. 'Oh no...'

Morwenna followed his gaze. A police car had come to a standstill on the road, its blue light flashing.

'I wonder if that's my old mate Rick come to tell us we're disturbing the peace... I bet there have been complaints about the noise.' Ruan winked. 'Or he'll have heard about the party. He can be a spoilsport.'

'Isn't Rick Tremayne too senior for Saturday night PC duties? He's a detective inspector now.'

'Oh, it's probably some of his minions,' Ruan grinned. 'You carry on taking more photos. I'll pop up there and talk to them'

'Thanks, Ruan.' As usual, Ruan was perfect when it came to practical situations. It was just the emotional stuff that was the problem between them. Morwenna exhaled. It would never change.

Morwenna wandered through the dancing groups, framing

and clicking, then she left the flashing lights behind her and meandered towards the ocean. She could hear the whisper of the waves and, as it always did, the sea tugged her forward. The ink of the water met the satin night sky, the moon slipping behind a straggling cloud. She breathed in the clean air, filling her lungs. Seeing Ruan always made her feel that they hadn't entirely moved on, either of them. It left her a little bewildered. She plodded on, deep in thought, the sand scrunching beneath her boots. The surf sucked in and rolled forward and Morwenna blinked and stared harder.

Someone was lying in the sand a few feet away from her, slumped over.

5

Morwenna hurried forward. The figure was almost lying down, twisted, as if trying to sit up, propped up on an elbow. She assumed the person was drunk and they'd fallen: as she got closer, she realised that it was a man. She noticed the smart suit, the tie, and she smelled the tang of cedar as she knelt next to Alex Truscott.

'Alex—are you all right?'

His face was contorted, his eyes wild. Then he swayed, as if he might pass out.

'Alex, can you speak to me?'

He gripped her arm and leaned forward, his weight crashing against her. She heard his voice, a low whisper that was taking all his strength. '... asked me to meet... by the seafront... quarter to ten...'

'What? Are you hurt?' Morwenna's eyes darted around for signs of what had happened, or for someone to shout to for help but there was darkness all around. Behind her, the noise of the party continued to jangle, booming music, high voices trailing through the cold air. She gripped her phone, ready to ring someone. She wasn't sure what else to do. 'Alex?'

He tried to speak again, but his lungs were weak. He wheezed, his voice a thin rasp, desperate to explain. '... I said I'd be here... to talk about the money... I heard someone behind me... they were late...' He clutched Morwenna's arm in desperation. 'The voice said... "parasite..." and something... hit me...'

He slumped on to his front and didn't move. Morwenna saw the object sticking straight out of his back, the dark stains on his jacket. She reached out, touching the stickiness of pooling blood, the cold hard blade of a knife. She recognised the ornate handle immediately. It was Tamsin's, the one from the tearoom that she'd brought down to cut the bread. Then the tide rushed in, soaking Alex's body and her clothes. She gripped the phone and pressed a button. Ruan was the obvious choice. He was on the road, talking to the police. He'd help.

* * *

Morwenna's head was thumping. She didn't normally have headaches; she hadn't had one in years, but right now she had the mother of all splitting heads. The intense fluorescent lights didn't help, or the incessant droning voice of DI Tremayne, or the fact that it was past three in the morning and her body throbbed with tiredness. He said her name again. 'Morwenna...'

She reached for the plastic cup of water and lifted it to her lips. It was empty. She slumped onto her arms. 'Can I have another?'

'I'll get you one,' a kindly PC said. Morwenna had already forgotten her name. She'd forgotten most things. She wanted to go home but here she was in the police station, dressed as a pirate, answering a barrage of difficult questions. She accepted the flimsy cup gratefully and swigged half the contents. It moistened her lips but did nothing to help with the headache.

'So, tell me about Alex Truscott again.' Rick Tremayne smelled overpoweringly of excessive aftershave and perspiration, and she felt suddenly nauseous.

'How is he?' Morwenna asked. She'd seen the ambulance arrive, the flashing lights – probably everyone in Seal Bay had seen them. The party had stopped and the pirates shambled together in awkward groups as the paramedics took Alex away on a stretcher. Morwenna couldn't remember if his face was covered with a blanket or not. 'Is he going to be okay, Rick?'

'DI Tremayne,' Rick pointed out sternly, indicating the recording machine. She gazed at his round face, his sweaty forehead, the white shirt stained under the arms. It had been a long night for him too. He probably wanted to get home to Sally and the kids. Sally Tremayne came in the tearoom sometimes with her two teenage boys; they were the image of their father.

'I think I've told you everything.'

Rick Tremayne waved a pencil. Morwenna was about to tell him that he should be using a PC. Then she saw the PC next to him and stifled a silly laugh. Her head was banging; she was so tired, she was close to hysteria.

'Let's go through it one more time.' Rick sighed and Morwenna flopped down on the desk, her head on her arms. He ignored her. 'So, there were how many people at the... gathering?'

'Twenty, thirty? I didn't count them, Rick.'

'Your daughter's engagement party.'

'Yes.'

'And were all the people there known to you?'

'Most of them – but it was in a public place, people passed by, there were stragglers.'

'And did you have permission for this gathering?'

'It was on the beach.'

So, did you invite Alex Truscott?'

'No, I didn't. But it was okay for him to be there.'

'Why?'

'Why what?'

'Why was it okay for him to be there?'

Morwenna groaned. 'It's a free world.'

'And he was there with his wife and son?'

'Pam and Simon. Yes.'

'You saw them both?'

'I said I did – twice.'

Rick scratched the inside of his ear with the pencil, then sucked the end. Morwenna pulled a face.

'Morwenna, you found the body.'

'Body? So – he's dead?' Morwenna heaved herself upright. Her mouth had gone dry and her heart was thumping. She felt her face grow warm and hoped Rick wouldn't think it was a sign of guilt. He gave her a cold stare.

Rick avoided her question. 'You found Alex Truscott?'

'Yes.' Morwenna put a hand to her head and realised how hot she was. She was feverish.

'And did you see anyone hanging around or running away while you were there?'

'No.'

'Did anyone see you?'

'No.' Morwenna was exasperated. 'Everyone was at the party.'

'And can you tell me how Alex Truscott was when you found him?'

'Lying in the sand, groaning. Then he slumped over.'

'Did he tell you someone had attacked him?'

'No, but it was obvious, Rick. There was a knife in his back.'

'The knife belonging to the Proper Ansom Tearoom?'

'Yes, I recognised it. But anyone could have picked it up. It was there to cut loaves of bread.'

'And it will have your fingerprints on it?'

'It will have everyone's fingerprints on it.' Morwenna rubbed her eyes. 'Can I go home? I'm shattered.'

'Just a few more questions,' Rick said and Morwenna groaned loudly. 'So, who would dislike Alex Truscott enough to put a knife in his back?'

'Take your pick – there were plenty of people at the party who didn't like him.' Morwenna shrugged.

'Did you hate him?'

'No, as a matter of fact, I didn't.' Morwenna met Rick's eyes. 'We're using the past tense. He's definitely dead, then?'

Rick shook his head. 'You'll read about it in the papers...'

'He wasn't a bad man,' Morwenna said sadly. 'He was what he was.'

'And what was he?'

'A businessman, an entrepreneur. He gave money to charity, the Lifeboats. He had his warm side.'

The PC spoke for the first time. 'He was an outsider, from London.' Morwenna tried to focus her eyes; the woman was fresh-faced, lean, hopeful-looking.

'He's been living in Seal Bay for ten years.' Morwenna remembered Simon's words in the library.

'And he's bought up a great deal of it from local people,' Rick added. 'That rubs people up the wrong way.'

'Are you sure *you* didn't stab him?' Morwenna lifted an eyebrow. She needed to go home now. She was too tired to monitor the words that came from her mouth and she had no idea what she'd say next.

Rick ignored her. 'I'm sure many people had grudges against

him.'

Morwenna shook her head. 'I wouldn't know.'

'The tearoom is the hub of Seal Bay – I bet you hear all the gossip,' the PC urged.

'I serve up tea and cakes.' Morwenna felt her shoulders sag.

The PC tried again. 'And you work part-time in the library. I'm sure you're aware of everything that goes on.'

'Books...' Morwenna's voice was a creak. 'I lend them out...' She raised her head, her eyes glazed. 'Look, Rick, do you think I did it? Is that why I'm still here?'

'No, but you were there with the body.'

'I'm in a teashop every day with scones and cream, but that doesn't mean I eat them.'

Rick Tremayne sighed. 'Look, Morwenna. I have a crime to solve and I'll be honest – I haven't a clue who did it. I know all the evidence is tenuous: it was Tamsin's knife, you found the body, your mother swears she'll kill Truscott. But I have nothing else to go on. I have to start with you and your family.'

'But you know we didn't do it. You're wasting time...'

The PC and Rick Tremayne exchanged glances. 'We'll need to talk again.'

'Talk all you want later, but I'm dog-tired.' Morwenna glanced up at the ticking clock on the wall. Three thirty-five. 'Can I go home? I'm dead on my feet.' She put a hand to her mouth – that probably wasn't the wisest thing to say under the circumstances.

'We need to catch the attacker as quickly as possible – the area's cordoned off on the beach. We have forensics out there now,' Rick said.

'Then I hope you'll find the person who did it, but don't waste your time on me. I can't help,' Morwenna said. 'No one in Seal Bay wants a criminal on the loose. Now, I need to sleep, please.'

'I'll escort you out,' the PC said. 'But we may ask you to come in again.'

'As long as I can sleep first, I really don't care.' Morwenna stood up, swaying dizzily. Rick scratched his ear with the pencil and stuck it in his mouth again. Morwenna thought she'd be sick. She followed the policewoman to the door and remembered her phone full of photographs of the evening. She wondered if she ought to mention it – the police might find it useful to identify who was at the party. But it would just end up with them all being interviewed and she recalled that another PC had taken everyone's names down on the beach. Then she remembered that Alex Truscott mumbled something to her before he fell forward – it was somewhere in the recesses of her tired brain. She suddenly felt very sorry for Alex and she wanted to cry. More than anything, she just needed to get her head down and rest.

* * *

Morwenna spent most of Sunday in bed, her limbs throbbing, her head full of jangling conversations, most of them featuring Rick Tremayne's droning voice from the previous night. But there were snatches of other things – Lamorna's argument with Alex on the beach, Pam's cynical sneer as she walked away from her husband. Images came back to her: Simon holding a glass of beer, swaying at the bar, eyeing Tamsin; Elowen dancing in her cabin boy costume. She remembered talking to Ruan, the awkward conversation about absolutely nothing, just empty platitudes. What had he said? 'None of us is getting any younger.' Morwenna groaned, rolled over and went back to sleep.

Much later, well after four, she woke up and realised she'd missed the sea swim. Her body needed to rest; she was tired, full of aches. Her brain was fuzzy now, thick with crammed thoughts. To be honest, she wasn't sure anyone would have turned up this morning, not after the events of last night. She thought about wandering down to the beach to help to clear up the detritus from the party, but the area would be cordoned off. She doubted she'd be allowed near the crime scene. That's what it was, a crime scene – a man had been killed, Alex Truscott, a man she'd known. She let the realisation sink in... He'd been murdered. He wasn't popular, that was an understatement, but no one hated him enough to kill him. She couldn't imagine who would do such a thing. The very idea made her head bang again.

Her stomach grumbled. Morwenna realised she was hungry. Her mouth was dry, her tongue furry. She was thirsty too. She rolled over and reached for her phone – a dozen messages: Tamsin, Lamorna, Louise, Ruan. She read Ruan's brief text.

Do you need me to call round?

Practical as ever, offering to come over. But there was no emotion, no softness after her ordeal. Morwenna told herself firmly that no, she didn't need him to call round. He was Tamsin's father, Elowen's grandad, he lived across the road – which was useful when she needed a cup of sugar – but that was all. She needed nothing from Ruan Pascoe, absolutely nothing. Zero, zilch, nada.

What she really needed was a shower, a cup of tea, a bowl of porridge; something normal, ordinary. She'd be all right then. She'd lounge in front of the TV for the rest of the day or read a book or go back to bed and sleep like a log. Then tomorrow would be Monday and she'd cycle to the library and the world would slowly get back to normal, back to how it used to be. She hoped.

6

Morwenna felt much more cheerful as she zoomed downhill towards the library on her bicycle with the breeze in her face. She'd decided at breakfast that Monday marked a new day, a new week, and she was going to be fine. It was an awful shame about Alex Truscott. The thought of what she'd seen on the beach still brought her to the brink of tears, but there was nothing she could do. She passed the pop-up knitting shop, pushing the image of Alex and his final gasped words from her mind. Today, Susan and Barb were perched in the window, their knitting held high, staring at the world like zombies. They raised their needles as Morwenna whizzed past and she was sure they were saying:

'She found the body, you know. Terrible thing, I reckon, to be stabbed with a bread knife...';

'We could have been standing right next to the murderer all evening and not known it!';

'A few inches more, and it might have been us lying on the sand.'

Morwenna imagined their chatter: it was a sad and serious business. She'd hear even more about it today in the library, where there would be theories and speculation. She was sure there'd be more people in Seal Bay wanting to borrow a book today than she could shake a skinny stick at.

She leaned her bike in the corridor and heaved her bag into the library. Louise was waiting there already, staring at Morwenna's hooped leggings and a baggy top as if somehow, she might have changed dramatically, having found a dying man. But she was still the same Morwenna. She held out her arms for a hug and Louise muttered, 'Are you all right, my lovely?'

'I'm good now, thanks.' Morwenna took in Louise's anxious face. 'Are *you* all right?'

Louise shook her head. 'It doesn't seem believable, Alex being killed, and at your party too. It's awful all round. Who do you think might have done it?'

'No idea,' Morwenna shrugged. She almost added 'it wasn't me', but she held back. She wondered if Rick Tremayne seriously thought she was a suspect, simply because she had found the body. She asked, 'Did you see anything at the party, Louise?'

'No. Nor did Steve. We went home just before ten thirty. He had to get up for work.'

'I'll ask Donald later, then I'll pop into Susan and Barb,' Morwenna said. 'Someone must have noticed something.'

'It would have to be someone strong, to put a knife in him like that. What do you think?' Louise was working on a theory already.

'I've no idea, honestly,' Morwenna said again, although she couldn't help searching for clues: a woman could have done it. Alex had enemies.

'Steve reckons it was Alex's wife Pam. She'll get all his money.' Louise took a breath. 'But Simon might inherit it all. Depends on Alex's will. Oh, it's such a mess.'

'It is.'

'And the police questioned you, did they?'

'They did, until the early hours of Sunday morning. I don't remember most of it, I was so shattered.'

'Poor love.' Louise was pouring tea. 'They are still down at the beach now. The area is roped off.'

'It's an ongoing investigation.' Morwenna took a mug with a black flag on it and the motto *Kernow bys Vyken* from Louise and muttered, 'Cornwall forever, eh? It's all happening in Seal Bay.' She slurped thoughtfully.

'I expect the police will sort it out.' Louise sighed. 'My Steve knows Rick Tremayne well. He says he's like a dog with a rabbit between his teeth...'

'He is.' Morwenna smiled at the image. 'He'll get to the bottom of it, I'm sure.' She remembered snatches of her interview with Rick. 'He's systematic... dogged...'

'Oh, I didn't tell you, what with everything else going on,' Louise began. 'Lady Elizabeth Pengellen has been at it again this weekend. I came in this morning and there were books all over the floor. And guess what?' She lowered her voice. 'They were all from the crime fiction section.'

'And...?'

Louise was serious. 'It's a *sign*, Morwenna. The books were scattered everywhere: Agatha Christie, Stephen King, Richard Osman...'

'Meaning that Lizzie is trying to tell us something?'

'She is. After all, there's a crime in Seal Bay and it needs solving. What do you think? We could be sleuths.'

Morwenna smiled. 'My life is crazy enough.' Then she stopped. Customers had started to file in. The Grundy sisters wanted to know what the latest word was on the murder, several teenagers sought out Morwenna to ask, 'Did you see blood spewing out?' and, at the back of the queue, a reporter from the

Seal Bay Gazette wanted a quote about how it felt to discover a body and 'was it true that Morwenna had seen a masked pirate rushing from the scene of the murder brandishing a cutlass?'

* * *

The entire morning was an opportunity to discover what people knew about the murder. Morwenna asked everyone who came in if they'd seen anything unusual, but people preferred to gossip rather than to offer clues. She was relieved when Donald Stewart arrived at lunchtime, patting her hand in sympathy, claiming he'd spent the whole evening on the beach dancing or standing at the makeshift bar talking to a doctor of physics about the paranormal. He suggested that they hold a séance to ask the ghost of Lady Elizabeth who the murderer was – after all, ghosts knew everything, they could eavesdrop without being noticed. Morwenna smiled, collected her bike and pedalled into the wind towards the tearoom.

* * *

Inside, Tamsin was rushed off her feet. Almost every table was full, people wanting coffee, cake and to discuss the crime. Morwenna thought that it was ironic that Alex's demise had led to a rise in custom at the tearoom. She wondered what Rick Tremayne's keen brain would make of that.

Tamsin was flustered; she tossed an apron in Morwenna's direction. 'Can you take orders for tables one, three and six, Mum? Coffees for table two. Someone's ordered a pot of Rooibos tea – I'm sure we have some at the back of the cupboard.'

'You carry on, my bewty – I'll look after the customers,' Morwenna said, determined to take the chance to talk to anyone who might have new information about Alex. She turned to see several pairs of keen eyes staring at her, all wanting to look at the woman who discovered the body on the beach. Morwenna kept her face straight and took a breath. 'Right, who's next? We have tea, coffee and cake, but I'm afraid sandwiches are off the menu today – the bread knife's gone missing.'

As the afternoon wore on, Morwenna and Tamsin felt their energy drain away. Tamsin had been on her feet since seven o'clock and Morwenna had done her best to sift information from customers. Everyone claimed to know Alex Truscott well, most people disliked him and theories abounded about who had killed him – Pam being the most popular choice – but no one had actually seen anything. Jack came home at four o'clock, whistling happily, in paint-spattered overalls. Elowen bounced beside him, back from Britney's house, chattering that she was looking forward to going to school because everyone wanted to be her friend now her grandma stabbed people with a bread knife.

Jack winked. 'Right, Tam, I'll take Elowen up to the flat to feed Oggy. He hasn't eaten a thing all day and Elowen's hungry too. Shall I put pasties in the oven?'

'Not for me,' Morwenna said. 'I'm off home in a moment.' Jack opened the door that led upstairs and Elowen rushed ahead, calling the dog. Morwenna remembered something. 'Jack – I must get those party photos for your mum printed off.'

'No rush,' Jack called back. 'Dreckly – isn't that what you Cornish people say, and then you get round to doing it a month later?'

'Exactly.' Morwenna grinned.

'I won't be long. I'm just tidying up,' Tamsin called after him. Then she placed her hand over Morwenna's. 'Mum, I haven't had a chance to talk to you. How are you? What happened at the police station?'

'They asked me what I saw and I told them straight.'

Tamsin's eyes were round. 'Who was it, do you reckon?'

'Could have been anyone.'

'Jack was upset. It was our engagement do.' Tamsin frowned. 'And Elowen was there too. I can't stop thinking, what if she'd found the body? I can't believe he was murdered here, right under our noses. I didn't like Alex Truscott much, but I hate the thought of it. Who'd kill him?'

'I've talked to dozens of people; no one has a clue.' Morwenna shook her head. 'It could be a passer-by, or a person with a grudge.' She didn't want to worry Tamsin, but her instincts told her it was someone Alex knew, someone she knew too. She was determined to puzzle it out.

Then the bell clanged and the door was flung open, revealing Lamorna leaning against the post, her face drained. 'Get me a cuppa quickly. And put rum in it.'

Tamsin was on her feet, moving towards the urn. Morwenna grabbed her mother's arm before she fell over.

'Are you all right, Mum? What's happened?'

'Rick Tremayne happened. I need to sit down. My legs are killing me and my hip aches something wicked.'

Morwenna eased her mother into a seat and Tamsin placed a cup of steaming tea in front of her, accompanied by a scone with butter. Lamorna dived in hungrily. 'I haven't eaten since breakfast.'

Morwenna said gently, 'Tell us what happened.'

'The police came round to my home and arrested me.'

'Arrested you? No!' Morwenna was shocked. 'They can't do that. Based on what evidence?'

'A PC asked me questions, then they took me to the station in a car to help with their enquiries. It was so embarrassing! All the neighbours came out and watched them drag me away. I even heard someone say, "they got the old crone who killed Alex Truscott." I could have swung for them!'

'Oh, Mum...' Morwenna said kindly. 'I wish I'd known. I'd have gone straight down to the police station and brought you home.'

'The thing is,' Lamorna wiped her lips and reached for the cup of tea. 'They questioned someone – Susan Grundy I think – who said she'd heard me tell Alex Truscott I'd kill him. Well, I did – say that, I mean, not really kill him.' Lamorna shivered. 'Do you think they'll arrest me for murder?'

'Everyone heard you *say* that,' Tamsin said kindly. 'No one believes you'd really *do* it. They can't arrest you based on a meaningless threat.'

'That's all they've got; Rick Tremayne told me that – he's a right miserable old tuss.'

Morwenna thought back to her own ordeal. 'I expect he's doing his job as best as he can.'

'He kept asking me questions. I told him straight, I said, "You won't find my fingerprints on that bleddy bread knife – I don't like bread much, it sits heavy on my gut."' She took a breath. 'I reckon I'm the only one in Seal Bay whose prints aren't on that knife.'

'Don't worry, Grandma.' Tamsin took the empty plate and cup to refill them both. 'You're back with us now.'

Suddenly, Lamorna covered her face with her hands and dissolved into tears. 'He's a bleddy bully, that Rick Tremayne. I've always liked his wife and his lads – they are polite and nice but him... he's a proper mean devil.'

She gave a shuddering breath and covered her eyes again. Morwenna looked at her mother's hands, the crimson nails, the gold rings, the tears seeping through the cracks between her fingers, and she wrapped an arm around Lamorna affectionately. Tamsin placed more tea in front of her grandmother, who reached out a hand for the cup. It rattled as she brought it to her lips. 'I'm their chief suspect. They haven't got anyone else lined up.'

'No way,' Morwenna said. 'That's rubbish.'

'You ain't off the hook either, my bewty.' Lamorna turned sharply to Morwenna. 'That's what Rick Tremayne said. He told me straight: "your Morwenna was at the scene of the crime." Then he said, "and you threatened him. Everyone knows he wanted to buy the tearoom and your family didn't want to sell." I couldn't believe the cheek of the man, saying that to me, an old lady in my eighties. As if I'd kill someone...'

Tamsin wrinkled her nose dismissively. 'That's nonsense, Grandma, no one kills someone because they don't want to sell them their business.'

'Rick Tremayne says I'm free to go for now because he can't find any evidence, but he wagged his finger at me. "Watch your back, Lamorna Mutton," he said and I told him straight, "Alex Truscott should've watched his own back." He didn't like it when I said that. But I was so jumping mad with him that he could think that me or my daughter could kill Alex. I'm not having it.' Lamorna's nostrils flared with anger, then the tears came back with a vengeance. 'Oh, I'm just proper upset by it all.'

'We'll stand by you,' Tamsin said loyally.

'Too right.' Morwenna pressed her lips together. 'Rick Tremayne is barking up the wrong tree if he thinks one of us did it. He's wasting his time chasing us when there's someone out there who really did kill Alex Truscott and whatever you think of Alex, he didn't deserve that. The police should be looking for the real criminal.'

'They should, Mum,' Tamsin agreed.

'The thing is...' A new gleam came into Morwenna's eyes. 'I reckon Rick Tremayne doesn't have a clue. But somebody's got to sort this mess out, haven't they? And if not Rick, then who's going to do a proper job?'

7

The papers were full of the news about Alex Truscott's twisted body lying at the water's edge with the Proper Ansom Tearoom bread knife stuck in his back. There had been no arrests. Many locals feared the 'perp' was still at large in Seal Bay, but the most popular theory was that Alex was murdered by a passing visitor who'd since gone over the Tamar Bridge back 'up north', or possibly an opportunist day tripper from 'the big city', Truro. Everyone in Seal Bay had their own opinion and Morwenna was keen to listen but, as yet, there was no real evidence. On Wednesday, Morwenna cycled down to the beach, where the area was still cordoned off with blue and white tape proclaiming *Police Crime Scene Do Not Enter*. She wanted to check on the location where the party had been, to see if anything jogged her mind. It was quiet at the seafront and she wanted to take time to rethink the chain of events.

She stood behind the tape, watching it flutter in the breeze, thinking. At least Rick Tremayne hadn't bothered her again; he hadn't visited Lamorna either, who was in a state of perpetual fear, claiming that everyone looked at her strangely when she went to the corner shop to buy a pasty. Morwenna continued to find opportunities to speak to anyone who'd been at the engagement party when they came to the library or the tearoom. She'd asked them all the same question: 'Can you remember anything unusual on the beach round about 10.45 p.m. on the ninth of September?' The answer was invariably no: everyone had been enjoying themselves, they hadn't noticed anything unusual, they were talking, dancing, sharing food. Morwenna was frustrated by the fact that she'd learned nothing new. But someone at Tamsin's party had killed Alex and she was increasingly suspicious. She was no sleuth, but she'd do her best to find answers.

She gazed into the ocean, recalling the chain of events. Late yesterday afternoon, Tamsin had been questioned in the flat above the tearoom while Jack went for a walk and Elowen stayed with Morwenna. She had sat happily, drinking lemonade and feeding morsels of chocolate cake to Oggy while Morwenna rushed around with tea, scones and sandwiches, cut with a brand new bread knife. At least for the time being, Alex's murder was still bringing in the customers, although they mostly sat for hours over one pot of tea, deliberating over the murderer. Morwenna sighed – the beach was strangely deserted, there was no one beyond the police tape. Just the sea lapping at the place where Alex had fallen. She might as well go home.

* * *

Early on Sunday morning, Morwenna came back to the beach again, but this time she felt much happier. It was time to swim. Despite the weather turning chilly, she felt uplifted; a biting east wind blew in from the ocean and she wondered when it would be cold enough for her wetsuit. The swimsuit she always wore was a specialist one, and she had a tow float around her waist today, petroleum jelly on her arms, but it didn't keep the cold out. Her skin was already mottled and she hadn't got in the water yet. Louise arrived, Steve dropping her off from the family car, and they huddled together, staring at the cordoned area.

'That's a blot on our landscape,' Louise observed. 'It's a good job the tourists have gone. All this drama might have put them all off coming here if it had been June.'

'Oh, I don't know...' Morwenna muttered between chattering teeth. 'Sometimes a murder pulls in the crowds. Human nature can be funny.'

'It can,' Louise agreed. 'No one else is joining us today. Barb Grundy has a cold and Susan is staying home with her. Donald's lagging his pipes.'

'Just us then,' Morwenna said. 'Shall we dive in?'

They ran together, feeling the wind and the icy water on their skin. Morwenna submerged her face and pushed her arms and legs strongly, swimming to the surface and spluttering.

'I love the water!' Louise yelled. 'I'm so close to freezing to death and yet I feel so alive!'

'It's good to be alive,' Morwenna replied and felt suddenly sad.

'Poor Alex Truscott,' they both said together.

Then Morwenna closed her water-filled eyes. A plan was forming. There was something she needed to do, that she should have done already. Her mind was made up. Yes, the visit to Seal Bay's number one suspect was long overdue.

* * *

Wearing a patchwork velvet coat and black leggings, Morwenna cycled up the hill, breathing hard. As a teenager, she'd cycle everywhere in Seal Bay, never giving hills a moment's thought, but now she listened to the bike creak, wondering if it was her knee joints cracking as she gasped her way to the top. The house stood alone, surrounded by hedgerows and large gardens overlooking the bay. She paused outside a double-fronted red-brick house with high gables and a grand oak door, and looked up. She'd expected the curtains to be closed but the windows were slightly open to let in the fresh breeze. Two cars were parked in the drive: a sporty Audi and a Range Rover. She'd seen Pam Truscott driving one or the other too quickly through Seal Bay. Two cars outside meant that someone had to be in. Morwenna leaned her bike against the wall, examining the pretty painted sign: Mirador. The Truscotts had given their house a new name when they first arrived – apparently it meant a beautiful view. Morwenna remembered with a smile that Lamorna thought the house was called Mordor, the realm of the evil Sauron in *Lord of the Rings*. She wondered what lay behind the doors now as she pressed the bell and heard it buzz.

Morwenna had her excuse ready – although it was the truth – as the door opened and Pam Truscott stood facing her in a blue linen suit. Her face was serious, but Morwenna wasn't sure if grief was etched there. Pam was surprised to see her. 'Morwenna?'

'Pam. I wanted to call in on you after what happened... to say how sorry I am.'

'You'd better come in. Goodness knows who's watching. Everybody seems to think my life is a peep show.' Pam led the way into a large room with billowing cream curtains and two shell-pink sofas. The smell of musky perfume surrounded her. Morwenna looked around for clues; there were beautifully framed photos, professional shots of Pam and her son Simon on every wall. She was in jodhpurs riding a horse or in a portrait being nuzzled by one; she was in a boat with huge white sails, smiling in a striped top. Simon's graduation photos took pride of place on the glossy mahogany dresser. There were no photos of Alex. In fact, the room definitely had a feminine touch, a delicate chandelier, a full-length ornate gold mirror, fresh blooms in vases. A wine bottle was open on the coffee table alongside a copy of Vogue, two empty glasses with dregs in the bottom. Morwenna frowned, wondering if Pam was drinking to help her cope with grief. But she wasn't drinking alone. Morwenna registered the extra glass and made a mental note. Pam noticed her gaze and read her thoughts.

'My cleaner hasn't arrived yet – and yes, I had someone round last night. It's not illegal.' She sat down, crossing her legs. 'So, what did you want to say?'

'Well...' Morwenna plonked herself down on the pink sofa although she hadn't been asked, realising that there was no chance she'd be offered a cuppa. She came straight to the point. 'I wanted to tell you how sorry I am about Alex. You know I found him on the beach and it must have caused you a great deal of distress, so I wanted to offer condolences.'

Pam fiddled with the gold chain around her neck, the diamond pendant. 'It was quite a shock. I know Alex wasn't popular, but I didn't know anyone hated him enough to stab him in the back.' She frowned. 'There must have been some venom behind it. The police said his lungs were damaged, his heart...' She swallowed. 'In truth, I'm surprised he had a heart.'

Morwenna noted the comment, looking for signs of anguish in Pam's face to see if her grief was real. She tried again. 'It must be hard...'

'Being a widow?' Pam almost laughed. 'I hardly ever saw Alex when he was alive. He was always doing business deals, or meeting up with his cronies or his...' Morwenna waited for her to continue and she was off again. 'You know Alex had another woman? It was always the same throughout our marriage, when we lived in London, before Simon was born. He had affairs. Making money and philandering were his two hobbies.'

'I'm so sorry.' Morwenna chose her words carefully. 'You don't think the other woman... you know... was there on the beach and—'

'Killed him?' This time Pam screeched a laugh. 'It's possible. There's a list as long as my arm of people who had a grudge. You should ask his mistress. I've no idea who she is; Alex thought I didn't know. Then there are the people he's taken money from in business deals.' She pointed a finger. 'You were one of them, Morwenna – he wanted to buy the tearoom, didn't he?'

Morwenna stared at her hands folded in her lap. 'He wanted a pizza takeaway for Simon.'

'Simon?' Pam flapped a hand as if she was swatting a nuisance fly. 'Simon's not interested in making money. Quite the opposite.'

'But his degree is in business,' Morwenna said quietly. 'I've lent him library books.'

'His only business is gambling, and he's no good at it.' Pam looked unconcerned. 'He has debts. His father's left him a trust fund in his will. I daren't think how long it will take to gamble his way through that little lot.'

Morwenna raised an eyebrow. So Simon spent money like it was going out of fashion. She wondered how she might delve deeper into the Truscotts' lifestyle.

'I wonder if it would be all right for me to attend Alex's funeral?' Morwenna said.

Pam frowned as if she'd just remembered. 'The undertakers are taking care of it. It's on the 22nd. They are releasing the body —poor Alex, just the thought of an autopsy...' Her lip trembled. 'I just want to get it over with.'

'I'm sure,' Morwenna said sympathetically.

'I imagine everyone in Seal Bay will be there; curious people who want to see what I'm wearing, if I cry or if I'm a merry widow.'

'People will want to pay their respects.'

'Perhaps...' Pam looked around. 'Alex had a way of treating me like just another possession. I had more than twenty five years of it... And now I can't even think about how I feel. It's too soon.'

'You stayed together, many don't.' Morwenna thought briefly of Ruan.

Pam turned to her sharply. 'Do people think I killed him?'

'I don't think so,' Morwenna said, examining Pam's expressionless face.

'I suppose I had the opportunity at your party.' She shrugged as if it was unimportant. 'We were just passing through. Alex did his usual trick, abandoning me, talking to other people. I spent time with Simon, but he was half-drunk and making no sense.'

'Who was Alex talking to?' Morwenna asked casually.

'No one and everyone...' Pam didn't seem to register her interest. 'I saw him chatting to you, your mother, and Damien Woon. There was someone else he was in deep conversation with, I can't remember who it was. I walked off on my own to have a cigarette. I've given up so many times, but the stress of living with Alex...' She took a deep breath. 'Afterwards, I went to the bar for a drink. Alex was nowhere to be seen. Then I saw the police car and the ambulance and, well, you know the rest.'

'I'm so sorry,' Morwenna said.

'Don't be. I'll miss him but hey, people would miss a wart if they'd had one for a long time.' She laughed and Morwenna thought it was a little too high. 'Perhaps that's all Alex was to me, a wart.'

There were tears in Pam's eyes. Morwenna wasn't sure if it was sadness or hysteria, but Pam seemed brittle. Morwenna said, 'I'd better go.'

'Can you see yourself out?' Pam reached for her phone and pressed buttons. She called out as an afterthought, 'Thanks for calling round.'

Morwenna hesitated in the large cream hallway, grand stairs sweeping up to a galleried landing, and listened. Pam was still talking, her voice low and confidential, as if speaking to someone she knew intimately: Simon, a friend, or a lover? She heard her say, 'Can you come over? I need you here now. You can be here from London in less than six hours.'

Fleetingly Morwenna wondered if Pam had killed Alex. She certainly had a strange way of grieving.

8

Morwenna had been busy since she left Pam's house. She'd visited more people in Seal Bay who'd been to the party, people she knew from the library, from the town, chatting to them casually about the events leading up to Alex's death. Had they seen anything? Had they noticed anyone behaving strangely? Again, she'd drawn a blank. No one had noticed anyone walking towards the tide with Alex, although lots of people wanted to mention something they were sure was a vital clue. 'Pam was looking proper shifty...' 'I saw a tall stranger in a dark coat watching from the shadows.' 'A fisherman I know who drinks in The Smugglers' Arms told me he hated Alex Truscott enough to stab him in the back.' Lots of talk but nothing of any use, Morwenna decided.

The rain was bucketing down as Morwenna whizzed through puddles in the town centre, dodging cars that failed to notice a drenched woman on a bike. As she struggled up the hill towards Harbour Cottages, she was conscious of a vehicle close behind her. She turned to see the bumper of a police car hovering inches from her back wheel. She waved an arm furiously, beckoning the car to overtake, but it remained stubbornly glued to her mudguard. Morwenna turned the corner to Harbour Cottages, glancing over towards number nine. It was past two. Ruan was probably home, although some Sunday afternoons he took Elowen to the trampoline place with the soft play area. He'd join in with her too – Ruan had always been fit, being a fisherman. Morwenna thought fleetingly of the taut muscles of his limbs, then she paused at the gate of number four and was unsurprised to see that the police car was idling by the kerb.

'Morwenna – a word.' DI Rick Tremayne hung an elbow through the open window.

Morwenna turned her back to him, pushing her bicycle towards the front door. Her silver hair, dark with rain now, stuck to her scalp and hung in straggly ropes. 'You can come inside, Rick. I'm not chatting to you out here in the rain.'

Moments later, they stood in her little living room. Rick Tremayne looked bulky in the compact space, his shorn head almost touching the beams. Morwenna hurried into the kitchen, bustling with the kettle and cups. 'Tea?'

'It's not a social call,' Rick replied.

Morwenna pulled a face. 'Well, I'm having one. I'm soaked to the skin and freezing. Do you want one or not?'

'I may as well.'

Morwenna returned with a towel around her neck, carrying two steaming mugs. She wouldn't offer Rick any biscuits. She couldn't remember a time in her life where she hadn't offered a visitor a biscuit with a cup of tea but, as the DI had said himself, it wasn't a social call. She plonked his mug on the table, then threw herself onto the squashy sofa near the fireplace and began to wring water from her hair. 'What can I do for you?'

'Alex Truscott.'

Morwenna nodded. 'What about him?'

'The thing is...' Rick looked at the mug as if it might contain poison. 'The thing is, we haven't found the killer yet.'

'Well, you'd better get a wriggle on.' Morwenna coiled her hair around her hand and twisted it into a bun, then dried her face with the towel.

'The problem I have is – you found the body and your prints are on the knife.'

'I bet half of Seal Bay's prints are on that knife.'

'And your mother threatened to kill him, in front of witnesses.'

'Meaning?'

'Meaning some might say it has to be one of you.'

'Don't be daft, Rick.' Morwenna sipped her tea carefully. It was scalding hot. 'You know perfectly well that it wasn't us.'

'You had the motive. He wanted the tearoom.'

'I want an electric bicycle – that doesn't mean I'd kill the man who reads the meter.'

Rick sighed as if his patience was wearing thin. Morwenna looked at his bulky frame, out of place in her small cottage, and wasn't sure if she felt annoyed or sorry. Both, in truth. She tried again. 'Look, you know it wasn't me or my mum who stabbed poor Alex. There must be other suspects you have your eye on, surely.'

'You called on Pamela Truscott earlier this afternoon. What did you want to talk to her about?'

'Knitting patterns, designer handbags.' Morwenna slurped loudly. 'What do you think? I wanted to offer my sympathy.'

'How did she seem to you?'

'Normal.'

'Not upset? Grieving?'

Morwenna exhaled. 'People show their grief in different ways.'

'Do you think she killed her husband?'

'Get on! So I'm a sleuth now, Rick? An honorary policewoman. I'll have to ask for a salary.'

'The thing is, Morwenna, I need to find the killer and evidence is thin on the ground. I have a beach party full of suspects who all claimed to be doing something else at the time of Alex's death, and a local woman who found the body, whose mother was threatening the victim with hell and high water. What would you do?'

'Me? I'd go home to Sally and the kids, have a hot bath, put my feet up and make a long list of suspects.'

'You Mutton women are too darned independent, too full of yourselves with your clever ways and your colourful clothes and your sharp tongues.'

'So having a tongue is a criminal offence is it, Rick? That's just about everyone in Seal Bay.' She saw his shoulders droop and felt immediately sorry for him. 'I'm not joking. Go home, rest, make a list. Ask the right questions. It'll come to you. But stop barking up the wrong tree, because it wasn't me and it wasn't my mum, right?'

Rick stared at the untouched mug of tea and shook his head. 'I'll leave the problem where it is for now. It's getting late.'

Morwenna muttered, 'Can you see yourself out? Don't hang about; this Cornish rain goes right through your clothes. You'll catch your death...' She put a hand over her mouth – she probably shouldn't be talking about death to the DI. She heard Rick scrape the front door open, then there were hushed voices.

'All right, Rick.'

'All right, Ruan.'

'You just going?'

'Yes, I am.'

'All right.'

'Right.'

The door closed with a creak and Ruan was in the living room. Morwenna shook her hair loose. It was still damp and Ruan said, 'You look like a mermaid.'

She grinned. 'Cuppa? Kettle's just boiled.'

'Don't mind if I do.'

Morwenna took the DI's mug into the kitchen and rinsed it out, stretching to the cupboard for a clean one. 'What can I do for you—' She paused abruptly, kettle in one hand. It had always been their conversation, 'What can I do for you, my luvver?' She couldn't say it now; they weren't lovers any more.

There was silence. Ruan was probably thinking the same thing. Then he said, 'I saw the police car. I wanted to make sure you were all right.'

Morwenna's heart expanded with gratitude. She gave him a mug of tea, a packet of chocolate digestives. 'Get yourself round these.'

They sat on the sagging sofa, one at either end, a gap between them, only the sound of Morwenna sipping tea and Ruan ripping the wrapper from the biscuits. Then he said, 'So, what did he want?'

'Rick?' Morwenna grinned. 'He was pretending that he thinks I killed Alex. Or that Mum did it. Both of us. He said we were too independent and we had colourful clothes.' She laughed. 'He'll make DCI yet.'

Ruan's brows knitted. 'Who do you think did it?'

'I've no idea. I can't get any clues from anyone at the party.' Morwenna finished the tea and put the mug on the floor. 'Rick kept asking me what he should do next. He thinks I'm a sleuth.'

Ruan met her eyes. 'He knows how intelligent you are.'

'Giss on!' Morwenna reached for the biscuits. 'I work in the tearoom and the library.'

'That's not the point.' Ruan made to stretch an arm around the back of the sofa behind Morwenna, then he thought better of it. 'You have more common sense than Rick and his whole team put together.'

'I wish.' Morwenna pressed her hands together. 'Mum's proper upset that they think it's her. As for me, I could do without the attention.'

'I reckon it could be Alex's missus.' Ruan leaned back and crossed one leg over the other. 'She has the most to gain.'

'I went to see her to offer my sympathy.' Morwenna closed her eyes for a moment, remembering. 'She seems hard as nails on the outside, but it's hard to tell if she's putting a brave face on. People always blame the spouse. Alex had another woman; did you know that?'

'I did, yes. Damien down at the boatyard told me he was carrying on with a woman who lives up Pennance Hill. Not that Damien knows her – it's just hearsay.' Ruan's voice was hushed. 'Alex always had some woman or other. It's not right.'

'Exactly.' Morwenna sighed. Ruan had always been faithful: loyalty hadn't been one of their problems. It was strange to think that they lived apart now; he stretched out his legs and pushed a biscuit into his mouth, just as he had when they'd lived together. He chewed thoughtfully.

'They aren't trying to blame Tam?'

'Not yet.'

'First you, then Lamorna.' Ruan was suddenly protective. 'They'd better not try pinning it on Tam.'

'Why would they?'

'It was her party. She's responsible for the tearoom. She was the one who'd lose out most if Alex bought it.'

They were silent for a while, then Morwenna said, 'Rick Tremayne can leave Tam alone.'

'Exactly, Ruan replied. 'We can't have that.'

'At least she's got Jack now.'

'He's a good lad,' Ruan agreed. 'And she needs a hand, looking after that little heller Elowen. She's a handful, what with her imaginary dog...'

'Oggy.' Morwenna grinned.

'I often think to myself, Elowen looks nothing like Tam – nor like us.'

'I expect she's like her dad.'

'Whoever he was,' Ruan said protectively. 'When Tam came back from holiday in the family way, I wanted to get hold of whoever left her in the lurch. I was so angry, I wanted to gut him like a fish.'

'Steady...' Morwenna warned with a smile. 'If DI Tremayne hears you, he'll pull you in for questioning.'

'They know I didn't do it,' Ruan said slowly. 'I was talking to the officer in the cop car when Alex was killed.' He smiled in realisation. 'I must be the only one at the party with a proper alibi. Didn't Alex say anything to you before he... you know...?'

'Wait on.' Morwenna ruffled her damp hair. 'He did say something...'

'What was it?'

She shook her head. 'I don't remember rightly. He was wheezing, bless him, and the world was spinning so fast. He was meeting someone though. I can't remember if he said it was a he or she.'

'It'll come back,' Ruan suggested. He turned to Morwenna, his eyes shining, and she thought how handsome he was.

She took a breath. 'So, everyone at the party is a suspect, right. Except for you, that is. I've talked to a lot of them, but what about people I don't know well? We can't rule out anyone who was on the beach at quarter to eleven.'

'I suppose so.' Ruan was thoughtful. 'Do we have a list of the people who were invited?'

Morwenna smiled. 'I can do better than that.' She reached for her phone, almost knocking over the empty mug. 'I took photos for Jack's mum. I have pictures of just about everyone.'

'Proper job.' Ruan leaned forward as Morwenna pressed buttons. 'So, let's have a look.'

Together they pored over the screen. Ruan's voice was hushed. 'There's Tam dancing with Jack and Elowen. Look, there's Simon Truscott at the bar, watching. Your mum's at the food table. There's Alex, chatting to Damien, and a woman just behind them?'

'Wait, let me make the picture bigger. Ruan, look – look at the breadboard...'

'It's just bread. And someone ripping chunks off. I know him. He comes on the fishing boats. He's called Milan—'

'But why's he ripping chunks off? Because there's no bread knife. Someone must have taken it!'

'To stab Alex?' Ruan's eyes were wide. 'Morwenna, shouldn't we be showing this to the police?'

'Maybe.' She hesitated. 'But would you trust Rick Tremayne with these pictures? After all, it was the tearoom knife.'

'But it's withholding evidence if we don't show him.'

'It might be... but perhaps it's simply a set of photos I took for my future son-in-law's mum?' Morwenna's eyes glowed. 'We should sit on these for a bit, Ruan.'

'Why would we do that?'

'Do you trust Rick to find out who the real killer is?'

'No. He's not the sharpest hook on the boat. And many of the lads think he can be a bit gung-ho.'

'So, we'll keep this between ourselves for now.'

Ruan was staring at her. 'Morwenna, are you trying to find out who did it? Beat Rick at his own game?'

'In one,' Morwenna grinned.

'Then I'm on your side,' Ruan offered gallantly.

Morwenna's mouth moved before she could help it. 'Not too close, I hope.'

She wondered why she'd said it. At the same time that she might possibly want him to come closer, she was pushing him away. It was confusing.

'I'll make us another cuppa.' Morwenna offered quickly.

'All right,' Ruan said and Morwenna fled to the kitchen.

She rattled the kettle, her mind racing. It would be hard discovering who killed Alex Truscott, but fathoming out her true feelings for her handsome ex was completely beyond her.

9

Morwenna was dog-tired on Monday morning. She'd stayed up half the night going through all the photos from the party, enlarging every single one on the screen, searching in dark corners for people she knew, or anyone she didn't: there was a woman in dark clothes watching from the shadows in two of the photos. She looked suspicious and Morwenna was determined to find out who she was.

Her head ached with thinking about each photo, analysing who was standing where, who was looking at someone else and what expression they had. There were several pictures of Alex, talking to so many people with the same confident smile on his face. There was no sign of an argument, except for one photo of him with Pam, who had turned away from him, fiddling with a necklace, looking unhappy. Simon was clutching a beer glass and was alone most of the time. Morwenna focused on the pictures of people by the food table, noticing again that the bread knife appeared in many photos, but in the ones she'd taken later, it was missing. There was no photo of anyone clutching it though, following Alex Truscott. It was frustrating that the pictures held no more clues.

The rain held off as Morwenna cycled to the library, but dark clouds spread like bruises beyond the cliffs. The ocean was brooding and turbulent, the waves crinkled. Today, she was wearing a red duffle coat, a yellow sou'wester against the bad weather, hooped leggings and purple boots. She was still thinking about Pam Truscott at Mirador, the grand house by itself on the cliff top overlooking the bay, wondering how she spent her time now she was all alone. She wondered who Alex's mystery paramour was. Ruan said she lived up Pennance Hill in a group of cottages just outside Seal Bay. That was another hill she'd need to cycle up. She'd leave the visit until after Alex's funeral on Friday – perhaps the secret lover would be there to say her final farewell. Morwenna would keep an eye out for her: she had an idea what she looked like from two of her photos.

She leaned her bicycle against the wall in the library corridor and hurried inside. She was surprised to see Louise in deep conversation at the counter with Donald Stewart, who was peering over metal-rimmed spectacles at a book they were sharing. He looked up and smiled with mild amusement as if she looked like Paddington Bear. She grinned back. 'All right?'

Louise was worried. 'She's been here again over the weekend.'

Morwenna was busy unpegging the duffle coat. 'Who?'

'Lady Elizabeth Pengellen.'

'Oh, our resident ghost.' Morwenna turned to Donald. 'You don't start until lunchtime.'

'The thing is...' Louise began.

'She's left us a clue.' Donald held up a book. 'See this – it was left on the floor this morning.'

'What is it?' Morwenna was puzzled.

'A novel by Christopher Landon.' Louise said, as if the implication was obvious. It wasn't.

'Meaning?'

Donald held up the book. '*Ice Cold in Alex*...'

'I know.' Morwenna moved to join them, staring at the cover. 'It's a novel about driving an ambulance through the desert in war-torn 1942. They made a film of it with John Mills. Ruan and I saw it years ago.' She paused. Louise and Donald's faces shone with a kind of reverence, as if they believed the ghost was real.

'It's a sign from the spirits...' Donald said in a monotone voice.

'How come?' Morwenna still didn't get it.

'Alex. That's Alex Truscott,' Louise explained patiently. 'And he's ice cold because he's...' She lowered her voice. 'Dead.'

'Isn't that a bit tenuous?' Morwenna asked.

Donald shook his head and his little goatee shook too. 'We're going to ask Lady Elizabeth to give us a sign to solve the murder.'

Morwenna stifled a smile. 'Well, you might have more success than DI Tremayne because he's getting nowhere.'

'I know,' Louise agreed. 'He asked me some questions in here the other day, but he wasn't really interested in what I had to say.'

'I can't stand the man,' Donald agreed. 'Boorish, that's what he is. A bungling sort of man.'

'Pressures of the job?' Morwenna suggested, making a mental note of the lack of confidence in the local DI.

'I don't know how Sally puts up with him,' Louise offered. 'Mind you, he probably isn't home much. Steve talks to him in The Smugglers' Arms sometimes and he's always complaining about the late hours he works. "You should drive the fish lorry up north three times a week," my Steve says.'

'So, back to business. I came in early to summon Lady Elizabeth herself,' Donald explained, his eyes round behind the glasses.

'She's not here yet then?' Morwenna looked around.

'She may be listening...' Donald lowered his voice. 'I'll talk with her now.'

'Really?' Morwenna began but Louise held a finger to her lips.

'Shh – Donald can communicate with those who have passed into the next world.'

'Then why doesn't he ask Alex directly?' Morwenna suggested, but Donald had raised his arms in the air and closed his eyes.

'Lady Elizabeth – we are your minions.' Donald intoned.

'I thought they were yellow animated creatures,' Morwenna whispered, but Louise signalled for her to shush again.

'Come to us now, my lady,' Donald continued. 'And give us a sign that you will help us.'

There was silence, then an ominous creak from the far corner. Louise looked suddenly terrified. 'Do you think she's here?'

'Aye, she's here,' Donald whispered. 'Give us a sign, O spirit from the nether world...'

'Nether world?' Morwenna mouthed, trying her hardest not to smile. Louise and Donald were staring at the far corner of the library, at the unmoving line of shelves, the orderly stacked books.

'Just show us that you will help us find the one who killed your friend Alex who is with you now in the unworldly realm.'

Morwenna started to shake her head, but Louise held her breath. There was a sudden loud creak behind them, the library door opening, and Louise almost jumped out of her skin. Donald leapt into the air and picked up the copy of *Ice Cold in Alex* as if he would use it to defend himself. Only Morwenna was calm as she smiled at Simon Truscott.

'Hello, Simon. How can I help? I'm so sorry about your dad.'

Louise suddenly began to stack books vigorously from behind the counter. Donald hadn't moved but his mouth was open.

'I brought my book back,' Simon began. 'Thanks, Morwenna. It's really weird at home without him.'

'It must be,' Morwenna said kindly.

'Mum's behaving like nothing has changed...' Simon shook his head. 'It just happened out of the blue. That policeman came round and promised he'd find out who did it but he hasn't done anything yet. The funeral is on Friday.'

'I know. Everyone in Seal Bay will be there to pay their respects.' Morwenna took the book he was holding out, The *Logic of Gambling*. 'Did you want to return this?'

Simon nodded. 'Yes – it wasn't much help. Have you got anything else on the subject?'

Morwenna thought for a moment. 'How about *So You Think You Can Win at Gambling*?'

'Oh, that sounds good.' Simon's eyes lit up. Morwenna rushed over to a nearby shelf as Simon rummaged in his pocket for his library card. She handed over the book. 'Thanks, Morwenna. I'm hoping it will take my mind off my dad.'

Morwenna thought his eyes looked red and tired; she wondered if he might cry. She offered a gentle smile. 'Pop in if you need anything, Simon. Or come to the tearoom one afternoon for a coffee.'

'I might,' Simon said, his mind elsewhere. 'Tam will be there and she's always good to be around... Well, thanks for the book, Morwenna. Have a nice day.'

'See you,' Morwenna replied as she watched him go. She turned to Louise and Donald. 'Poor lad. It must be tough.'

'It must,' Louise sighed.

'Not at all.' Donald was breathing heavily with excitement. 'Don't you realise what just happened? He's the killer!'

'He's what?' Morwenna wrinkled her nose. 'How did you work that one out?'

'He came in just as I asked Lady Elizabeth for a sign. She sent him in, to show us who the killer was. It's him, it's Simon Truscott.'

'Well, I suppose witches were burned for less,' Morwenna said matter-of-factly.

'Oh, I'm not sure, Donald,' Louise muttered. 'He seems a nice lad. I mean – why would he kill his father?'

'He's the killer, you mark my words,' Donald said, his tone serious.

'I've no idea if he is or if he isn't, poor lamb,' Morwenna replied, thinking about the book Simon had just borrowed and what Pam Truscott had said about her son's gambling debts. She offered a smile. 'Well, we can't stand about here, gassing all day. Anyone for a cup of tea?'

* * *

Later on, Morwenna cycled back to the tearoom. A stiff breeze blew in harshly from the sea, ruffling her hair. As she slowed the bicycle, Jack came down quickly from the ladder that leaned against the outside wall, paintbrush in his hand. 'Well, what do you think of my handiwork?'

'Nice and clean and bright.' Morwenna surveyed the fresh blue and white walls. 'Very good.'

Jack was proud of himself. 'Tam wants me to do the flat next. Elowen wants a yellow bedroom. But I've got some work next week, starting Monday. Pam Truscott asked me to wallpaper her bedroom.'

'Oh?' Morwenna was interested. 'What sort of paper?'

Jack laughed. 'It used to be plain magnolia walls in there but she's picked this really racy design. It's like a repeated pencil print of red puckered lips like you see on teacups, the mark left by lipstick. Funny choice, if you ask me.'

'It is,' Morwenna agreed, wondering why Pam would change her bedroom wallpaper. 'Well, I'm glad you've got work. Oh, by the way, I'll send you these photos of the party.'

'Yes please.' Jack grinned. 'I'll finish up here and then I'll get off to pick up Elowen from school at half past three. Poor Tam's had a hell of a morning.'

'Oh?' Morwenna was concerned.

'That policeman came back and told her he had some more questions. He was very interested in the bread knife and Tam was really worried. He said she'd have to go down to the station after work and talk to him but I helped out serving teas for half an hour so she could pop upstairs to the flat and talk there. She was very shaken when she came down.'

'Was she? I'd better see if I can help. Thanks, Jack.' Morwenna locked her bicycle outside the tearoom and headed inside. It was quiet – an elderly couple were sitting at a table sharing a cream tea and a mother and her toddler were eating sandwiches. From where she stood, Morwenna guessed they were crab paste and mayo.

Tamsin rushed over, her face troubled. 'Mum, it's been awful...'

'Jack said Rick Tremayne has been here...'

Tamsin lowered her voice. 'He kept harping on about the bread knife and why I chose to take it to the party. I explained that it was just to cut the bread with, and he kept on repeating, "Why didn't you cut the bread before you brought it down for the party? Why did you take a lethal weapon on to the beach? Why did you insist on crusty bread – why didn't you just take loaves of plain white sliced?" He was acting like I committed the murder.'

'Oh, for goodness' sake,' Morwenna gasped. 'He'll be interrogating Elowen next.' Morwenna gritted her teeth.

Tamsin was upset. 'Do you think so, Mum?'

'No, I'm just being daft. Tam – go and get a break. I'll hold the fort in here.'

Tamsin sighed. 'It's gone quiet in here now. After the initial burst of interest, no one's bothered about the tearoom now. All the tourists have gone, there's just a few locals and they don't buy much. Maybe Alex was right... maybe I do need to sell.'

Morwenna put a hand on her arm. 'It'll be fine. Go on now – get yourself something to raise your blood sugar, and come and sit. I promise you, it'll sort itself out in time. Pay no mind to that silly tuss Rick Tremayne. He's doing his best.'

Tamsin nodded and moved towards the urn, selecting a mug. Morwenna watched her and for a moment, her heart lurched. Tamsin was her baby girl, even though she was grown up, and at this moment, she seemed vulnerable. Both she and Lamorna had been subject to Rick Tremayne's energetic questioning and it had left them fragile.

Morwenna watched Tamsin sit at the table, shoulders hunched, and she yearned with all her heart to support her daughter. Tamsin had Elowen, a business to run, a new fiancé, and she looked so tired. Morwenna felt her hands clench. She would defend her child; she'd protect all the women in her family. Ruan had been right. She needed to step up and sort it all out. He'd offered to help her, and she'd accept his assistance. He was Tamsin's father, after all.

If Rick Tremayne was looking in all the wrong places for Alex's killer, then she'd better start looking in all the right ones.

10

The crematorium chapel was packed full to bursting on the 22nd; local people who knew Alex Truscott crowded into the building in sombre clothing. The library and the tearoom were closed: almost everyone from Seal Bay who wasn't working was at the funeral. At the front by the coffin, whispering to the vicar at the pulpit, was Pam Truscott, wearing a yellow silk dress and a wide-brimmed hat. Next to her, impeccable in grey, was Simon. Morwenna glanced around; the Grundy sisters were in the second row, their heads together, pointing and whispering. Louise and Steve Piper were in the row behind; Donald Stewart was there, and Damien Woon from the boatyard, who nodded in her direction. Morwenna was glad that Elowen was spending the afternoon with Carole Taylor and Britney; they were going to the pictures to see a Disney film. Carole thought a funeral wasn't the right place for small children and Tamsin agreed.

Rick Tremayne and one of his PCs were seated right at the back, conspicuous in ill-fitting suits. Morwenna recognised most members of the congregation, but two people caught her eye. One was the large man she had photographed at the party, breaking pieces of bread – he was a fisherman called Milan, apparently. She reminded herself to ask Ruan about him. And the woman in a pew directly opposite wearing a black dress and sunglasses looked familiar. Morwenna knew exactly where she'd seen her before; she was elegant, her dark hair tied back. She wore a gold necklace with a diamond pendant exactly the same as Pam Truscott's: it had to be Alex's mistress from Pennance Hill. Morwenna decided she'd keep an eye on her to see how she reacted.

The organ began to play the opening notes and everyone stood to sing 'Dear Lord and Father of Mankind'. Morwenna glanced at Lamorna, Jack and Tamsin to her left, holding up service sheets, and Ruan on her right. He whispered, 'Pam Truscott looks like she's dressed for a wedding.'

'Some people celebrate a life with bright colours,' Morwenna said.

Ruan leaned closer. 'Do you think Alex's killer is here?'

Morwenna shrugged. 'Could be...'

'They reckon a killer often likes to revisit a crime – and they can lord it at events like this to show off. It's called narcissism, it's part of their psychological make up.'

'How do you know that?' Morwenna whispered.

'I watch *Killer in My Village*,' Ruan said with a wink.

'You need to get a life,' Morwenna replied affectionately.

'So did poor Alex...' Ruan's lips were next to Morwenna's cheek. 'We should keep an ear open, especially after the service. You never know what the killer might reveal without intending to.'

Morwenna noticed his mischievous grin, the cute lines around his mouth, and it took her back for a moment to happy days. She whispered, 'TV Crime series have a lot to answer for.' Then she lifted the service sheet and joined in with the singing.

It was only respectful to do so. The woman in the adjacent pew wasn't singing though. She was snuffling silently into a white handkerchief, her head down.

Everyone sat down again and a man Morwenna assumed to be his brother was speaking about Alex, how wonderful he was, how he donated lots of money to charities, how he was a self-made man. Then Pam, standing tall in the yellow silk dress, sashayed to the front of the congregation and read a poem in a tremulous voice. Morwenna had never heard it before – it compared a dying person to a leaf falling from a tree. The chapel was silent as Pam returned to her seat, heels clacking against the stone floor, chin tilted upwards. Then Simon took her place, clutching a book, his hands shaking, and began to read.

'That man is a success who has lived well, laughed often and loved much... loved... much...'

That was as far as he could go before his face crumpled. He lowered his head, shaking where he stood. Pam rushed over to him and enveloped him in her arms. In the opposite pew, the woman in black was sobbing audibly now. Morwenna and Ruan exchanged glances. A cough could be heard from the back row and, even though she didn't turn round to look, Morwenna guessed that it was DI Tremayne.

After the service, everyone walked outside into the fresh air and stood around, talking to anyone they could find just to bring themselves back to a sense of normality. Ruan was chatting to Tamsin and Jack. Lamorna patted Morwenna's arm, 'I'm going straight home. Someone from Tregenna Gardens is giving me a lift. I don't like funerals.'

'All right, Mum.' Morwenna pecked her cheek.

'Come up for your tea on Tuesday. I could use a bit of company.'

'I'll be there.' Morwenna watched her go, then she stared

over the rows of houses down to the sea. It was a calm day, the sky a dishwater grey, the sea creased like tinfoil. She'd walk home; she hadn't brought the bicycle, but it was a pleasant enough day. The wind blew her hair and rearranged it badly. There was a voice at her shoulder. 'You're Morwenna Mutton.'

'I am.' Morwenna turned to see a small woman dressed in black, sunglasses over her eyes. She was the woman from the opposite pew, the mystery woman in the photographs at the party, who was standing in the shadows.

'I'm Beverley Okoro. It was you who found Alex on the beach, wasn't it?'

'It was, yes.

'Alex and I were – friends. I need to know about his last moments...' Beverley hesitated as if wondering what to say, then she exhaled.

'Do you want to go down the pub? We could talk there,' Morwenna suggested.

'I could use a drink. My cottage is in the other direction. I brought my car.'

'Right...'

Beverley gripped her arm. 'Will you come with me? I'd like to talk about Alex. I need some... closure...'

'Of course.' Morwenna was pleased to have the chance to find out more about Beverley.

'My place is on the edge of town... I'm an artist.'

'All right.' Morwenna glanced over her shoulder. Rick Tremayne was watching her, hands in his pockets. She waved to him, offering a mischievous smile.

The journey to Pennance Hill took no more than fifteen minutes, and most of that time was spent negotiating the traffic on the roundabout out of Seal Bay. They paused by a row of little stone houses. Beverley parked the car and led the way into one of the middle ones, along a path flanked with bushes, green foliage sprouting high. The front door boasted leaded lights in the design of a night sky, and a sign said Half Moon Cottage. Beverley pushed the key into the lock and breathed, 'I'm gasping for a drink.'

Inside, there was a strong smell on the air, oil paint and turpentine. The cottage was dark and cramped, furnished with a heavy sofa and a red Persian rug, next to an open fireplace. Morwenna was surprised: she thought artists needed light, but perhaps Beverley's studio was at the back. Beverley strode over to a cabinet and opened a whisky bottle. 'You'll have to get the bus back. I won't be able to drive by the time I've had a few of these.'

'That's fine.' Morwenna gazed around the sitting room at the paintings on the wall. Beverley was certainly prolific. And it was clear that she was Alex's lover – the paintings were mostly of him in the nude, reclining on a bed, lying in a field of daisies, a smile on his face. There was one just of his torso and private parts; she was sure it must be him based on the other pictures. Morwenna imagined him posing, while Beverley lovingly waved her brush. She suppressed a smile and said, 'I'm guessing you did all these.' Her eyes fell on an oil painting of Alex and Beverley together, their backs turned, skin against skin and arms entwined, their bottoms bare.

Beverley took a huge gulp from a heavy glass and Morwenna noticed how her hand shook. There was a delicate tattoo on her arm, a naked angel. She passed another glass to Morwenna and picked up the bottle. Her shoulders slumped, she took off her sunglasses; her eyes were red from crying. 'Alex and I were lovers.'

'I guessed as much.'

'He always said he'd leave her – his wife. It was just a matter of time.' There was bitterness in her tone, anger.

'How long were you together?' Morwenna asked gently.

'Two years, off and on...'

'Off and on?'

'I kept threatening to leave him unless he left his wife, and we'd row, then we'd get back together.' Beverley gulped whisky and sank into the sofa. 'He wasn't fair. Alex was full of promises, but he'd always let me down.' She refilled her glass. Her voice was unsteady, suddenly irritated. 'Why am I telling you this? It's got nothing to do with you.'

'You must be finding everything so difficult,' Morwenna said, noticing how quickly Beverley's mood changed.

'You've no damned idea.' Beverley stood up quickly, her expression clouding. Morwenna took an involuntary step backwards. She wondered if Beverley was capable of violence. She spoke calmly.

'I found Alex on the beach. I'm still traumatised by it.' She perched on the edge of the sofa and touched the glass against her lips, pretending to drink, to be as shaken as Beverley. The whisky was sharp: she wouldn't drink much, she needed her wits about her. 'It was terrible, what happened.' Morwenna said quietly.

'You were there.' Beverley seized her hand and gripped it. 'Tell me what you saw.'

'It was dark, near the water's edge.'

'Did he say anything?'

'Not really.' Morwenna certainly wasn't going to tell Beverley anything. She seemed unstable, erratic.

'Did he mention me?' Beverley was insistent, near to tears now. 'I need to know...'

'It was very quick.' Morwenna glanced around the room; in the corner on a desk there were paints, a palette and several knives. One had a curved blade like a cake slice, the other was a scalpel. Morwenna registered that artists were used to handling knives.

'So he didn't say anything about me? A final message?' Beverley's voice trembled as she poured a second whisky. Her eyes were glazed. 'Did you see anyone nearby? Who do you think did it?'

'I've no idea, honestly,' Morwenna said.

'I know who it was.' Beverley was shaking with anger, the glass gripped in her fist.

'Oh?' Morwenna studied her carefully for clues. 'Who do you think could have attacked him?'

'It's obvious,' Beverley spat. 'His wife Pam. The bitch. She'll get all his money. There will be nothing left for me. You see how I live, in this tiny cottage, and she has the big house on the cliff. Alex loved me. He gave me this necklace.' Beverley tugged at the pendant and her expression changed to one of sadness. 'She has one exactly the same. I bet he bought them together, buy one get one free. Perhaps that's how much he really thought of me. Perhaps he was lying all the time. Perhaps he deserved everything he got.' Then she was trembling. 'No. He loved me, I know he did.'

Beverley's face was streaked with tears. The hand that held the bottle shook as she refilled her glass. It was time to leave. Morwenna spoke gently. 'Can you get some rest, Beverley? It's been a hard day.'

'I hate her so much.' Beverley stared ahead, not listening. 'She has his house, his name, his money. What am I left with? Nothing. No one even knew about us – it was our secret.'

'Is there someone who could sit with you for a while, a neighbour?' Morwenna was already thinking about the journey home. There would be a bus along three times an hour.

'I hope she dies a slow painful death. I hope she kills herself while driving that flash car or that she gets disfigured under a surgeon's knife. She has Botox regularly, you know. And those boobs aren't her own...'

'You're hurting.' Morwenna noted the vicious words as she laid a gentle hand on Beverley's shoulder. 'You've been through a lot today.'

'Pam Truscott needs bringing down a peg or two. I'd like to slap her face hard, wipe that smug expression off.' Beverley's fury became tears again. 'Do you think I'm dreadful, Morwenna? The bitter, twisted mistress who's been left all on her own? Is that what you think?'

'You're grieving,' Morwenna soothed. 'Now if I was you, I'd get a hot bath, drink something calming. Then maybe you can get a friend to come round?'

'Friend?' Beverley nodded, draining her glass. 'Perhaps you're right, yes. Thanks – thanks for coming back with me and talking about Alex. I need to talk, I loved him. We'd have been together one day, if... Despite the fights, we cared about each other.'

'Ah, I understand that,' Morwenna said sympathetically. She was thinking about Ruan. So much silence, then the final argument, like a car crash. 'I'll let myself out. Take care, Beverley.'

'Thank you,' Beverley said weakly and reached for the bottle again. Morwenna put her full glass down on the table and turned towards the door. She wanted to get home, back to her own cottage. Beverley was volatile, passionate, she drank too much. Morwenna had a lot to think about.

11

On Monday morning, Morwenna woke early, dressed in purple leggings and a baggy fisherman's jumper, an old one of Ruan's, poured hot tea in a mug and sat in her living room, a pencil and paper in front of her. She'd already made a list, and she wanted to look at it again. The first name was Pam Truscott. Morwenna recalled the way she'd read the poem at the funeral, not quite in control. She wondered if it was an act or if she was heartbroken. She thought again about her visit to Mirador, the feminine living room that contained no evidence of Alex.

The second suspect on her list was Simon Truscott. Morwenna puzzled over his relationship with his parents. Pam was protective. Alex had wanted to buy the tearoom for him, to set him up in business. Simon seemed a gentle soul. She'd find the opportunity to talk to him again. Morwenna checked the wall clock: it was eight o'clock. She had plenty of time before she needed to leave for work. She thought fleetingly that Ruan would be at sea now. She'd never get out of the habit of timing her day around his fishing trips, hoping he'd get back on time and safely.

Morwenna's thoughts moved to Beverley Okoro. Her erratic behaviour was down to grief, wasn't it? She'd lost the man she loved. Morwenna suddenly wanted to check something, and she grasped her phone, thumbing through the party photos she still hadn't sent to Jack. That was the one: Alex talking to Damien Woon from the boatyard and there, in the shadowy background was Beverley, watching. Morwenna studied her face, the angle of her body. Beverley clearly didn't want to be noticed. She stared at the photo to see if she was carrying a knife, but it was too dark to be sure.

The list of suspects was in front of her, but it was no good without more information. So many questions buzzed in her mind. And there were people she hadn't spoken to yet, Damien Woon and Milan the fisherman. It was time to grab a bite of breakfast and then off to the library. Morwenna wondered if Lizzie the ghost had been busy over the weekend.

As soon as she arrived, Morwenna knew her suspicious were right. Louise was sitting in the seat at the counter, looking extremely perplexed. 'Morwenna...'

'What's happened?' Morwenna rushed over. Louise was staring at the laptop.

'That's very odd.'

'What's odd?'

'I came in this morning and the screen was on. It's set to go off after eight hours.' Louise shook her head. 'Do you think Lady Elizabeth was here?'

'Did she send you an email?' Morwenna joked.

Louise sighed. 'She may be the only one who can tell us for sure who killed poor Alex. The funeral was awful, wasn't it?'

'It was,' Morwenna agreed. 'It seemed awkward, having half the Seal Bay police force in the back row. I wonder if they expected the killer to break down and admit to everything.' She thought for a moment.

'Poor Pam and Simon. And do you know, there are people who think it might be one of them...'

'Lady Liz, for one.'

'Oh, Morwenna.' Louise looked worried. 'It's hard to sleep at night, thinking there's a killer in our midst.'

'Alex might have been killed by a stranger, maybe someone was after his wallet, and then left the area.'

'Steve said someone in the pub told him that Alex wasn't robbed.'

'I'd love to know what's truth and what's rumour. I have a few ideas of my own. But I'm sure Rick Tremayne will arrest someone at some point,' Morwenna soothed.

'Steve reckons he'd arrest anyone just to say he's found the killer,' Louise said. 'He doesn't have much confidence in Rick – no one does. Everyone says he's been wasting time questioning local people and not looking at evidence.'

'The evidence is pretty thin on the ground, in fairness,' Morwenna replied. She was wondering what Rick Tremayne would make of Beverley Okoro and the naked paintings of Alex on the wall. She'd talk the possible killers through with Ruan. It was always good to bounce ideas off someone else. Or if not Ruan, then Tamsin, or Lamorna tomorrow when she was going round for her dinner.

'Shall I make us a cuppa?' Louise suggested and Morwenna nodded just as her phone buzzed. It was Tamsin.

'All right, Tam?'

'Mum, I'm stuck in the tearoom and Jack is up at the Truscotts' house, wallpapering. I don't suppose you could go to school and fetch Elowen?'

'Is she poorly? What's happened?'

Tamsin's voice was small in Morwenna's ear. 'She's been suspended.'

'What? She's only five years old...'

'The teacher wouldn't say much over the phone. I've got to go and bring her home and she'll explain when I get there. I'll have to close the tearoom unless you can sort it out and I've got customers in.'

'Leave it with me, Tam. We're not busy. I'll go and get her.'

'Thanks, Mum, you're a star.'

Morwenna turned to Louise. 'I just have to pop out for a bit – is that okay?'

'Of course. Is everything all right?' Louise was concerned.

'Something's happened at Elowen's school... I have to go.'

'If you're held up, don't worry. It's always quiet on Mondays. Just text me.'

'All right,' Morwenna said thankfully as she rushed through the door and grabbed her cycle.

* * *

Seal Bay Primary was ten minutes from the town centre, up another hill. Morwenna puffed her way to the top, clambering from the bicycle, breathing hard. These hills seemed to become steeper. She paused to stare at the brick-built school beyond the railings and the playground. She'd been a pupil there herself over fifty years ago. The place hadn't changed much, although there was a new building out the back, and a shiny blue and white school sign with a Cornish coat of arms and the motto *One and All.* A smart reception graced the entrance where a secretary sat behind a desk to meet and greet visitors. Morwenna pushed her bike in that direction, leaning it against the wall, wondering what trouble lay ahead. She took a deep breath and went inside.

It was quiet in reception. The woman behind the desk adjusted green-framed glasses. 'Morning, Morwenna. I'll just let someone know you're here.'

'Morning, Daphne. No problem.'

Morwenna waited in reception, gazing at the display of photos on the wall, children doing gymnastics, performing in the Christmas show. There was a sign saying, *You are Unique: YOU Matter* and another, *We Are All Part of One World Community*. Morwenna heard the sound of clacking heels approaching and Ms Parker pushed open the glass doors and swept through, a tall woman in a long skirt and with pale hair. Morwenna nodded a greeting. Elowen was behind her, carrying her school bag, sucking her index finger. She saw Morwenna and smiled. 'Hello, Grandma. Are you taking me home? I've been distended.'

'Suspended,' Ms Parker corrected. 'I'm afraid Elowen hit another child...'

Morwenna held out a hand and Elowen pushed her small fingers into the waiting palm. 'I did – it was Billy Crocker. He said my mum killed Alex Truscott at her engagement party and so I stuck one on him, just like Great Grandma says I should do if someone bullies me.'

'Ah...' Morwenna gave the teacher an apologetic look.

'Elowen will stay away from school for the rest of the day to consider the consequences of her behaviour,' Ms Parker said matter-of-factly.

'The thing is, Grandma, Billy Crocker is a big-mouthed tuss and when he said that about my mummy, everyone else laughed and then he said I was a murderer too. Oggy wanted to bite him – he was in my school bag growling – so I hit Billy because everybody knows a dog bite is worser than a punch on the nose.'

Imelda Parker lowered her voice. 'Then there's this invisible dog thing... it's non-stop...'

'Thanks for your time, Imelda.' Morwenna wondered if she should have used the teacher's first name in school. Then she couldn't help herself. 'I'm assuming Billy Crocker has been suspended too?'

'For getting a punch on the nose?' Ms Parker frowned.

'No, for bullying. I'm sure that's not allowed.'

'Oh...' Ms Parker seemed surprised.

'I suggest you have a word with him,' Morwenna said and tugged at Elowen's hand. 'Come on, my bewty, let's take you to the tearoom.'

'Can Oggy and I have cake?'

'We'll do a bit of reading first,' Morwenna suggested. 'I'll push my bicycle and you can ride on the seat.'

'Oh, that's 'ansom.' Elowen lowered her voice. 'Much better than school.'

Once in the playground, Morwenna held her bicycle while Elowen scrambled onto the saddle. 'Am I in trouble, Grandma?'

Morwenna took a breath. 'You shouldn't have hit Billy Crocker. You'll have to say sorry. Violence doesn't solve problems.'

Elowen's brow puckered beneath the dark hair. 'So why did someone kill Alex Truscott? That's violence.'

'I don't know, Elowen. Sometimes adults do bad things.'

'Mummy didn't kill him though.'

'No.'

'So... who murdereded him with the bread knife?'

'I don't know...'

'Mummy says Grandad and you are going to find out who did the murder before the policeman does because he's a silly tuss.'

'Ah.'

'So are you going to, Grandma?'

'What?'

'Find out who murdereded Alex?'

'Yes, I am,' Morwenna said simply. 'Is Oggy comfortable on the bike?'

'I put him in the basket at the front. He's 'ansom there.'

'Then let's go home, shall we? We can have a drink, read a book and then we can talk about Billy Crocker and why the way of peace and harmony is better than the way of violence...'

12

'Right then, who are your chief suspects?' Lamorna asked cheerily on Tuesday evening, placing a plate piled with a pasty, potatoes, mushy peas and gravy in front of Morwenna, another for herself. 'I reckon it's Pam Truscott. She didn't look as if she was grieving to me in that yellow dress and the big hat at Alex's funeral.'

'Could be, Mum. I'm not sure though. I need to dig a bit deeper.'

'How are you going to do that?'

'I took some photos at the party – I just need to eliminate everyone who doesn't have a beef with Alex. Then I need to ask the right questions.'

'Have you spoken to all the people at the party?'

'A lot of them. I have a couple more to visit. There are some people higher up the list than others.'

'Big job that. I think you might need some assistance.' Lamorna gave Morwenna a crafty look as she shovelled up a forkful of steaming pasty. 'I'm sure Ruan wouldn't mind tagging along.'

'Yes, he's been helpful.' Morwenna noticed her mother's sly smile. 'What's going on in that brain of yours?'

'You looked pretty cosy at the funeral.'

'We were sharing a service sheet.'

'That's not what I meant.'

Morwenna put her knife and fork down. 'What *are* you saying, Mum?'

Lamorna sighed. 'I wasn't a great role model, was I?'

'You're a brilliant role model.' Morwenna gazed at her mother, sitting on the chair opposite with one foot tucked beneath her, wearing a long dress, no shoes, a fancy hairgrip with a flower holding her hair from her eyes.

'No...' Lamorna shook her head. 'After Freddie Quick left when you were little, I played the field a bit.'

Morwenna shrugged. 'You stayed with Bob Allen for five years. Uncle Bobby. I liked him. He taught me to play chords on the guitar.'

Lamorna was thoughtful. 'Yes, I probably should have hung on to him. Or Morrie Edwards. He thought the world of me. He wanted to get married, you know – a Christmas wedding, that's what he set his sights on, just like our Tam's going to have with that shifty emmet she's picked. I nearly said yes too, but...'

'Why didn't you?'

'Freddie broke my heart, with his silky hair and his lovely smile. After him, no other man was the same. You remind me of him every day.'

'I'm sorry.'

'No, no...' Lamorna prodded a mushy pea with her fork. 'But I always think, there was me flitting about, one man after another. Do you remember the actor who had a thing for me, Daniel Kitto, with that lovely husky voice? He's still acting, apparently.

Oh, I had no staying power. Maybe that's what influenced you to leave Ruan.'

'Of course it wasn't...' Morwenna gazed at her plate; her appetite had gone now. 'Ruan and I were good together, then we weren't. Tam was grown up and Ruan was working all hours and I was either in the library or the tearoom or by myself. Then he came home each day and I was still by myself.'

'Is that why you broke up?'

'Not really, we were rumbling along all right over the years. Then one day it just blew up. I said some daft things and he said some daft things, and it was like a volcano exploded in the space between us. We reached a point of no return.'

'How's that? You've never said... not really.'

'I always think of it like a car crash. I told him he didn't make me happy any more and he told me he didn't know how to be any different and I told him it wasn't enough just to carry on as we were. I knew I was saying the wrong things; I could hear myself digging a big hole and he was doing the same. We had a furious argument and he said, "Do you want me to leave?" and I didn't know how to mend things, so I said, "You may as well." He didn't know how to reach out either, so he just said, "All right then, if that's how you feel," and I said, "I do, Ruan." Then he got hold of the little cottage opposite, moved in on a Friday evening and I cried myself to sleep alone in the big bed we'd slept in together for years.'

Lamorna sighed and poked the pasty. 'Can't you ask him to come back?'

'Too much water's passed under the bridge.' Morwenna was surprised at the lump in her throat. 'Things are best left as they are. We get on fine this way.'

'I don't know so much,' Lamorna said. Morwenna didn't know either. There were times when she woke up at night and reached out to touch a cold space in the bed. She wasn't sure what to think. She and Ruan were at an impasse, and she didn't know how to put a wrecked car back together. There were too many dents, too much damage. She'd leave it on the scrap heap where it was – it was the safest place.

Lamorna forced a smile. 'Well, at least our Tam's got herself a bloke.'

'Jack seems very fond of her.'

'He's fitted into Tam's life a bit too quickly. Oh, I don't know what it is...' Lamorna said, digging into the pasty again. 'I'm being harsh, maybe. He's had a hard time of it. He told me his mum had a stroke and she was all by herself, living up country in Greenwich.'

'Gloucestershire, Mum, and she has diabetes.'

'Oh, right.' Lamorna nodded. 'Well, if Tam must marry him, a Christmas wedding will be the proper job. We can have the reception in the tearoom and...' She gave a small laugh. 'As long as it's not on the bleddy beach. We don't want another murder.'

'No,' Morwenna agreed. 'But I'm quite keen to solve this one. It's been bothering me. Just before he passed, Alex muttered something to me about how he'd heard a voice, but he didn't say if it was a man or a woman. My mind was whirling so fast, I can't remember most of it. But I was there. I feel I owe it to him to find out who killed him. Plus...'

'You don't want that silly tuss Rick Tremayne pestering us.'

'He's only doing his job, Mum. It must be difficult, everyone in Seal Bay looking over their shoulder to see if someone's standing behind them in the supermarket queue clutching a bread knife. Alex's death has disturbed everyone. Even Elowen has been a bit more feisty than usual, and I don't want things getting out of hand. I had to have a long talk with her. You know she was suspended from school for hitting Billy Crocker. She'll be back tomorrow – we had a long talk about it.'

'She's a chip off the old block,' Lamorna agreed. 'You were just the same at her age, too much energy, too sure of yourself on the surface, but sensitive and generous to a fault.'

'Nothing's changed.' Morwenna was playing with her food. 'I'm going to have a swim at the weekend, get the cogs in my brain whirring,' she said thoughtfully. 'Then I'm going to work out who stabbed Alex before Rick does, you see if I don't.'

* * *

The wind was bitterly cold the following Sunday as Morwenna stood on the beach in a yellow swimsuit, wrapped in a towel, with a bag containing her clothes, a flask of tea and two bars of chocolate. It was October, just, and the sky hung low, heavy and grey with gloomy clouds. Louise couldn't come: Steve wanted to take her out for lunch because it was his birthday, and the weather seemed to have deterred the Grundy sisters and Donald. She'd go into the ocean alone. She gazed at the water, choppy as broken glass. It was just what she needed, a sudden burst of cold, a rush of energy. There would be a clue somewhere, she knew it.

She was about to run towards the water when she heard someone shouting from the road. A woman clambered from a car and hurtled towards her, wearing a wetsuit, carrying a large bag. Morwenna thought the woman looked familiar: she was young, cheerful, her face shining with optimism. Then it came back to her. She was the PC who'd been with Rick Tremayne when he'd interviewed her after the murder in the early hours of the morning.

The woman smiled. 'Are you going in?'

'I am,' Morwenna said.

'Do you mind if I join you?'

'Not at all.' Morwenna looked at the woman in her brand-new wet suit. 'Are you used to swimming in the sea?'

The woman shook her head. 'It's my first time.'

Morwenna grinned. 'You'll be fine. We'll make the first dip short and sweet.'

The woman held out a hand to shake. 'Jane Choy.'

Morwenna smiled. 'We met at the police station.'

'I was hoping to pick your brains.'

'Only if I can pick yours...' Morwenna began to walk towards the water.

Jane was a step behind her. 'Thing is, we've drawn a blank with our investigations.' She was ankle deep in the cold ocean. 'No fingerprints on the knife that wouldn't have been there already – nothing. No marks of trainers in the sand because the tide came in.' She gasped as an icy wave rushed over her head. Then they were both swimming, buoyed by the surf. She squealed, 'This is freezing! It's like crabs gnawing at my skin. There aren't any crabs here?'

'No, you're fine, Jane. Just try to relax and enjoy the thrill of it all.' Morwenna rolled in the water, floating on her back. 'Ahhh. This is exhilarating. And so, so cold.'

Jane thrashed about, her teeth chattering. 'The thing is...'

'You know no one in my family did it.' Morwenna gasped, a mouth full of water.

'Yes, of course,' Jane agreed. 'And I'm sure DI Tremayne thinks the same thing.' As an afterthought she added, 'Morwenna, I can't tell you anything about our side of the investigation.'

'I know. Off the record, though,' Morwenna said. 'I'm going to find out who killed Alex. And I'll do it before Rick Tremayne does because I'm not sure he will, and I won't have him pestering my family.'

'As long as you don't do anything illegal.' Jane was shivering. 'And this person is dangerous. They've killed once.'

'They won't be a danger once Rick locks them up.' Morwenna dived in deep and then resurfaced. 'I'm just talking to a few people who were at Tam's party. I won't arouse any suspicion.'

'Be careful, though.' Jane pushed her arms into the water, a steady crawl. 'I wanted to ask you about the night you found Alex. You were a bit dazed at the time, and you couldn't remember anything. But something must have come back to you?'

'I'm guessing you want to find out independently of your boss?' Morwenna gave a mischievous grin. 'You could do Rick's job better than he can.'

'Maybe one day,' Jane conceded with a smile.

'And you want my help?'

'Off the record.' Jane was treading water.

'If you've got my back, then I'll help you,' Morwenna bargained. 'You never know when I might need a bit of inside support...'

'All right.'

A huge wave rolled in, splashing over their heads. Morwenna felt a slap of salt in her face that stung her eyes. She was sucked down into the icy depths, and she pushed her arms hard to come up again. Then it came to her, clarity – there she was again, crouched beside Alex Truscott at the water's edge, seeing the knife in his back for the first time, listening to his voice.

Morwenna surfaced, gasping air. 'He said he was meeting someone and they were late...'

'I wonder who?' Jane was trembling now. 'I'm so cold.'

'We've had enough – I'll race you back to shore.' Morwenna

pushed her arms, staying afloat, trying to warm herself, her words tumbling out as she shivered. 'Alex Truscott – it's coming back to me now. Alex had arranged to meet someone at a quarter to ten to talk about money… that's what he said.'

'Male, female?' Jane turned in the water and followed Morwenna who was swimming strongly back to shore.

'He didn't say.' Morwenna breathed deeply. She was trembling now. 'But it was someone he knew.'

They were standing on the beach now, shaking violently, skin mottled. Morwenna threw a towel to Jane. 'Wrap up, quick as you can. I walked down here – I was planning on walking back. But can we jump in your car – go back to my house? I'll make hot chocolate and we'll share everything we know about Alex.'

'Yes, please… that's a great idea. I live alone; I've nothing to rush home for.' Jane nodded exaggeratedly as if her head was loose on her neck. 'Anything to keep warm… I'm freezing – but that was such a blast.'

13

Monday was extraordinarily busy. For some reason – perhaps it was the onset of autumn, the biting wind from the sea and the prospect of darker evenings – many people came to the library to borrow books. Or perhaps some of the residents of Seal Bay had heard the rumour that Morwenna intended to find out who had killed Alex. Certainly, almost every customer asked for her opinion. Apart from Simon Truscott, who was quiet, his head down as he brought back his book on gambling and borrowed a lifestyle book, *How to Live When You Could Be Dead*. Louise commented after he'd left that it was hardly an appropriate title.

Late in the afternoon, after a burst of activity in the tearoom because Tamsin had decided to offer a free roll with each bowl of soup to bring in customers, Morwenna finally had a moment to settle herself down in the corner with a cup of tea. It was almost five o'clock. Tam was checking the daily takings; Jack had collected Elowen from school a while ago and they were sitting at another table. He was helping her with her homework: *Draw your favourite animal and write its name.* Elowen impatiently drew a banana, said 'That's Oggy,' and asked if she could go down to the beach. Jack was patiently helping her copy the four letters but she was much more interested in being outside.

Morwenna was working on her own list as she sipped hot tea. The long chat she'd had with PC Jane Choy yesterday afternoon hadn't left her yet. Neither of them had a prime suspect. Jane thought that Simon had a motive: everyone knew about his gambling. And he could have stolen the knife and slipped away easily for a meeting with his father. Morwenna had studied the photos; anyone at the party could have done the same thing. There were other people who had feasible motives of their own.

'Think outside the box. Think...' Morwenna muttered to herself.

'Refill, Mum?'

'Yes please, Tam.' Morwenna stared again at the name Beverley Okoro. She'd leave her on the list for now. Who else was there at the party? Damien Woon. Morwenna had seen him talking animatedly to Alex Truscott, minutes before he was killed. They could have been arranging to meet to talk about money. Damien owned a boatyard; it had been in his family for a long time. His business seemed profitable: he certainly sold lots of boats. Morwenna wondered if there was some connection with Alex. Morwenna decided that she'd ask Ruan, who was friendly with Damien. She wrote the name Damien Woon on her list and then added, 'visit the boatyard'.

She recalled the Captain Pugwash lookalike standing hungrily by the trestle table ripping pieces of bread apart with his fingers because there was no knife. What did Ruan say his name was? Milan something, a local fisherman. She knew of the family vaguely. Morwenna grasped her phone and flicked back through the photos she still hadn't sent to Jack. Yes, there he was, a tall burly man tearing hunks of crust with his bare hands.

Where was the knife? A thought occurred to her. 'Tam, can I find out what time a photo is taken on my camera?'

'Yes, it's on info – give me a minute. I'm just sorting out the money, then I'll be over.'

Jack called from the other side of the tearoom. 'I'll help. Elowen, run up to the flat and grab your coat and scarf, then we'll go down the beach for a walk.'

'With Oggy,' Elowen yelled as she rushed upstairs. Jack was by Morwenna's side. He took the phone from her fingers.

'Oh, that's all the pictures from our party. That's Milan Buvač, filling his face.' Jack smiled. He pressed a button and handed the phone to Morwenna. 'There you go, hit info, and it tells you the picture was taken on September the ninth at ten thirty-five.'

'Right. Thanks, Jack.'

'No problem.'

'Your mother hasn't seen them yet...'

'Anytime.' Jack grinned good-naturedly, and held out a hand as Elowen rushed downstairs in a warm parka.

'Don't be long, you two.' Tamsin smiled and Jack pecked her cheek.

'We'll be back in half an hour, then we'll cook tea.'

'Oggy wants sausages,' Elowen chirped happily, then the door chimed and she was skipping towards the beach, her hand in Jack's.

'He's so good with her.' Tamsin smiled dreamily. 'More tea, Mum?'

'No, I'll get off back home in a minute.'

'You could stay on?'

'I have things to do.' Morwenna's eyes went back to her list. She added the name Milan Buvač, then she picked up her phone, enlarging the photo in case he had stuffed the knife up his sleeve. But there was no knife in the picture at 10.35 pm – it had been taken already. She was clutching at straws. But there were several leads she could follow, Beverley, Damien, Milan. Simon, Pam. And there might be others...

The door chimed as Susan and Barb Grundy banged into the tearoom. Tamsin looked up from the money she was counting. 'We've just closed. But I've got hot tea if you need some?'

'No, we popped into see Morwenna,' Susan Grundy said, seating herself next to Morwenna at the table.

'We won't keep you,' Barb reassured her, scraping the chair, making herself comfortable.

'We couldn't make the wild sea swimming yesterday,' Susan said. 'It was too bleddy cold.'

'But we heard you were there, swimming with the policewoman.'

'So, Barb and I thought, you're working with the police now to find out who killed poor Alex Truscott, that's what's going on.'

'Are you working with the police?' Barb asked.

'Only everyone in Seal Bay is saying that you're busy finding out who the killer was.'

'Who told you that?' Morwenna was surprised.

Susan tapped the side of her nose with a long finger. 'Ask no questions...'

'But people who come into the pop-up shop like to talk,' Barb added.

'And most people think it was Pam Truscott who stabbed him.' Susan leaned forward eagerly.

'She has most to gain,' Barb agreed. 'Everyone is surprised that Rick Tremayne hasn't arrested her straight off.'

'Although, truth be known, half of Seal Bay wanted to put a knife in Alex Truscott's back.'

'Definitely, Susan. So many people owed him a lot of money, one way or another.'

'Did they?' Morwenna was surprised. Initially, she'd been concerned by the Grundy sisters' desperation to share gossip but it occurred to her that no news slipped by their sharp ears. They'd be useful. 'Who else owed Alex money?'

'Most of the fishermen, for starters. They fall on lean times when the fishing isn't good, and I heard Alex lent them money to get their families through until payday,' Barb explained.

'But they have to pay back with interest,' Susan added. 'Alex was a crafty businessman.'

Morwenna thought for a moment. 'Do you know a fisherman called Milan Buvač?'

'Oh, yes, a big chap, nice wife, six kiddies, teenagers mostly and a little one, I think,' Susan chimed.

'A lot of mouths to feed,' Barb nodded.

'They live on Lister Hill, not far from where your mother lives in Tregenna Gardens, don't they, Barb?'

'Number forty-two.' Barb folded her arms. 'A lot of the fishermen live up there. She keeps it very clean, Rosie Buvač. There isn't much money in the house.'

'That might explain why he was so hungry, eating all the bread.' Morwenna looked at the name on her list, Milan Buvač, and wrote 42 Lister Hill next to it.

Two faces were staring at her when she looked up, eyes narrowed. Barb said, 'Is he a suspect?'

Morwenna laughed. 'Not at all. But...' She leaned forward. 'Can you do me a favour? I need an ally – two, in fact.'

'Anything,' Susan agreed, her expression serious. 'Is it to do with the murder?'

'It is.' Morwenna lowered her voice. 'Now you've got to keep things very quiet. Don't breathe a word.'

'We won't,' Barb promised.

'I want you to keep your ears close to the ground. I'll call into the pop-up knitting shop to buy something for Elowen, and you can tell me everything you hear.' Morwenna's tone was thick with conspiracy. 'Anything that sounds suspicious or anything you think that might help me find out who killed Alex – just let me know.'

'We will,' Susan said.

'I still think it was Pam Truscott,' Barb added.

'We need to keep open minds – and say nothing to anyone, right? This is between us three.' Morwenna whispered.

'Ah, right, I got it. Like we are your assistants.' Susan agreed.

'Miss Marple and that woman Jessica in *Murder She Wrote.*' Barb smiled.

'Exactly.' Morwenna smiled. 'You'll do that?'

'Of course we'll do it, won't we, Barb?'

'And not a sound will pass our lips, although our eyes will be peeled.'

'Thank you both,' Morwenna purred. 'I feel so much better knowing you'll share all your wisdom.'

'We will,' Susan said as she and Barb clambered out of their seats, their arms linked.

'Our lips are sealed,' Barb added with a wink and the door clanged shut behind them.

Tamsin burst out laughing. 'Mum, what are you like?'

'They'll be really useful. I've got at least five suspects.' Morwenna said simply. 'But I can't help but think I'm missing someone important. Who knows? I'll check a few more people out over the next few days.' She sighed. 'Someone silenced Alex, and I'm going to find out who.'

'Be careful though,' Tamsin said anxiously. 'You know what it's like in Seal Bay. Tongues wag, people talk. And if Rick Tremayne finds out you're doing a better job than he is, he won't be at all pleased.'

14

Morwenna was asleep beneath the warmth of the duvet. It was almost five, the room full of shadows, when something woke her with a start. She sat up straight in bed. There was silence now, but a single muffled sound had come from the hall. She wondered if there was a burglar in the house. She listened hard, her body tense. Nothing but swirling shadows. Holding her breath, she padded downstairs, standing in the grainy blackness of the living room, afraid to exhale. Her heart thumped. She switched on the light and the room was immediately familiar, everything where she had left it the night before, her phone, a fluffy blanket she'd wrapped around herself, the list on the table, the pencil. She walked silently to the hall and turned on the light. The door was bolted. On the welcome rug lay a piece of paper, folded in half. She picked it up and read the scrawled letters.

BACK OFF MORWENNA OR YOULL GET THE SAME AS ALEX TRUSCOTT THIS IS A WARNING

Morwenna caught her breath and tried to work out the clues. Capital letters. No punctuation. She thought about the language: 'back off...', '...you'll get the same...' Who would speak like that? She unlocked the door, top bolt and key, standing in the doorway in pyjamas. The wind buffeted her face. A figure moved on quiet feet in the darkness across the road and Morwenna inadvertently stepped backwards.

A voice called, 'Morwenna? Everything all right?'

'Ruan?' He stepped beneath a streetlight and she took in the oilskins, the woollen hat pulled down over his hair. She'd forgotten how sexy he looked in fishing garb.

'I'm on my way to the boat. Are you all right? What are you doing out this early?' He examined her expression and was suddenly anxious. 'What's happened?'

'I got this.' She handed the note to him and watched his face as he frowned.

'Who's it from?'

'I've no idea. It was just pushed through the letter box.'

'Didn't you see anyone?'

'No.'

Ruan was puzzled. 'Why would someone send you this?'

'More anonymous than sending a text?' Morwenna forced a smile. 'Maybe I'm getting closer to who killed Alex. The writer doesn't sound like a fan.'

'It's just scrawl. All capitals. No punctuation.'

'Someone's not happy with me.'

'Can I come in?' Ruan asked.

'I don't want you to be late.'

'I won't be. I just want to make sure everything's all right. The door was locked, I suppose?'

'Yes.'

'Windows all closed?'

'I think so.'

She walked back into the house and Ruan followed her. She stood in the living room as he checked the catches on the windows behind closed curtains, and again in the kitchen.

'All look fine.' He scratched his head thoughtfully. 'I wonder who posted that note?'

'Did you see anyone outside?'

'Not a soul,' Ruan said. 'Someone could have pushed it through the letter box and run off down the hill. Or they could have driven away, but I didn't hear an engine. I'll put the kettle on.'

'I'll do it,' Morwenna offered. 'Do you have time?'

'A quick one.' Ruan met her eyes.

Morwenna glanced away awkwardly. 'Thanks for coming over.'

'I wanted to.' Ruan stopped himself. 'I mean, I'm glad you're all right.'

Morwenna poured hot water from the kettle into a teapot. 'I feel a bit shaky. Someone's angry with me enough to threaten me.'

'Everyone knows you'll find the killer. Even Damien asked me about it in The Smugglers' Arms the other night.'

'Did he? What did he say?'

'That you should keep your nose out.' Ruan admitted. 'He thinks it's dangerous. He's not wrong.'

'Is that what he said?' 'Morwenna carried two mugs through, sitting beside Ruan on the squashy sofa. She indicated the list on the table. 'Go on, read the names.'

Ruan picked it up and perused the contents. 'So, Damien's on your list...'

'He was talking to Alex at the party moments before he died, and I wondered if they did business together?'

'I think he sold Alex a boat once,' Ruan said. 'He's a good bloke. It's worth popping round to the boatyard for a chat.'

'What's he like? I don't know him well, just enough to say hello.'

'He's a decent sort, a bit abrupt around women, especially since his marriage went sour.' Ruan glanced at his hands.

'And Milan Buvač. Do you know him? Is it true that Alex used to lend fishermen money?'

'I just know Milan from fishing. You might ask him if he saw anything that night,' Ruan agreed. 'He's a gentle giant though – I'd be surprised if he's the murderer.'

'There must be someone I haven't thought of yet.'

'Well, it might just be Simon.' Ruan tugged his phone from his pocket and pressed a button, handing it to Morwenna. 'I just got this text from one of the lads, before I left the house.'

Morwenna read it aloud. '"Have you heard they arrested Simon Truscott last night for the murder of his old man. Rick Tremayne has found evidence."' She frowned. 'Really? So, if Simon killed his father and was arrested last night, then who sent me the note minutes ago?'

'You have a point...'

'Unless Simon is working with someone else?' Morwenna suggested.

'Simon doesn't seem the type, although appearances can be deceptive.' Ruan met her eyes. 'But if he's not the killer, someone's out there, threatening you. You should take the note to Rick Tremayne. Perhaps you'll find out more about Simon at the same time.'

'I don't trust Rick with it – he'll tell me off for interfering. I know just the person to share it with.'

He finished the mug of tea. Morwenna wondered how he

could drink it so quickly; it was scalding hot. He stood up quickly. 'I'd better get off.'

'Right.' Morwenna shot to her feet and their bodies were inches apart. She didn't move. For a moment she was transfixed. 'Thanks.'

'I wondered,' Ruan began and Morwenna's eyes were locked to his. 'Will you come round to mine later? For dinner?'

Morwenna flopped back into the squishiness of the sofa. 'Why?' She thought immediately it was the wrong thing to say.

'I want to make sure you're all right.' Ruan took a step backwards. 'I want to hear about how your investigation is going.'

'Oh.'

'And…' Ruan turned to go. 'I'd like to make you dinner.'

'All right.' The words were out before Morwenna could stop them. 'This evening then.'

'Good. I'll see you about seven.' Ruan had already disappeared into the hallway. 'I'll let myself out. Lock the door behind me, Morwenna.'

'I will,' she called after him. 'Then I'll go back upstairs and try to have another hour's sleep.' She heard the front door click.

Morwenna sat where she was, knowing she should bolt the front door, push the threatening note in her bag, finish her tea, go upstairs and lie down for an hour before her day started properly. But she couldn't move, not yet. She was wondering about having dinner with Ruan, and whether it was a date, and how she felt about it. She was formulating some interesting thoughts about Alex's killer, and where she'd go next. But when it came to Ruan nowadays, she hadn't a clue.

* * *

After her shift at the library, Morwenna cycled up the steep hill to the police station. She'd texted Jane Choy earlier, asking if she could make time for a brief meeting and Jane had said she'd pop out in her lunch break at 12.45 pm. Morwenna was on her way, cycling past the pop-up shop. Susan and Barb Grundy were knitting at the window, watching the world go by, looking for clues. They greeted her with a complicit thumbs up and Morwenna waved back. She was glad they were on her side. Jane Choy was a useful ally too. She wondered what the PC would say when she showed her the threatening note. She slowed down opposite the police station and waited on the other side of the road, outside Autumn Wind, the residential home set behind tall gates. She could smell McDonald's just down the road, the aroma of burger and cooking fat heavy on the air. She didn't feel at all hungry, but it reminded her that she'd need to be quick. The lunchtime rush at the tearoom would have started already, and today's soup was leek and potato.

Jane appeared furtively through a side door and waved a hand, indicating that Morwenna should stay where she was. Jane crossed the road, shoulders hunched against the cold breeze, weaving through traffic.

'Morwenna. Sorry I'm a bit late. It was hard to get out – I usually have a sandwich at my desk. Shall we talk here?' Jane said hurriedly, pointing to the large open gates of Autumn Wind. They slipped inside, taking refuge behind a tall oak tree. 'What was it you wanted? I haven't got long. The DI has Simon Truscott in the nick, and it's hard going. We've been at it all morning, going back and forth about Tamsin's party and the bread knife and why he'd want Alex Truscott dead.'

'Do you think it's Simon?' Morwenna asked.

'Rick thinks so. We took his phone to look at what he'd been doing, and he'd sent Alex some angry messages.'

'He gambles a lot.' Morwenna shook her head. 'That doesn't mean he killed his dad.'

'Rick believes it's as good as a confession. Simon's in tears in there. The poor kid says things weren't going well between him and his dad – he'd been drinking and arguing with his father over his money problems, and he sent Alex some rash threats in a moment of madness. Rick's like a cat with a mouse though. I feel sorry for Simon.'

'It mightn't have been him.' Morwenna rummaged in her bag for the note. 'Look. This was pushed through my letter box at five o'clock this morning.'

Jane opened the note. The strong breeze almost took it from her hands. Then she said, 'If the murderer posted this to you this morning, then it wasn't Simon. We brought him in late yesterday. He's been in the cells overnight.'

'Exactly what I thought,' Morwenna agreed. 'Unless he got someone else to deliver it.'

'It's possible,' Jane said. 'He's a vulnerable young man.'

'Do you think someone has a hold over him?'

Jane sighed. 'Rick can't charge Simon – there's no real evidence against him apart from a few ill-advised texts to his parents.' She clutched the note in her fingers. 'Can I hang on to this?'

Morwenna prised it away. 'It's probably best that we don't let Rick know we're talking to each other. And it's only a matter of time until he lets Simon go.'

'You're right,' Jane conceded. 'Okay, I'll get back to my desk. Give me a couple of minutes to cross the road, then ride away. If Rick thinks we're sharing information, he won't be pleased.'

'I agree.' Morwenna nodded.

'He already thinks I have far too much to say for myself. He told me that this morning after I suggested that Simon wasn't a suspect simply because he'd called his father a fascist bastard who deserves to rot in hell.' Jane grinned; she'd said enough. 'Stay in touch.'

'I will.' Morwenna watched her rush away, dodging between two fast cars, disappearing into the side door that led to the police station. She glanced at the time on her phone – she was running late. A visit to Damien Woon at the boatyard might reveal some evidence, but she'd need a motive first. She wondered how she could approach Milan Buvač – she could visit his wife, perhaps. There were so many more questions buzzing in her head, and she was certain that she'd pick up some important clues from the people on her list.

15

It was a busy afternoon at the Proper Ansom Tearoom. Customers came and went in a steady stream until four o'clock. Morwenna was too busy to stop and chat with Tamsin but she instinctively felt that her daughter had something on her mind. Then Jack arrived home with Elowen and they sat quietly, reading, talking in whispers. Morwenna served the few customers who'd come in for tea and cake and Tamsin slipped into the kitchen at the back and busied herself making soup for the following day. Morwenna followed her as the time drew closer to five o'clock, cleaning surfaces and placing dirty plates in the dishwasher. What she really wanted was a chat. She offered a warm smile.

'I hope Elowen's doing better at school now?'

'Mmm.' Tamsin hovered over the cooking range. 'I think she's settled down since she punched Billy Crocker. She's a bright kid.'

'She is.'

'The invisible dog is worrying me though, Mum. I thought she'd keep it up for a day or two and then she'd forget it. But it's Oggy this and Oggy that. Do you think I should get her a dog? Is she lonely? Jack thinks if we had a baby it might help. He's desperate for us to get married.'

'There's no rush for either – there'll be time to talk about babies after the wedding.' Morwenna gave her daughter a searching look. 'Is that what you want?'

'Sometimes I think another child might be good for Elowen but...'

'But?

'I have my hands full with the tearoom. Jack's job up at Mirador is almost finished and he's got no more work lined up. He doesn't sleep well. We're not making enough money. Jack suggested retraining as a chef; he thinks we could turn the tearoom into a restaurant, but that's all pie in the sky.'

'We'll pull through, we always do.' Morwenna smiled. 'Just don't rush into anything.'

'Well... we were talking. We're not sure we can afford to keep you on.'

'Oh? I see. But – let's not worry now – it's a family problem. We'll work something out.' Morwenna hadn't seen that coming. 'Maybe more painting and decorating work will come Jack's way.'

'I hope so. He's very good. He made a lovely job of the flat and Elowen's room.'

'He did.' Morwenna looked at her hands, submerged beneath suds. 'Are you really worried about the tearoom, Tam?'

Tamsin grunted. 'Maybe if Jack gets work, we'll be all right for a bit. But most people in Seal Bay do their own DIY. I'm thinking I might do a big Hallowe'en push soon for the kids, half term and a few spider cakes and spiced pumpkin milkshakes.'

Morwenna moved towards her daughter, opening her arms for a hug. 'Something will turn up.'

'I wish I'd sold the place to Alex now. Jack and I could have started again. Besides...' Tamsin turned from the range and her eyes glistened. 'Our wedding's supposed to be in December... How are we going to pay for that?'

'Your dad and I will help out.'

'Thanks, Mum.' Tamsin fell into the hug and Morwenna could smell the sweetness of shampoo in her hair.

'Hang in there, Tam.'

Tamsin glanced up at the clock. 'It's time you went home. It's half past five. I can't afford to pay you, let alone give you overtime.' She gave a brave laugh, but Morwenna could see the anxiety etched in her face.

'Right, I'm off, things to do.' Morwenna kissed Tamsin's cheek. 'Have some downtime tonight with that gorgeous little girl.'

'I will. Jack's cooking us spag bol.'

'I'll see you tomorrow then,' Morwenna said soothingly 'And try not to worry. We get through these things as a family. We always do.'

Tamsin nodded, but her eyes were filled with sadness. 'Right. See you tomorrow.'

* * *

Morwenna rode her bicycle up the hill to Mirador; despite the biting wind, she felt warm inside the red duffle coat, standing hard on the pedals as she pushed her way up the slope. The sun was dipping behind the cliffs, the ocean turning a burned orange merging with bruised purple clouds. It would be dark when Morwenna returned to Harbour Cottages; she was glad she had a good bicycle lamp and reflectors. A streetlamp flicked on outside Mirador and the windows glowed yellow behind closed curtains. Someone was at home.

Morwenna braked, placing one foot on the kerb as she heard

the front door click. She heaved her bicycle closer to the privet hedge, listening to a car door slam and an engine roar. Then the Range Rover edged towards the road with Pam driving, and pulled out. As Pam turned to descend the hill towards town, Morwenna followed at a distance. She had no idea why she was following Pam Truscott – she was probably only going to the supermarket, but Morwenna could pop in for teabags and initiate a chat if need be. It was a chance, and she'd take it.

The Range Rover signalled right; Pam wasn't going into town; she was making for the harbour. Morwenna followed as she drove slowly down a narrow, twisting road, grateful that there were no hills to climb, past a few straggling fishermen's cottages and watched as the Range Rover accelerated through the gates of a boatyard. The sign said:

D. WOON, BOATS.

'Interesting,' Morwenna muttered to herself. 'What's she doing here?' She wheeled her bicycle through the tall gates, leaving it against one of the sheds as she sidled along the path towards another group of outbuildings. In the distance, little sailing boats bobbed. Morwenna could see the light reflecting on the water, a wriggling yellow sheen like shot gold. There were huge buildings to the right; Damien Woon's boat sheds where he repaired and rebuilt all sorts of craft. The smell of diesel fuel from the boats hung lightly on the air. Morwenna sidled towards the end of a building and listened. Pam clambered from the Range Rover and she was met by a tall, broad-shouldered man with a dark beard. He gave a short laugh, his voice a resonant burr.

'I wasn't expecting to see you. I was just going down The Smugglers.'

'I wanted to catch you, Damien. It's about what we discussed on the phone.'

'I said I'd do the job.' His voice was low.

'The thing is, I need it done quickly. There can't be any reminder of how it was before Alex died. I want to move forward.'

'I can see why you'd want that,' Damien Woon said. 'Shall we go and have a look at her?'

'That would be lovely.'

Morwenna watched Damien and Pam stroll towards the boats but she could no longer hear what they were saying. She gazed around. If she was agile, she could skirt around the side of the boatyard and clamber on one of the nearby decks. She'd hear better from there. Her boots scrunching against gravel, Morwenna tiptoed carefully across the yard, moving like the Pink Panther. She stopped and held her breath as Pam's voice lifted on the air.

'I want a complete change. I need her to be fresh, brighter.'

Morwenna wriggled onto a nearby boat and moved carefully around to the other side as it rocked in the water. She clung to the mast and slithered down to a crouching position. Pam and Damien were close enough now for her to hear every word. They were looking at an old sailing boat. Morwenna hoped the darkening sky and the looming shadows would conceal her.

Damien spoke in his warm burr. 'So let me get this straight. You want to get rid of all traces of the past, right?'

Morwenna leaned forward, holding her breath.

'I do. It wasn't as if Alex liked the boat – he just chose the design. I want to make it my own now.'

'In which case I'll repaint it completely, upgrade the deck, new sails, the whole package.'

'I want *The Pammy* ready for spring so I can get out on her.'

'I understand. It can be hard to move on. I was at the party when Alex was killed. It was tragic.'

Morwenna heard Pam sigh. 'I used to joke with him that it was only a matter of time until someone gave him his comeuppance.' Her voice seemed to falter. 'And we'd had the almightiest row before we went to the party. About Simon. About his gambling.'

'Simon didn't get on with his father?'

'Oh, Simon's a little bit obsessive.' Pam's voice became even lower. 'I have my own opinions about what happened though...'

'Really? And what are those?' Damien moved closer to Pam. Morwenna needed to hear what they were saying. She stuck out a leg, straddling the gap to the next sailing boat. It rocked a little and she stayed where she was, holding her breath, leaning towards the murmuring couple. She found it hard to hear them clearly, then Damien said, 'Have you spoken to the police about it, Pam?'

'Rick Tremayne's been round. He just sat in my living room drinking tea, talking about how he knew everyone in Seal Bay. He didn't believe Alex had a mistress because I couldn't tell him her name. She sent me a letter, you know, anonymously.'

'I heard something about Alex having an affair. The fishermen talk in The Smugglers sometimes. Why would she write to you?'

'She wanted me to know that she loved Alex more than I did. That he intended to leave me. She wrote that now he was dead she's got nothing to remind her of him. To be honest, it felt like she was making demands.'

Morwenna edged closer, leaning as far to the right as possible. The boat teetered beneath her and then she was balanced again.

'So do you know who she is?'

'She didn't sign her name. But I won't let her threaten me. She was at the Muttons' beach party, you know. I could tell by the way Alex was behaving. He kept looking around. I saw him smile at someone when we were by the food table. It was a woman – I saw her watching us. So I walked off and left him to it. I went to talk to Simon.'

'So, do you believe this woman killed Alex?'

'Why not? Do you think I should tell the police – show them the letter?'

'It might be best to leave things as they are... sleeping dogs...'

Morwenna leaned further right and tried to adjust her balance. Her foot slipped on the glassy surface of the boat and she toppled, falling into the water with a yell. The heavy duffle coat dragged her down, and she pushed her arms and legs with all her might. The bows of the boats loomed above her, shifting shadows. Morwenna lunged towards them, then her head was above the water and she was gasping and spluttering. She grasped a rope and clung to it, heaving herself upright, blinking water from her eyes. The brightness of a torch blinded her and she heard a quiet growl. 'Who's this then?'

Morwenna looked up into the face of a bearded burly man, a woman in a heavy coat glancing over his shoulder. Damien Woon reached out a strong hand. 'Come on, let's get you out of there.'

Morwenna saw the tattoo on his forearm, an inky shape. She let him tug her upwards, clambering out with some difficulty, and stood on hard concrete, shivering and dripping. She put a hand to her face and felt something slimy.

Damien recognised her. 'It's Ruan Pascoe's maid, Morwenna Mutton.'

Morwenna hunched beneath the heaviness of the wet duffle

coat, the water squelching in her boots. She offered a smile. 'The thing is, Damien, I was thinking about getting a boat...'

'You're in the right place.' Damien seemed perplexed, but Pam was glaring. Morwenna offered her an angelic smile.

'Yes, I was just having a look at a couple, when I fell in. Lovely boats...'

'What do you want, Morwenna?' Pam snapped.

'Oh, it's too late now to be discussing business; I can see you're busy and I have things to do, so I'll get off. Maybe we can talk boats another time, Damien, when you haven't got customers? Nice to see you, Pam.' Morwenna turned on her heel and squelched away.

16

Morwenna stood at the sea green door of number nine, her silver hair shining, wearing a long tube dress that was at least twenty years old. He wouldn't recognise it. Ruan would remember what day it was when he'd caught a sixteen-pound bass and which direction the wind had been blowing, but he'd never remember from one day to another what Morwenna was wearing. He inhaled sharply. 'You look...' She watched him select the word, dispensing with 'beautiful' and 'gorgeous.' It was the wrong vocabulary for their relationship now. Instead, he said, '... nice.'

'Thanks.' Morwenna thought Ruan looked very nice too in a black T-shirt and skinny jeans. She thrust a bottle of Merlot into his hands and followed him inside. It was impressive, the way he'd done up number nine, the kitchen and living room now open plan, a soft sofa, a bookshelf, a woodburning fire. It was brighter and more modern than number four with all its clutter and haphazard décor. She noticed photos on the far wall, one of Ruan holding a huge fish, several more with Tamsin and Morwenna over the last thirty years, one of the two of them together during a holiday on the beach, their arms around each other. The picture always brought a lump to her throat; she swallowed it and forced a smile.

'Something smells good.'

He was pleased. 'I've made bao buns.'

Morwenna had no idea what they were. 'Do you mean lardy cakes?'

'No, steamed dumplings filled with all sorts of things – you eat them with sauces and pickles.'

'Oh, all right.' Morwenna was secretly impressed. Ruan had pushed the boat out. He stood behind her chair and she sat down, then he presented her with a plate of fluffy semicircles of dough stuffed with different fillings. There were little bowls of pickles, dipping sauce, cabbage, avocado. She ignored the chopsticks by her plate, lifting a small dumpling between two fingers, nibbling it carefully. 'What's this? Tofu?'

'It is.'

'Since when have you eaten tofu?'

'It's good for you.'

Morwenna grinned. 'It's delicious. What have you done to it?'

'I baked it in breadcrumbs.' Ruan filled her glass.

Morwenna stared at him. 'All you used to cook me was fish fingers.'

Ruan said, 'I was worried about you after what happened this morning. I wanted to make sure you were all right. And I didn't think fish fingers were the right choice for tonight.'

'Oh?' Morwenna met his eyes. 'Why not?'

'You're a sleuth now. I thought I'd cook you something sophisticated to go with your new job.'

Morwenna sighed. 'I might need a real new job soon. Tam's struggling in the tearoom.'

'I know. I had a drink with Jack the other night in The Smugglers' Arms. He thinks they are in for a tough winter. He said life is even harder in Seal Bay than it is in Guildford where he grew up.'

'Gloucestershire,' Morwenna corrected him. 'We'll make sure they are all right somehow. And they have the wedding coming up.'

'Jack's worried about that too. Tam's trying to put it off until next year and he's desperate to marry her.'

Morwenna reached for another bao bun. 'What's this one?'

'Shiitake mushroom,' Ruan said with a smile.

'It's yummy.' Morwenna sipped her wine. 'I could get used to this.' She realised what she'd said. 'I mean, I need warm food after what happened to me after work. I went to Woon's Boatyard and Pam Truscott was there talking to Damien.'

'I know.' Ruan said kindly. 'Damien texted me and said you fell in. I was a bit worried but when you came to the door, I knew you were all right.'

Morwenna laughed. Ruan and his friends were in constant communication: there was very little he didn't know. 'The water was like an ice bath and I had my duffle coat on. It was soaked. I think it's past recovery.'

'As long as you're not hurt.'

'I'm fine.' Morwenna found it hard to drag her gaze away. Ruan's eyes glimmered, a soft light not unlike love, and she was transfixed for a moment. Faced with the fatal combination of tenderness and her ex, Morwenna changed the subject.

'Pam was talking about Beverley Okoro. She doesn't know her name though. Apparently, Beverley sent her an anonymous letter saying that Alex was going to leave her.' She was thoughtful for a moment. 'So, could Beverley have done it? What would her motive have been? She loved Alex – it was Pam she hated.'

'I suppose she could've had an argument with Alex. She was

on her own at the party, so she had the opportunity.' Ruan was thoughtful. 'Who do you think it was?'

'Whoever put the note through my letter box this morning wanted to make a point. And they don't want me to know who they are. So, it must be someone I know.' Morwenna reached for another bao bun and dipped it in sweet sauce. 'Could it be Pam? She was talking about getting her boat repainted, whatever the expense which seems an odd priority for a grieving widow. I don't think her heart is broken.'

'Damien said the same to me: she has all Alex's money and now she's getting the boat ready for some solo sailing.'

'Do you think she's got a lover? When I was round her house, I heard her on the phone to someone. Did she want Alex out of the way?'

Ruan shook his head. 'Who knows?'

Morwenna offered a secret smile. 'I'm working through the suspects, and I need to have a chat with your two pals.'

'Let's forget the murder, just for tonight.' Ruan held up the wine bottle and Morwenna nodded. She was feeling relaxed, mellow. Another glass wouldn't hurt. She was enjoying the evening and at the moment, after drinking one large glass, she was quite happy for the evening to unravel however it would. She would go with the flow, unravel with it. She noticed Ruan's eyes on her, and she asked, 'What are you thinking?'

'I'm not sure I should say.'

'Why not?'

'We're having such a nice time. I don't want to spoil it.'

'You won't.' She leaned her chin on her hand. 'Go on... what's on your mind?'

'I'm enjoying being with you.'

'Me too.'

'It just seems sad that we... lost each other.'

Morwenna's eyes closed dreamily. 'Mmm.'

'We were good together.'

'Before the car crash.' She forced herself upright. 'I mean, before the arguments. Perhaps that's why we get on so well, because we live apart.'

'I don't know so much,' Ruan said. 'I'm not sure there would ever be anyone else for me...'

'We have Tam,'

'We have more than that.'

Morwenna was tugged into the deep gaze again and she felt herself weaken. She thought about reaching across the table, putting her smaller hand into his large one, feeling the roughness of his palm. His fingers were inches away. She sighed. 'This is lovely.'

'It is.'

'I haven't enjoyed myself so much in a long time.'

Ruan took her hand between his. Morwenna could feel the heat. His voice was the whisper of a new flame. 'Morwenna...'

She felt herself slipping into the invisible blanket that was enveloping them. She closed her eyes and waited for the meeting of their lips.

A sudden noise split the silence. Someone was rapping at the front door. Ruan was on his feet when Morwenna opened her eyes. 'I'll get it.'

He came back in seconds later, his face closed, as Rick Tremayne followed him into the room, a burly shape in a greasy jacket that had once been expensive, and an off-white shirt. Rick stared at Morwenna, his brows low. 'You weren't at number four. I came here to ask Ruan if he'd seen you.'

'We're having dinner,' Ruan said, making it clear that Rick Tremayne was interrupting.

'I need talk to you, Morwenna.'

Morwenna smiled sweetly. 'I'm fine, Rick. Thanks for your concern.'

'DI Tremayne,' Rick corrected her. 'I'm here on a formal matter. I've just been talking to Mrs Truscott.'

'Oh? Is she all right?' Morwenna asked innocently.

'I went round to update her on current proceedings and we had a very interesting conversation. Apparently, you went to Woon's boatyard. She seemed to think you were spying on her before you fell in the water.'

'Is that what she said?' Morwenna gave a high laugh. 'I went to have a look at a boat.'

'And why might you do that?' Rick grunted.

'Our daughter is getting married,' Ruan said quickly. 'We were thinking about hiring one for the ceremony.'

'Ah,' Rick stammered.

'Damien will bear that out. He and I spoke earlier this evening.' Ruan placed a protective arm on the back of Morwenna's chair. 'Was there anything else, Rick?'

DI Tremayne wasn't sure what to say for a moment. He folded his arms. 'Morwenna, you have to leave solving Alex Truscott's murder to me. Stay away from trouble, do you hear?'

Morwenna smiled. 'It was a boat, Rick. I was trying it out for size. It was dark – I fell in the water.'

Rick muttered to himself and shambled towards the door. Ruan followed him and she heard him say, 'Give my best to Sally and the boys,' then she heard the door close with a clunk.

She was suddenly tired. The memory of falling in the chilly water had set her shivering. Morwenna stood up as Ruan came back into the room.

'Ruan – if you don't mind, I think I should go. I'm a bit tired after my unplanned swim.'

He understood. 'I'll walk you to your door.'

'No, it's fine.' Morwenna was sure if he came to number four with her, they'd end up kissing and she'd invite him in, and then...? Her head was already muddled. She needed to go to bed, on her own, to sleep. Tomorrow would be a new day and she'd rearrange her thoughts when she was less tired. 'Thanks for a lovely meal.' She was almost drawn into the hypnotic gaze again. 'We must do it another time.'

'We will.' Ruan held the door open. 'Stay safe, Morwenna.'

'You too,' she added. 'Are you out fishing early tomorrow?'

'Out with the tide, as ever.' He grinned, then she was gone across the road, fleeing for the safety of number four, ready to fall into a warm bed.

She opened the door and rushed inside into the gloom. She was unsure whether she'd just had a narrow escape or missed a wonderful opportunity. She would probably never know.

* * *

The next day she cycled to the library to find Louise waiting outside next to a police car, in conversation with PC Jane Choy. Morwenna knew why instantly as she clambered from the bicycle. She caught Louise's anxious expression and asked, 'Did Lizzie the ghost do this?'

The three of them gazed at the red bricks of the library. Someone had sprayed blue paint across the side of the building, huge capital letters.

BACK OFF BITCH THIS IS A WARNING.

Jane Choy touched Morwenna's arm. 'There's no name but it's obviously meant for you.'

'I thought it might be for me.' Louise slumped back against

the library wall on weak legs. 'I can be a bit harsh when books aren't returned on time...'

'The message is public,' Jane said quietly. 'Whoever wrote this is making sure everyone in Seal Bay knows.' She thought for a moment. 'Although the word 'bitch' could be aimed at anyone.'

'It's for me,' Morwenna admitted grimly. 'No punctuation again, and capital letters, just like the note in my letter box.'

Louise was alarmed. 'Is it a message from Alex's killer? Morwenna, you need to be careful.'

'I'm not worried,' Morwenna said quietly. 'But *bitch*, though. That's a bit teasy.'

'It's a direct threat and I'm taking it seriously.' Jane pressed a hand against Morwenna's shoulder. 'You and I will stay in touch, so that I can make sure you're safe.'

'Thanks, Jane.' Morwenna felt a small sense of relief. 'So, shall we all go swimming on Sunday morning?'

'Count me in,' Jane said. 'As long as I don't have a shift, I'll be there.'

'Me too,' Louise said, but she sounded nervous. 'We'll have to close the library for today and get the paint removed.'

'Good idea,' Jane agreed. 'We don't want it to be visible to the public for long.'

'Shall I ask Jack? He might be able to help. I know he's low on work and he'd appreciate it,' Morwenna suggested.

'Let me make a phone call first to check the council will let me go ahead.' Louise said. 'We do need it covered up quickly.'

'*Bitch* is one of those words not everyone uses,' Jane said. 'It's only aimed at women. I wonder what sort of person would choose to paint it on a building. Do we have a clue here?'

'Might a man say it when he's angry with a woman?' Louise suggested. 'The graffiti artist must be a man.'

'Do you think so?' Jane shook her head. 'When women call

each other bitch – it's a challenge, a call to fight, to see who's the hardest. No, I think it's a woman.'

'But women wouldn't spray paint on a municipal building, would they?' Louise countered.

'They might,' Jane argued.

'Mmm...' Morwenna was quiet, thinking – a light had gone on in her head. She was good at remembering voices and she could hear one now, as clearly as if it was yesterday. The last time she'd heard the insult was clear in her memory: "...the wife Pam, the bitch – she'll get all his money."

Morwenna grabbed Louise's hand. 'Are you all right here? I mean, if the library is closed. Can you hold the fort for a bit?'

'Of course.' Louise said. 'I'm fine. Why – where are you going?'

'There's someone I need to call on. I just need to check something out.' Morwenna was astride her bicycle already, leaning forward, one foot on the pedal. 'I'll text you both later.' And she was on her way, silver hair flying, weaving through traffic towards the road that led out of Seal Bay.

17

Morwenna parked her bicycle by the garden gate and walked up past dense foliage to the leaded light door of Half Moon Cottage, knocking lightly. Music drifted from inside the house, loud jangling guitars, a complex potpourri of sounds. Morwenna rapped the knocker harder. The music continued to meander and Morwenna hammered the door for a third time, so loudly that she was sure she'd disturb the neighbours. There was no reply from within so she wandered to the window.

She peered inside. Beverley Okoro was painting at an easel, her back to the window. Her hair was swept up in a colourful scarf, tendrils hanging down, and she wore a long layered floral dress to her ankles. Morwenna watched for a moment as Beverley lifted her paintbrush like a magic wand, standing back to survey her strokes of bright blue, returning to paint again. Then she bashed the window hard with her knuckles and Beverley turned round, her face frozen in fear. She gave a little wave to indicate that Morwenna should hang on, before rushing to the door, flinging it wide.

'Hello,' she said, looking quizzically at Morwenna before her face flooded with recognition. 'Oh, we met at Alex's funeral, yes. What do you want?'

'I wanted to check that you're all right – you were upset.' Morwenna said kindly.

'Do come in. I thought you were the police.'

'Why would I be the police?' Morwenna was intrigued as Beverley led her inside. There was a light smell of oil paint and turpentine in the air.

'The thing is – I suppose I can tell you...' Beverley whirled round, out of breath. 'I've been silly. I wrote something I shouldn't have. I'd had a drink.'

'Oh?' Morwenna remembered the graffiti on the library wall. She glanced at Beverley's painting. It was a depiction in blue lines of two bodies, their arms and legs wrapped around each other in the throes of passion. The man was Alex – she recognised his face, although she'd never seen the expression of ecstasy on it. The last time she saw him, he'd been gasping in pain. The woman had dark hair hanging over her eyes. Morwenna assumed it was Beverley. Her mouth was deep red, smiling as if she'd never been happier. Beverley had printed her name, BEV O, in one corner. Morwenna scanned the canvas. 'That's a very powerful picture. I like the blue colour.'

'The colour of his eyes. It's how I remember him,' Beverley said sadly. 'While I'm painting us together, I can feel his presence. It's as if he's with me now, his arms around me. Do you know what I mean?'

Morwenna didn't, but she said kindly, 'That must be comforting.'

'It is.' Beverley stood in front of the painting, mesmerised. 'It's all I have of him now. I truly loved him. We should have been together. We should have left Cornwall and gone somewhere else... I always said we should go to Tobago, buy a large house with big windows, and live there.' She almost smiled. 'We used to walk round the house naked all the time. We loved the freedom of being together naturally, honest and unfettered, no pretences, no lies.'

'Apart from his wife?' Morwenna glanced towards the old CD player. The music had reached a grinding crescendo. Beverley reached out an arm and turned the volume down. 'Grateful Dead,' she shrugged and Morwenna was puzzled, then she realised it was the name of the band.

'So, Beverley – what did you write that you shouldn't have? You said you were worried that the police might come round?'

'I sent a letter to Alex's wife. I told her exactly what I thought of her. The police clearly don't know anything about me or they'd have called on me already,' Beverley said confidentially. 'Alex and I spoke to each other at the party before he died, you know. That was our last time together. He promised we'd leave Seal Bay before the end of the year. Of course, he'd said that so many times. We had a little tiff on the beach – I called him a liar.'

'Ah.' Morwenna knew.

'I went there because I was sure he'd be with her. I wanted him to see me, to be aware of the fact that I was never far away, that I was watching him. I loved him much more than she ever could. And she knew I existed, but she pretended I didn't.'

'She?'

'The bitch, Pamela.' Beverley clenched her teeth.. 'I was so angry. Since he died, it's as if Alex and I never existed. So I wrote her the letter.'

'What did you say?'

'I told her what I thought of her, clinging to a man she didn't love just for his money. She has someone else, you know.'

'I didn't,' Morwenna admitted, recalling her earlier suspicions.

'She goes sailing with him. It's been going on for ages. She and Alex had a boat, but Alex was more of a dry land man. She's always out in it with this man, throughout the whole summer. It gave Alex more time to spend with me.' She indicated the painting with a wild slash of her arm and Morwenna thought she might smash it or dissolve into tears.

'Do you know who he was, Pam's lover?' she asked gently.

'Alex didn't say a name. I just remember him saying once, "she's out on the boat again, with *him*."' Beverley shrugged. 'To be honest, I couldn't care less about Pam. I hate her more than I can say. I wish she was dead.'

Morwenna gazed around the room, taking in the painting and the bitterness of Beverley's words. Beverley was watching her, eyes narrowed. Morwenna offered a kind smile to diffuse her rising temper. 'So, I suppose you wrote the letter because it made you feel better?'

'I felt better once I'd pushed it through her letter box and driven away. It told her that I'd lost everything. She ought at least to give me something of his to remember him by. I told her the truth.'

'The truth?'

Beverley's face hardened and her eyes glinted. 'She has everything: the house, the money, the cars, the boat. I didn't even have an old jumper of Alex's that I can hug at night while I cry myself to sleep, so that I can smell that earthy scent of him in my arms.'

'I do understand.' Morwenna remembered sleeping in Ruan's arms. She knew exactly what Beverley meant; the scent of a man was so soothing. She'd been unaware of it all the years they'd spent together but once he'd gone, she missed the smell of him like an ache.

Beverley was still shaking. 'I wanted to hurt her; I was furious. I told her I hope someone will do the same to her as they did to Alex. I said she had it coming.'

'You're clearly grieving,' Morwenna said kindly. 'So, you went to the house? Do you go there a lot? Have you ever been inside?'

'Not inside. But I often drive there to look at it. Mirador, where he lived with her, with their son. Where I should have been living, in her place. I went there early this morning to stare up at the windows. One was wide open – it was the room he shared with her. I cried my eyes out.'

Morwenna nodded. 'It must be so difficult.'

Beverley was livid; she was breathing rapidly. 'And the police might come round if they find out that I wrote to her. You mustn't say anything. Say you won't breathe a word.' Her brow clouded. 'But it's not a crime is it, to be in love and to be angry with the woman who killed him?'

'Do you really think Pam Truscott did it?'

'I'm sure she did. What if her lover helped her? They hated Alex. And he probably said he was about to leave her for me.'

Beverley's lip trembled and a tear rolled down her face. Morwenna assumed she knew in her heart that Alex would never have left Pam. He'd used Beverley as he'd used so many other people; that was just the way he did business.

Morwenna placed a gentle hand on Beverley's shoulder. 'Can I get you a cup of tea?'

'Whisky,' Beverley said. 'I usually have one about this time.'

Morwenna glanced at the clock. It wasn't eleven yet. She said kindly, 'Shall I leave you to your painting?'

'Thanks.' Beverley nodded, gazing towards the cabinet. 'It was nice of you to call round. Do you want a drink?'

'I won't – I'm cycling,' Morwenna said, making her way to the door. 'Take care of yourself, Beverley.'

'I will,' Beverley replied automatically, but she was already pouring whisky into a tall glass and taking a desperate gulp.

Morwenna closed the door behind her, her thoughts buzzing.

* * *

Morwenna arrived at the Proper Ansom Tearoom after a long bicycle ride through busy traffic, stuck behind a Korrik China Clay lorry for a mile and a half as it chugged out thick black smoke. Jack's white van wasn't parked outside. She turned towards the sea. She loved Cornwall, Seal Bay, this stretch of beach, whatever the season and the weather. She inhaled the fresh salty bite of the wind and gazed as the surf rolled in, seeping across the sand, tugging away again. The ocean stretched towards the blue line of the sky where fluffy lambs' tail clouds curled like hieroglyphs. A harsh gust of wind blew and she shivered.

Inside the tearoom, she found Jane Choy dressed in her uniform, seated at a table with her hat next to her, drinking tea. She smiled as Morwenna came in. 'Perks of the job. Do you have a minute?'

Tamsin called from behind the counter. 'You're early, Mum, but the lunch rush will start soon. I'm on my own. Jack's got some work cleaning up the library. Apparently, there was some graffiti.'

Jane raised an eyebrow. 'We haven't found who sprayed the paint but there's been another development.'

Tamsin placed a cup of tea in front of Morwenna who muttered thanks, then she leaned forward. 'What's happened?'

'Don't let on to Rick that I've told you, but it will be all over Seal Bay by this afternoon anyway.'

'What will?' Morwenna saw the anxiety on Jane's face.

'Pam Truscott went out shopping early this morning. She

gave Simon a lift to the betting shop. When she came home later, her house had been broken into.'

'Thank goodness she wasn't there.' Morwenna breathed.

Jane tutted. 'The upstairs window had been left open. The whole bedroom was ripped apart, jewellery taken, money, all sorts of valuables.'

Morwenna lifted her mug, thinking. 'Do you think this is connected with Alex's murder?'

'It would seem so.' Jane lowered her voice. 'Whoever did it went into Simon's room, folded up some of his clothes beneath the duvet so that it looked like a body and stuck a knife through it. It must be some kind of threat...'

'A knife again?' Morwenna recalled her conversation with Beverley that morning. Then another thought came to her. 'Or is it a grudge? And someone stole jewellery that Alex would have given to Pam. Perhaps they wanted something to remember Alex by?'

'Is it opportunism, or to make a statement?'

'Or is the knife a message saying "back off"?' Morwenna asked. 'So how is the robbery linked to that? If it's about passion and jealousy, then why the knife in clothing?'

'Do you think Alex's mistress broke into Pam's house?' Jane asked.

'I wouldn't rule her out.' Morwenna pressed her lips together.

'Simon wasn't back from the betting shop when I left Mirador. Pam said she wasn't going to tell him about the knife in the duvet. She didn't want to worry him.'

Morwenna was quiet for a moment. She put her fingers to her lips, thinking. 'Is it a genuine robbery? Or could Pam or Simon have staged it?'

'They could.' Jane pushed her plate away. 'I really value your perceptive mind, Morwenna.'

'I need a dip in the ocean, to get my brain churning. Will you join me for a Sunday morning sea swim?'

'I'll be there, bright and early,' Jane agreed. 'We need inspiration.'

'We do,' Morwenna agreed. 'There's something that doesn't quite add up, but I'm working on it. As soon as we've joined the dots, it'll be as clear as daylight. Then we'll have our man – or our woman.'

18

On her way to the library on Saturday morning, Morwenna called into the pop-up knitting shop. Susan and Barb were surrounded by their wares. There were colourful scarves, mittens, bobble hats, pyjama cases, and tea cosies. Morwenna chose a large, knitted dog with a cute purple face: Elowen would love it. She rummaged in her purse.

'I got some news for you, Morwenna,' Barb said. 'Hot off the local gossip machine. We've been your assistant sleuths, just like we promised.'

'We've been keeping our ears close to the ground,' Susan added.

Morwenna handed them a ten-pound note. 'What have you discovered?'

'We think Pam Truscott has been playing around. She's had a lover for a long time – word on the street is that there's been a man hanging around at the house, long before Alex was killed. He drives a Jaguar. It could be him – the man with the bread knife.' Barb said, making an exaggerated wink of complicity and sticking up a thumb.

'I'd heard something...' Morwenna recalled being in Mirador, two empty glasses on the table, and Pam's words echoed in her ear. 'I had someone round – it's not illegal.'

'Ah, but we've got his name for you.' Susan was pleased with herself.

'He's called Barnaby Stone,' Barb blurted. 'Aren't we just super cool detectives, Morwenna?' She did the thumb sign again. Morwenna picked up a tea cosy: she'd better buy that too, as payment for their information.

'He's not local?' Morwenna pulled her purse from her bag again.

'He's from up north, London.' Susan held out a woollen scarf and Barb offered up the matching bobble hat. It was the same design as the tea cosy. 'He's a plastic surgeon, a real babe magnet, apparently.'

'He does her Botox,' they chimed together as Morwenna paid for her purchases, stuffing the woollen items in her bag. Susan added, 'That's how they meet in secret – he's her plastic surgeon and they have weekends together.'

'Thanks, Susan, thanks, Barb. That's very interesting.'

'Will you get Rick Tremayne to arrest him?' Barb asked smugly.

'I might have a chat with him first. Barnaby Stone, you say?' Morwenna winked. 'Keep your ears close to the ground for me.'

'You'll have to buy everything in the shop as payment,' Susan cackled.

'It's all for the Lifeboats: it's in a good cause.' Barb added.

* * *

Morwenna left her bicycle in the corridor in the library and found Louise poring over a book. Morwenna joined her. 'What have you got here?'

'John Donne's *Metaphysical Poetry...*' Louise turned wide eyes on Morwenna. 'There's been another message from Lady Elizabeth.'

'Has she taken to writing poems?'

'No, the book was lying on the floor when I got in, five minutes ago. Open at this page. Look.'

Morwenna read aloud. 'Death be not proud, though some have called thee

mighty and dreadful, for thou art not so.'

'It's a message from the grave. She's warning us: someone else is going to die.'

'It's a poem about God and the afterlife.'

'I'm serious, Morwenna.'

Morwenna turned the page. 'It's a good job the book didn't land on the next poem – it's called *The Flea* – we'd be phoning Rentokil.' She sniffed. 'Come to think of it, there's a very funny smell in here.'

'It must be the chemicals from the work Jack did yesterday, sorting out the graffiti.'

'I don't know.' Morwenna sniffed the air again. 'It smells like damp to me.'

'Maybe Lady Elizabeth has an aura? Maybe the scent of the damp ground in the graveyard accompanies her wherever she goes?'

Morwenna hugged her. 'You have a great imagination, Louise. You should write books, instead of lending them out...'

* * *

Several hours later, Morwenna arrived for her shift in the tearoom. The lunchtime soup was proving popular; families congregated around tables dunking free rolls, and Morwenna rushed around with trays, clearing away the empties. They served the regular customers with lardy cakes and tea and Morwenna was busy again, sweeping up the crumbs.

There was a quiet five minutes just after four o'clock. Tamsin rushed out with mugs of tea. Morwenna took hers gratefully. 'Where's Elowen?'

'She's at a party – the birthday girl has invited half the class. Gran took her. She won't be back until five.'

'And Jack?'

'He's gone to Woon's boatyard. He's hoping Damien will give him some work painting boats.'

'That'd be useful.'

'Oh, it really would, Mum,' Tamsin said sadly. 'Poor Jack has been down in the dumps about it all. He came here to make a fresh start. He loves Cornwall, and we met and...' She twisted the engagement ring on her finger. 'He's great with Elowen and everything was going so well. But now the tearoom is only just breaking even and I'm not sure we'll be able to pay for a Christmas wedding even with you and Dad helping us. We only want something simple but – it's my wedding, Mum. I want it to be right.'

'Of course,' Morwenna said, her voice full of sympathy.

'A few days ago, I suggested that we move the wedding to next summer and Jack actually cried. He was so upset, Mum. I want a wedding I'll remember, with my friends, a nice dress, the works, but he doesn't care about the extras, he wants to be married now. He has this old-fashioned idea about providing for me. He thinks it makes him more of a man, although I've told him that's rubbish. He had no dad as a youngster, no role model, and his mum had it tough, what with her breakdown.'

'Poor Jack. It might make sense to move the wedding back though. It would give you more time to save.'

'He hates us being poor. He wants to buy me presents. I told him that's not important but he's desperate to do the right thing and to be a proper dad to Elowen. That's why he's down at Damien Woon's now, begging for a job.'

'Oh, Tam.' Morwenna patted her hand. 'It's so unfair, isn't it?' An idea came to her. 'Why don't I have Elowen tomorrow? I'll take her out for the day. Then you and Jack can have some special time together.' She recalled her evening with Ruan. 'Your dad has a great recipe for bao buns. You should make some, share a romantic meal.'

'Oh, I could. But yes please to taking Elowen for a few hours!' Tamsin threw her arms around her mother. 'You're the best.' She gazed around. 'We're a bit quieter now. You can get off early if you like. I'll finish up here.'

'I may as well stay and help. Elowen will be back soon and I have a woollen toy for her.' Morwenna produced the purple-faced dog.

'A friend for Oggy.' Tamsin laughed. 'You could give it to her yourself. She is up at Lister Hill, with Grandma. It's Maya Buvač's birthday party.'

'Oh, all right.' Morwenna was already on her feet, rushing towards the door. 'Then I will. Yes, it will be nice to see Mum and Elowen and it would be good to meet the Buvač family at last...'

* * *

Morwenna slogged up Lister Hill on her bike, the purple-faced dog in her basket, stopping at number 42. She rang the doorbell and a cheery-faced woman answered, holding out a hand to shake. 'Hello. It's Morwenna Mutton, isn't it, Elowen's gran? We've never actually met properly. I'm Rosie. Come on in and have a cuppa and a piece of birthday cake.'

'Thanks, that would be 'ansom.' Morwenna gasped, still out of breath. 'Cycling up that hill nearly killed me...'

Rosie led the way through a narrow hall that smelled warm, of baking, and an underlying aroma of fish. There were coat pegs on the wall, fisherman's oilskins, shoes placed underneath, a tidy shelf, and rows of wellington boots. They paused outside the living room. Captain Pugwash was in there in full regalia, complete with tattooed arms, a skull-and-crossbones hat, waistcoat, breeches and a red and black striped shirt. He was surrounded by a dozen small girls and boys who were staring at him, entranced. Morwenna watched in admiration as Milan Buvač waved his hands theatrically, recounting a dramatic pirate story in an accent half-European and half-Cornish, while the kids gazed at him open-mouthed. Rosie whispered, 'He'll have them quiet for another half an hour yet, so come on into the kitchen.'

Morwenna followed Rosie into the kitchen where Lamorna was sitting at the table drinking tea. She lifted the pot. 'Cuppa?'

'I will, thanks,' Morwenna said gratefully.

'How do you know Rosie, Mum?'

'From the school gates – when I pick up Elowen, I talk to all the mums. Sometimes I get a lift to the teashop with Elowen or back up to Tregenna Gardens – I can't manage the steep hills now, not with my hip. The bus does me fine, mostly.'

Morwenna could imagine Lamorna chatting easily with all the twenty and thirty-somethings, giving them the benefit of her life story in exchange for a warm ride home. Rosie plonked herself down. 'Ah, this is nice. I can take the weight off my feet.

It's been a busy afternoon, singing 'Happy Birthday' and passing the parcel.' She smiled. 'I wouldn't swap a minute of it though.'

Morwenna sipped from the cup Lamorna handed her. 'Milan is amazing with the kids.'

'He's a gifted storyteller,' Rosie agreed. 'He's wasted as a fisherman – he always wanted to be a magician.'

'I've never met a man who didn't,' Lamorna said cryptically.

Morwenna smiled. 'You mean like my dad – the disappearing act?'

'Exactly.' Lamorna winked. 'Our Tam thinks she's found a good lad, though I'll believe it when I see it.'

'He's up at Woon's boatyard,' Morwenna explained. 'Looking for work.'

'I used to go out with Harry Woon, Damien's uncle.' Lamorna rolled her eyes, remembering. 'Or would it be his great uncle? I'm not sure. Great kisser, Harry Woon – lips like suction pads. Do you know, we were on the number 72 bus once and we kissed all the way from Seal Bay Post Office right down to the last stop on the seafront. Twenty minutes that kiss took. My lips were numb for three days.'

'How old were you, Mum?'

'Fourteen.' Lamorna sniffed once. 'He's dead now, poor Harry. Years ago. He won't kiss again.'

'I hope Jack can get some work,' Morwenna said thoughtfully. 'I was down at Woon's boatyard the other night.'

'I heard about it.' Rosie smiled cheerily. 'Didn't you fall off a boat into the water? Pam Truscott told me all about it.'

'Oh?' Morwenna was interested.

'Yes, I do her cleaning three times a week. Beautiful house, she's got. And the extra money really helps.'

Morwenna recalled Pam saying something about her having a cleaner. 'Pam Truscott has a boat, doesn't she?'

'*The Pammy*. Alex bought it for her as an anniversary gift, I think. Mind you, Alex never liked sailing much...'

Lamorna looked from Morwenna to Rosie. 'Who does she go sailing with, then?' Morwenna had exactly the same question on the tip of her tongue.

'That'd be Barnaby Stone.' Rosie said straight away. 'He's a charming bloke. He and Pam share a love of sailing.'

'Do you see him often up at Mordor?' Lamorna wanted to know.

'Mirador, Mum.' Morwenna marvelled at the ease with which her mother asked the questions she needed answers to, although she knew her mother well, so had no reason to be surprised.

'He comes down from time to time. Such a nice, well-mannered man. And he and Pam do so much good work for the fishermen.'

'Oh? I thought Alex was the one who helped—'

'Not at all.' Rosie folded her arms firmly across her chest. 'Alex gave a few pounds to the Lifeboats and he let everyone know about it. But Pam and Barnaby have always been good to the fishermen and their families. When times are tight, they help out with a loan between wages just because they can, and they never ask for interest. Some people can't pay them back and they often just let it go and pretend they've forgotten. Barnaby puts a lot of money into helping ordinary Seal Bay folk. And Pam's always been concerned about the Cornish fishermen and their families, what with her love of boats.'

'So you didn't like Alex Truscott?' Lamorna asked, with a glance to Morwenna.

'I couldn't stand him. Milan hated his guts. We rented this place from Alex. You know, one of the first things Pam and Barnaby did after Alex died was to put the rent down on all the fishermen's cottages. No, Milan had no time for Alex Truscott.'

Morwenna recalled the image of Alex's final moments on the beach. She finished her tea and tried a different angle. 'Do you know Barnaby well?'

'Of course.' Rosie picked up the teapot to refill the cups. Lamorna was slicing cake into wedges. 'He's been coming to visit for years. He and Pam are thick as thieves. I don't think Alex cared for him much and, to be honest, I think the feeling was mutual.'

'I'm not surprised Alex and Barnaby didn't hit it off.' Morwenna accepted the smallest piece of cake, gazing at the blue icing and the yellow-haired edible mermaid on top.

'Oh, he's a lovely man, Barnaby. And he does Pam's Botox – brilliant surgeon, they say. And he sings while he works, you know, all the pop songs.' Rosie bit into the cake.

'Barnaby stayed at the house with Alex living there?' Morwenna was surprised.

'All the time – he's been visiting since they moved down from London.'

'That's very open-minded,' Morwenna had to admit. 'What with Barnaby being Pam's lover.'

'Her lover? That's the funniest thing I've heard in ages!' Rosie broke into peals of laughter. 'You must have misheard someone. Pam and Barnaby aren't lovers. He's her brother.'

19

On Sunday morning, while she was still snug in bed, Morwenna received two texts. One was from Louise, saying that she couldn't come to the early-morning swimming session because she and Steve were going to Truro to visit his mother. Louise joked that she didn't know which would be the iciest, the ocean or the reception she'd get from her mother-in-law, who always said her son had married the wrong woman. The second text was from Jane, who had been called into the office to cover a sick colleague's shift, so she couldn't make the early-morning swim either. Morwenna rolled over into the warmth of the mattress and thought for a moment, then she replied to both friends.

How about a night swim instead?

Jane replied straight away: she'd meet her at the usual spot on the beach at nine thirty. She'd take her car and give Morwenna a lift home. Louise replied next: she'd probably still be listening to her mother-in-law complain about how thin Steve looked since he'd married Louise; how he should have married that nice girl Patsy Lenton instead; and how the fish you bought in the supermarkets were less tasty nowadays than they'd been in the nineteen seventies. Louise admitted she'd rather be up to her neck in freezing water, although it wasn't a very charitable thing to say, and she'd see Morwenna on Monday morning as usual in the library.

Morwenna clambered out of bed, grabbed a piece of toast for breakfast, tugged on star-spangled leggings, a purple top, ankle boots, a yellow fleecy coat and cycled down the hill to the tearoom. Elowen was waiting by the door, clutching the purple-faced dog, jumping up and down excitedly.

'Come in, Grandma. Mummy and Jack are upstairs having breakfast. They are eating boiledy eggs and I've had mine already and so has Oggy and Oggy Two.' She flourished the knitted dog. 'And you and me and the dogs are all going out for the day with Grandad.'

'With Grandad? Are we?' Morwenna asked. She stepped into the cafe to see Ruan, dressed warmly, seated at a table and smiling.

'Tam said you were taking Elowen out, so I thought we'd all go in the van,' Ruan offered. 'We could go up to Pettarock Bay, stroll on the beach, walk along the coastal path overlooking the sea...'

'We could,' Morwenna agreed. She felt a little annoyed. She'd planned a day with Elowen, just the two of them, and Ruan had barged in without so much as a 'May I come too?' She felt her jaw clench; it was typical of Ruan to do something kind-hearted without thinking that she might have other plans, and she was taken back to the very worst days of their relationship, near the end, when they'd argued about the pettiest things.

Morwenna took a breath: she was being unfair. Ruan was Elowen's grandad. He'd be very welcome to spend the day with them. In fact, he'd be great company. And the van would be useful; they could get out of Seal Bay for a change. So she grinned and said, 'Thanks, Ruan. That would be really nice.'

Then Jack appeared at the door, bleary-eyed, wearing an old T-shirt and shorts. He was damp from the shower, freshly smelling of shower gel. 'Thanks for taking Elowen.' He smiled, glancing at Ruan. 'I want to treat Tam to a really special day. She doesn't know yet, but I'm taking her out to lunch at the Royal Duchy Hotel.' He noticed Morwenna's surprised expression. 'Don't worry – I have a job with Damien at the boatyard as of now. I'm going to help him with a bit of painting and he said he'd let me do a bit of welding and mechanical stuff too. I can do that all right – I did a few courses back in Gloucestershire.' He was pleased with himself. 'I'm doing two hours overtime for him tonight. And he's given me a week's money in advance.'

Morwenna wondered if he shouldn't be saving it to pay bills, but she could see the pride in his face. He clearly wanted to spoil Tamsin.

'You have a lovely day. We'll bring Elowen back about five o'clock.' Morwenna patted his arm. 'I'm going for a swim in the sea later on.'

'In the dark?' Jack shuddered. 'I can't even swim. I have a shower twice a day – that's enough water for me. I can't imagine how cold it is...'

'That's part of the thrill of it,' Morwenna explained.

'Grandma, can we go now?' Elowen tugged her arm. 'Oggy and Oggy Two want to go to Pettarock Bay to see all the other pets.'

Ruan smiled, ruffling her hair. 'There are no pets there, my lovely – but lots of rocks and a beautiful beach and an ice cream with your name on it.'

'Can I have bubblegum flavour? I had bubblegum icing at Maya's party and it was lush.'

'Come on, my bewty, let's go.' Ruan took her hand. He turned to Morwenna and she wondered if he'd take hers too. She was glad he didn't. She'd have had no idea how to react. He offered a charming grin instead, handsome as ever. 'Your chariot awaits.'

* * *

Pettarock Bay gleamed in the October sunshine, white stone houses clustered together, craggy cliffs and glittering coves. Ruan drove the van down to the seafront to park behind a line of Sunday visitors, and they clambered over the wall and walked towards the rushing waves. The beach stretched for over a mile, and was a popular place for surfers in the summer. It was quiet now, a few people braving the sea in wetsuits, one or two dog walkers. Morwenna glanced over her shoulder at their boot prints on the golden sand washed clean by the Atlantic. Elowen ran on ahead, clutching the woollen dog, calling over her shoulder, 'Oggy's in the sea already. Come on, Grandma, Grandad, we can splash.'

'We should catch her up.' Ruan broke into an easy run, and Morwenna watched his fluid movements before she pushed herself forward, trotting to keep up, shouting, 'It's a good job we brought wellies...'

Ruan gripped Elowen's hand and they began to jump waves, the small girl squealing with delight. 'Hold my hand, Grandma, then I can *wheee*.'

Morwenna grasped the small fist and soon she and Ruan were lifting Elowen above surging waves as she kicked out her feet and yelled in excitement. Inevitably, one of her red wellingtons flew off, arcing in the air and falling with a plop in the ocean. Elowen laughed, 'Oggy will swim out and get it.'

'I'll give him a hand,' Ruan offered and he rushed forward, plunging an arm into the frothing tide, plucking out the welly which he turned upside down, watching the water spill out in a steady stream.

'Your jeans are wet,' Morwenna said, and Ruan looked down, noticing for the first time.

'They'll dry in the wind.' He rolled them up to his knees before heaving Elowen on his back. 'What shall we do now?'

'Oggy wants to play *thwackit* on the sand,' Elowen insisted.

'I'll pop back to the car and get a ball and some spare shoes,' Ruan offered with a smile.

They played a game with strange rules that Elowen seemed to make up as she went along. Oggy and Oggy Two were in goal, and the object of the game was to hit the ball past them with your fist or foot. Elowen decided that she and Ruan would be one team and Morwenna would be the other. Morwenna spent the next hour running down the beach to collect the ball every time it sped past Oggy, who never seemed to save the ball because Elowen claimed that he had no teeth any more, so he couldn't catch the ball in his mouth. The score was 29–0 and Morwenna was dead on her feet. 'I'm too old for this.'

'That's because you're sixty-one and I'm only five,' Elowen said.

'Let's get ice creams,' Ruan offered and half an hour later the three of them were sitting on the sea wall in a line, licking creamy cones.

Elowen had blue ice cream on her nose. She grinned. 'I love being with you and Grandad, Grandma. Can we do it every day?'

'It's been good fun,' Ruan said. 'We can come here whenever

we like, but don't forget that you're at school, I'm a busy fisherman and your grandma always has so much to do.'

'Looking for the bad man who hurted Alex Truscott,' Elowen said. 'Everybody in my school knows that you'll find him before Rick Tremayne does. Billy Crocker calls him PC Ploddy-Plod. Billy says he won't find the killer because he's too fat and my grandma couldn't catch a cold because she's too old, and I wanted to punch him but I didn't, so I won't get distended again.'

'Your grandma's not too old. She's perfect as she is...' Ruan said with a grin.

Elowen sniffed defiantly. 'That's not the worst thing Billy Crocker said to me. He said Jack's not my proper daddy because my real one ran away when I was bornded because I'm so ugly. Then he said I'm still ugly and everyone will leave me because I look like a pig's bum. I thought about punching him in the nose but Oggy told me not to, so I didn't.'

'Oggy's a good dog,' Ruan said. The ice creams were finished. He took Elowen's hand and Morwenna took the other as they strolled towards the cliffs where the tide was rolling away.

'And you're a good girl for not listening to Billy's nonsense.' Morwenna could hear the strength in her own voice. 'It's silly when people call someone ugly. No one's ugly. Everyone has their own beauty and you're beautiful inside and out, Elowen.'

'I know.' Elowen broke into a skip. 'Oh look – there are rock pools by the cliffs. Can I go and see if there are any crabs, Grandad?'

'Yes, go on...' Ruan let her small hand go and watched Elowen run into the distance, his face gentle with love. 'She'll be all right.'

'Yes, she will. She's a bright kid, full of beans. A proper Mutton maid.' Morwenna noticed Ruan's slightly surprised reaction and she added, 'Well, she's a Pascoe too.'

'She reminds me of you,' Ruan agreed. 'Full of get-up-and-go, feisty. I like that.'

Morwenna said nothing as they walked along. She was lost in thought for a while. She and Ruan had walked along the same beach so many times. They'd even walked to the rock pools on Pettarock Bay when she was expecting Tamsin. They'd chosen her name on this very beach: Tamsin Madeline Pascoe. Tamsin had been Ruan's choice, a good Cornish name, although he'd also liked Tegen; it meant pretty. Morwenna wanted the name Madeline because she thought it was strong, beautiful and romantic. Those were good times – there had been so many.

Ruan sensed her thoughts. 'Morwenna...' She noticed him look ahead. Elowen was kneeling next to a rock pool, Oggy Two pushed inside the top of her anorak. 'I've been thinking.'

'Oh? That's dangerous, Ruan...' She gave him a warm smile.

'I'm enjoying spending time with you. Today's been nice. And dinner the other night was lovely.'

'Yes, it was,' Morwenna agreed. She was a little concerned where the conversation was heading. She pushed her hands deep into the pockets of her fleecy coat, just in case.

'We could spend more time together, you know, walking on the beach, dinners...'

'We'll always be Elowen's grandparents, Tam's—'

'I meant just me and you. I'd like it if we got to know each other again.'

'Mmm.' Morwenna wasn't sure. She wondered what would happen if they slipped back to the old ways, the silences, the arguments. But this was very pleasant, walking side by side. Perhaps it wouldn't do any harm. 'Maybe we could.'

'I wish we hadn't...' Ruan paused, thinking. 'The way we split up wasn't right. I shouldn't have let it happen. You told me to go and I went. But we'd been so close before that, so good together.'

Morwenna sighed. 'We rattled along so well for years and then we hit a pothole in the road and over we went, just like that.'

'I regret it all going wrong,' Ruan said quietly.

'I do too...' Morwenna began, then she didn't know what else to say.

'Let's spend time.'

'We could.'

'I always thought you'd find someone else,' Ruan muttered. 'You still might...'

'I might, but I can't see it.' Morwenna glanced at him. 'You might find a pretty Cornish maid.'

'I had the best one.'

'I don't know so much, Ruan.'

'Let's take it slowly, see what happens.'

'That was one of our problems,' Morwenna said with a half-laugh. 'You were laid back and I was rushing around everywhere. We were so different.'

'But good together... we were good,' Ruan insisted. Then Elowen was waving her arms and yelling.

'What is it?' Ruan called.

'I found one, Grandad, a big brown crab with massive wiggly legs and a hard head like a Klingon. Shall I pick her up?'

'Wait there – we'll come and see!' Morwenna yelled. She glanced at Ruan. 'Race you to the rock pool, old man.'

He grinned back. 'Last one to reach Elowen buys the pasties,' and they were off at a steady lope, rushing into the cold air, smiles on their faces.

20

Ruan and Morwenna dropped Elowen off at five o'clock as promised. Tamsin was happy to see her. A day with Jack and lunch at the Royal Duchy Hotel had done her good. She looked happy, her eyes shining, as she invited Morwenna and Ruan in for a cuppa. Jack was just leaving for the boatyard to help Damien for an hour or two. Morwenna felt instinctively that her daughter wanted some quality time with Elowen, so she hugged her and promised to see her soon.

Ruan stopped the van beside number four Harbour Cottages and leaned across. 'It was a lovely day.'

'It was,' Morwenna agreed. 'We'll do it again.'

'We will.'

There was a pause, both wondering how to end what had been a perfect time in Pettarock. Ruan tried first. 'You could come into number nine for dinner. Or I could come into number four.' He examined her expression. 'Or maybe another time – you're off swimming tonight.'

'I am.'

'Morwenna, you'll be careful, won't you?'

'Swimming in the dark? I've done it before.'

'No, I mean, you've had two threats now, the note and the library.'

'I'll be with a police officer.'

'I don't want anything to happen to you.'

'I'll be fine, Ruan. Anyway, the best way to deal with it is to catch Alex's killer and lock him or her up. Then we can all rest easy.'

'Who's at the top of your list now?' Ruan asked.

'I keep coming back to the money thing – I'm sure that's at the heart of it. Whoever Alex was meeting at the beach, he knew them. He trusted them. More than that, he wanted to talk to them urgently, or he wouldn't have agreed, he'd have put it off to another day.'

'Not Pam then, or Simon?'

'I'm not ruling them out.'

'And Beverley?'

'She's on my list. Whoever threatened me twice means they know I'm getting closer.'

Ruan took her hand. 'I'll help.'

She kept her hand in his. 'I know. Thanks.'

'I'm up early tomorrow, off fishing, but I'll text you. Maybe we can have dinner again, talk things through – Alex's killing, I mean.'

'I'd like that.' Morwenna leaned over and kissed his cheek briefly. 'It's been lovely. Goodnight, Ruan.'

''Night.'

She slid out of the van and he called after her. 'I bet the water will be freezing cold...'

'That's the whole point,' she laughed, rushing down the path and disappearing behind the front door, closing it quickly behind her with a thump.

* * *

When she arrived at the beach at half past nine, Jane was already there, sitting in her car with the radio on, waiting. Morwenna rapped on the window and Jane looked up – she'd been a long way away, deep in thought. Jane tucked her car keys under her clothes in the footwell – everything would be safe for the short duration of the swim. She clambered out, already in her wetsuit and Morwenna tugged off her clothes and bag, bundling them into the passenger seat, closing the door with a crisp clunk.

Jane grinned. 'How was your day? Have you found out anything more about Alex's killer?'

'No. I had a family day. I went with Elowen to Pettarock.' Morwenna decided to leave out the bit about Ruan. She shivered, the cold sea breeze lifting her hair. 'How about you?'

They were surrounded by darkness, leaving the twinkling lights behind them as they rushed towards the sea that whispered in the distance, their feet cool against damp sand. 'I paid Woon's boatyard a visit this morning,' Jane said. 'It was very strange.'

'How so?' Morwenna was breathing rapidly in the cold. Running fast was already hard work.

'Damien was a bit aggressive, to be honest.'

'Were you in uniform?'

'Yes, I was in the car and he wasn't happy to see a police vehicle in his yard. I went for a snoop around, to ask a few questions, how he got on with Alex Truscott, but...' Jane caught her breath as the chill of seawater snapped against her ankles and calves. 'He was there painting a boat. He told me not to waste my time visiting him again. He mentioned you, too.'

'Oh?' Morwenna heard the shiver in her voice. The water was deep now, and she pushed her arms hard. She felt the familiar kick to the heart as the warmth was sapped from her body, the exhilarating ache in her limbs, the wind whipping against her skin as she braced herself against the rush of another wave.

Jane shrieked with the sudden drop of temperature. 'Damien Woon said Pam Truscott was a good customer. He told me to tell you to stay away. He said he'd been polite because you were his friend's ex, but he wouldn't be so accommodating if you came back again.'

Morwenna leaned back into the cool clasp of the water. 'That doesn't bode well. I'll have to go back and have another look around.'

'He was uncooperative, to say the least.' Jane said between chattering teeth. They dived under, swimming in the inky darkness, staring up at the stars. Then Jane blinked water from her eyes.

'Morwenna, my muscles are like chewing gum. I'm going to have to get out and run back to the car.'

'Right. You go on and I'll follow you in five minutes.'

Morwenna watched Jane swim away back to the shore, then it was too dark; she was just a shadow on the beach. The moon slid from behind a cloud overhead and the ocean was rippled with shimmering silver. The sky and the sea melted into black velvet as Morwenna plunged beneath the surface of the water, catching her breath with the fresh cold. She needed a few more moments alone to think.

She tried to go through each suspect methodically, but everyone at the party except Ruan was still a possible killer and she felt instinctively that the motive was money. She recalled Jane's anxious words about Damien Woon, how difficult he'd been when she paid him a visit. His threat could be simply defensive: he had a business to run, Pam was a valuable customer. A police presence wouldn't help his reputation;

Morwenna couldn't imagine any other reason why he might be hostile to Jane. She wondered whether Damien had an in-built distrust of the police, or women, or both. She'd ask Ruan if there was a darker side to him. She was becoming too cold in the water now, so she struck off back to shore, pushing through rippling moonlight.

Morwenna's feet touched sand and she scrabbled upright, rushing forward, her skin a hard shell of shivering goosebumps. She rubbed salt water from her eyes, gazing towards Jane's car, parked by the sea wall. There was no light on inside – she could see only a shadowy outline. She surged blindly on and almost fell over the hump in the sand. She paused, confused, bending down over a slumped body in a wetsuit. It was Jane Choy. It was almost too dark to see properly, but Morwenna placed her fingers at the throat and felt the quiver of a light pulse. She touched Jane's shoulder and her fingers came away sticky.

Adrenalin pumped through her body; Morwenna was ready to rush to the car, to where her phone was, when someone grabbed her from behind. Her heart leaped, seized with the fright of the moment, and she fought and writhed for all she was worth, twisting round. A hand fumbled at her neck, across her body; she felt the roughness of a dark coat. There was a flash of flesh in the moonlight, a tattooed arm, and she smelled sweat and something else, the warmth of someone close, hot breath on her skin. Then a hard object hit her on the head. She fell like crumpling cards on the dense sand and struggled to open her eyes. She was being dragged along, heaved across the beach, then she was sinking, water was rising around her face, cold lapping waves, and for an instant consciousness left her.

Morwenna wasn't clear what happened next. Her mouth was full of salt water, her brain muddy, her lungs heavy, and she was sinking beneath rough waves. She pushed her arms instinctively, swimming hard, gulping fresh air, then her legs shook and she was upright, running along the hard sand of the beach, gasping and shivering, towards the sea wall. Tugging open the door of Jane's car, she reached shaking fingers into the footwell and grasped her phone. She wrapped a towel around her shoulders, huddled into the warmth of the seat and tried to press numbers. It took an immense effort to ring 999, then she was gabbling, shaking violently, saying random words while a calm voice in her ear repeated questions over and over.

Morwenna hunched in the car, water streaming from her swimsuit, blood covering her face, her lungs and limbs aching, and she searched for Ruan on WhatsApp, pressed the phone and his gravelly voice said her name.

'Ruan – I've been attacked – Jane too – I'm all right, I think.... I'm by the beach, in her car. I phoned the ambulance.'

'Are you at the usual place?' She could hear him moving already. 'I'm on my way. I'll find you.' Then she was holding the phone, trembling with fear and cold, coughing and spluttering seawater from her lungs, reaching with numb fingers to find anything she could hug around herself, clothes, a coat. She ought to go to help Jane, but her muscles had stiffened and she couldn't move. She shivered with the cold and fear.

A car approached, blinding headlights, slowing down, stopping. Ruan was next to her and she felt the warmth of his arms. Morwenna gulped hot tears as he wrapped a blanket around her and she heard her voice shake as she mouthed the words, 'Jane's out there, on the beach...'

He held her against him as a siren wailed and blue flashing lights were so bright that she closed her eyes. She heard Ruan talking to someone, telling them Jane needed help on the beach. Voices were speaking hurriedly, bodies moving, fumbling, rushing. Then a woman was beside her, saying her name, touching the wound on her head. She felt a sharp burst of pain; she tried to answer the questions that filled her ears over and over, but her brain was swirling. Sleep tugged but her limbs caught fire and raged for a while, then she was suddenly numb, slipping away.

Someone helped her to her feet and Ruan was holding her as she stumbled towards an ambulance. There were loud voices, more screaming sirens, whirling lights; the ambulance doors closed with a metallic clunk and she was sitting with Ruan and a woman in green uniform. Then the world folded in and everything was pitch dark.

21

Morwenna tried to open her eyes, but white lights glared overhead and she kept them closed. She tried to remember where she was and what had happened, but consciousness came and went. She felt a rough hand against hers, Ruan's voice murmured her name and her eyes flickered open for a second. It was all too bright. Her head throbbed, a dull ache, and her limbs were burning. She stopped trying and let sleep tug her away.

Hours later, she looked directly into Ruan's gaze. She was in a small, white-walled room. He stood by the edge of the bed, smiling. 'You're all right then?'

'I might be...' Morwenna tried to remember. She recalled images of being wheeled into a room, a fluorescent glare overhead, concerned voices, someone wrapping her tightly, someone else treating a wound on her head. It was almost as if she was watching from a distance – it had happened to someone else. Ruan sensed her confusion.

'They kept you in overnight to monitor you. You had signs of hypothermia, you'd swallowed some water and the bump on your head needed dressing, but the doctor said you'll be fine.'

Morwenna remembered. 'You got to me quickly.'

'I went in The Smugglers for half a shandy but none of the lads were there. Damien didn't show. Milan Buvač came in just as I was leaving. Thank goodness I was down the road.'

Morwenna felt the support of deep pillows behind her head. 'Did you stay with me all night?'

'I wanted to be here when you woke up,' Ruan said simply. 'Lamorna's coming in soon. She took Elowen to school – she's been helping at the tearoom. Tam sands her love – she's worried about you. It's just her and Elowen in the flat – Jack took off straight after he finished overtime on Sunday night. He drove through the night to visit his mum and got back first thing, happy as Larry. He said she recognised him for the first time in ages and she gave him a few quid for the wedding. He's started work at the boatyard, so things are looking up.' He reached over and took her hand in his. 'How are you feeling?'

'Woozy.' She thought for a moment. 'And hungry.' She pressed light fingers against her temple, beneath her hair, feeling padding, micropore surgical tape. 'Ouch.'

'The wound has a few stitches in it. The doctor says they'll dissolve.'

'Someone hit me. They dragged me into the water.'

Ruan's hand squeezed her fingers encouragingly. 'You dragged yourself out again. You're made of strong stuff.' She noticed the concern etched on his face. 'Thank goodness you did.'

Morwenna half-closed her eyes. For a moment, she was back on the beach. Someone had an arm around her neck, tugging her. She remembered the sharp smell of warm breath and something else: as she tried to wriggle away, she glimpsed a tattoo beneath a heavy sleeve. 'The person who attacked me had a tattoo.'

Ruan sighed and hauled up his sleeve, showing an inked compass. 'I have one – most sailors do.'

Morwenna tried not to move her head. There was an ache that moved constantly between her eyes. 'Damien Woon has one.'

'He has several. A tattoo won't lead us to whoever assaulted you.'

'What's he like, Ruan?'

'Damien? He keeps himself to himself. He lives on his own since his wife left. He drinks a bit, has a bit of a temper on him, but I guess that's due to unhappiness.'

'Because his wife left him?'

'He ploughed lots of money into the boatyard and it's not done well over the past couple of years. His ex-wife took her share. He's hoping that taking Jack on will improve business. Damien's always busy but he's very thorough, a perfectionist; he takes too long to finish a job, so having an extra pair of hands should help him catch up.'

Morwenna wondered if Damien had attacked her on the beach, or if it had been someone else who'd pulled her into the water. Women had tattoos too. She racked her brain to remember if she'd seen one on Pam Truscott. The suspect needed to have at least one tattoo on their arm. She still felt cold beneath the sheets, yet her muscles constantly prickled as if stabbed with hot needles.

Ruan was right. Tattoos weren't huge clues. She needed to focus on working things out, logic. The person behind her who attacked her – they were taller than she was. Morwenna forced a smile – that was everyone on her list. She was a novice sleuth but she was learning fast. What else could she remember? Strong hands, the hands of someone who used them every day, perhaps – for work? Damien, even Beverley. Or Pam – she'd be strong from sailing? And there was a smell on their skin as they held her from behind – what was it? A strong smell, thick, lingering.

The image of Jane Choy flashed into her mind lying on the sand and she gasped.

'Are you all right?' Ruan moved closer.

'How's Jane?'

'I'm not sure,' Ruan said. 'The paramedics were dealing with her last night as the ambulance took you away. I haven't heard anything.'

'Do you think she's here, in the hospital?' Morwenna asked. 'I have to find out.'

'We'll ask – a doctor should be calling in on you soon.'

'Will they let me go home?'

Ruan shook his head. 'You'll need to take it easy.'

Morwenna glared at him. 'Someone attacked Jane, then me. Of course, it's the same person who killed Alex.' She shivered, a violent spasm. 'I'm so lucky to be here.'

Ruan's eyes filled with tenderness. 'Yes, you are.'

'Do you think I should let this all go, Ruan? Let someone else look for the killer?'

'Yes, but you won't,' Ruan said gently. 'I know you. You won't leave it until you find the person responsible.' He squeezed her hand again. 'I'm here to help.'

She looked at him and with pure affection. 'Thanks, Ruan.'

He shifted, pushing his hands in his pockets. 'Should I go and find you some food? You said you were hungry.'

'I bet Mum brings me something,' Morwenna grinned. 'A pasty wrapped in a cloth, and a flask of tea.' She tried her legs, stretching a calf. It didn't feel too bad. 'I need to go home soon.'

'You shouldn't. And you ought to give the library a miss for a day or two. Louise and Donald can manage. And...' Ruan's face was concerned. 'You should probably stay out of the water for a while.'

'I was thinking of going for a swim this afternoon,' Morwenna said playfully, watching the concern on his face change to a smile.

'You're pure badness.' He grinned.

Then a burly man marched into the room without knocking and stood at the end of the bed, hands on hips. 'Well, well, well, Morwenna Mutton. You're lucky you're not dead.'

'Rick,' Ruan said by way of greeting. Rick Tremayne pretended that he hadn't noticed him. He was glaring at Morwenna. 'What business did you have, being on the beach that late at night? It was all your own fault. You and Jane Choy.'

'How is Jane?'

'Her condition's all down to you and your thoughtless behaviour. It's a wonder she's still alive.'

'We were swimming in the sea. We had every right to be there.' Morwenna leaned forward. 'How is she, Rick?'

'She has a stab wound to the shoulder. It missed her lung but she has internal injuries. It'll take her a while to recover from that.' Rick clenched his teeth. 'It's all your fault, dabbling in police business.'

'No, it's not, Rick,' Ruan said gently. 'It's the fault of the person who attacked her. Morwenna called the emergency services. You should be thanking her.'

'If you'd caught the person who killed Alex, then Jane would be all right now,' Morwenna said. She was quiet for a moment, thinking. 'The person who attacked me must have stabbed Jane first, surprised her from behind. It was so dark; it was hard to see. I didn't notice anyone come up behind me. She or he must have been hanging around on the beach the whole time, watching us.'

Rick was suddenly professional. 'Can you give me a description, Morwenna? Can you recollect anything about the assailant's appearance?'

'Averagely strong, I'm guessing – I twisted free and they couldn't hold me, but then he or she hit me hard with something. A stone, maybe, or the handle of a knife.' She turned to Rick. 'Was a knife found at the scene?'

'We're looking, but so far we've found nothing. A few trainer prints, different brands,' Rick admitted. 'Did you see his face?'

'It could have been a man or a woman, I don't know. I did see a tattoo on their arm, beneath a coat or jacket.' Morwenna glanced at Rick, whose white shirt sleeves were rolled up. On his left forearm there was a mark in colourful ink, some sort of bird, an eagle perhaps. Morwenna couldn't remember the design she'd seen on the beach; it had been a brief flash in the moonlight, nothing more.

Rick noticed her staring at his arm, and he coughed awkwardly. 'So, shall I assume that the blow you had to the head has knocked some sense into you and you're not going to meddle in police business again?'

Morwenna met his eyes. 'What ward is Jane in? I want to go and see her.'

'I've no idea,' Rick said glibly.

'Then I suggest you find out and get down to visit, take her some flowers and ask her how she's feeling.' Morwenna glared at him. 'A bit of professional concern wouldn't go amiss, DI Tremayne.'

'And some common sense wouldn't go amiss, Morwenna. So, you listen up. Stay out of police business from now on or I'll be calling round to see you.'

'For a few tips on how to get the job done?'

Rick's face was blotched crimson. 'I'm sure I can find some

sort of charge, such as obstructing a police officer in the execution of his duty.'

'Is that a threat?' Ruan asked from behind Rick's back.

'Rick, is this interview over?' Morwenna flopped back against the propped pillows. 'The thing is, I've just suffered a nasty attack that you can't get to the bottom of by yourself and, unless there's anything else you want to ask, I really need to rest. As soon as I'm well again, I have plenty to do – as I'm sure you do now.' She opened one eye. 'And please give Jane my best. I'll pop in and see her as soon as I can. There's no time to waste.'

The door banged open and Lamorna hurried in, carrying a huge bag of clothes for Morwenna, puffing hard. 'Morwenna, oh, bless you, I'm so glad you're all right. The nurse on the desk said the doctor would be here dreckly and if you're well enough, they might let you come home. I've brought you a nice Cornish pasty too, and a flask of tea – I bet the tea in here is weak as well water and you need a nice strong – oh, hello, Rick.' Lamorna fluffed her hair, preening herself. 'Have you found my daughter's attacker yet? Because if you haven't, I'll want to know why a big, strong, rugged police officer such as you is still standing around here doing nothing when there's a murderer on the loose, stabbing all and sundry in Seal Bay.'

'Lamorna, look here,' Rick began.

'I need to sit down. My hip kills. Will anyone tell me off if I sit on the edge of the bed?' She eased herself down. Lamorna ignored Rick, her eyes only for Morwenna. 'How are you, my bewty? I heard you'd had a knock to the head and a couple of stitches. Everyone in Seal Bay is talking about how brave you've been. Susan and Barb Grundy came into the teashop this morning, gushing all over me, saying that you'd dragged yourself out of the freezing water, half-dead, blood dripping from your head, and you'd found the PC lying on the sand stabbed, and you had hypothermia, but you still phoned 999... and Elowen sends you her love, and Tam and Jack. Oh, and Louise. Apparently, the smell of ectoplasm in the library is getting worse. Louise said you'd know what she means – I haven't got a clue what she's on about.' Lamorna turned back to the two men who stood behind her. 'Hello, Ruan – nice to see you, my lovely. Thanks for looking after Morwenna... Are you still here, Inspector?'

Rick Tremayne frowned. 'I had to conduct an interview.'

'Are you done now?' Lamorna asked. 'Only my daughter's had a serious head injury and she needs to rest.'

'I'm finished – for now.' Rick shrugged uncomfortably. 'But I'll be back.'

'What did the Terminator say when he took up playing the piano?' Lamorna laughed. 'I'll be Bach.'

She didn't notice Rick sloping out through the door. She was emptying her basket, lifting out warm pasties wrapped in a tea towel, and a large flask. She began to pour tea. 'I hope they don't mind if you bring your own food in here,' Lamorna muttered to herself. 'I brought you a pasty too, Ruan, because I knew you'd been here keeping an eye on Morwenna. Lord knows, she needs someone to look after her.' Lamorna turned back to her daughter. 'Proper proud I am of you. You're some maid, and that's for sure.'

Morwenna felt suddenly tired. 'Thanks, Mum. I definitely need a cuppa. I'm worn out.' She accepted the drink gratefully. 'Help me sit up a bit here. Do you think the doctor will come soon? Once I get the all-clear, I can go down to whichever ward Jane is on.'

'You should rest here,' Ruan said quickly.

'I want to be at home.' Morwenna's eyes flashed with determination.

'And straight to bed, I hope,' Lamorna added quickly.

'Well, I thought I'd prop myself up on the sofa with a few cushions and go through my list again.' Morwenna sipped her tea, glancing from Ruan to Lamorna. 'Now give me a hand – I need to see the doctor, get discharged and then I can get on and find who the killer is once and for all.'

22

Morwenna was quiet as Ruan drove the van away from the hospital. Ruan focused on the late-afternoon traffic, giving her space to think. She was still reeling from her visit to Chervil Ward where she'd spent ten minutes with Jane. It was when she first saw the PC lying in bed, inhaling oxygen, swathed in bandages, a drip in the back of her hand, that she realised how fortunate they had both been. Jane was conscious but not making much sense, drifting in and out of sleep, her eyelids heavy. Ruan said on the way out that the body recovered by resting, taking things slowly. But Morwenna had expected Jane to look better, to be able to remember things and answer questions. The nurse told her to come back tomorrow; Jane needed time to heal. Morwenna recalled that Jane lived alone, and she felt immediately sorry that she had no one to rush to her bedside. Morwenna was blessed; Ruan and Lamorna had been quick to support her and Tamsin had sent so many texts.

She resolved to ring the hospital first thing tomorrow to ask how Jane was progressing. She wondered if Rick Tremayne would organise flowers. She gazed out of the passenger window;

they were passing the beach, the place where she and Jane had been attacked.

Morwenna muttered, 'Can we call in at Woon's?'

'I'd rather you went straight home. It would have made sense to stay in hospital where they can look after you.'

'I have things to do, Ruan.'

'Please. Go home and sleep first.'

'Sleep afterwards?'

There's no talking to you when you've made your mind up.' Ruan replied, taking the road away from the hill to Harbour Cottages. 'What's worrying you?'

'I don't know.' Morwenna shook her head. 'I just want to see if anything jogs my memory.'

'All right – just for a few minutes, then home.' Ruan took the road to the boatyard, past tiny fishermen's cottages, driving through the tall gates and across gravel, stopping near the outbuildings. Morwenna clambered out carefully, conscious of the bandage on her head. Her limbs ached. She took a few tentative steps forward towards the boats; most were moored in the water at the quayside, tied with thick rope, but *The Pammy* had been lifted out on a crane, and was now stored upright on a stand. Jack was sitting on a stool, painting the hull below the waterline.

Ruan called out. 'Jack, how's it going?'

'I'm putting some anti-fouling paint on.' Jack stood up slowly. 'How are you doing, Morwenna? I'm sorry to hear about what happened. Tam told me. Are you all right?'

'I'm fine.' Morwenna put a hand to her head, touching the bandage. 'Are you enjoying working here?'

'Oh yes, and Damien is giving me even more overtime. There's so much to do. It's great for me and Tam.'

'Is Damien about?' Ruan asked.

'In the office, I think.' Jack watched as Ruan walked away, along the quay towards the little wooden office. 'How's your friend, the policewoman?'

'She'll be fine.' Morwenna hugged her coat, the one Lamorna had brought into the hospital. She was still feeling the wind's bite; her bones were still brittle with the ocean's cold. Then she remembered something. 'Jack, I'm so sorry. I haven't sent your mum's photos yet. I promised I'd get them to you and it's been ages.'

'That's not a problem really.' Jack looked down at his feet. 'To tell you the truth, Mum's more poorly than I told you. I popped up to see her but she can't have visitors for long. I don't really feel comfortable talking about it. I only saw her for half an hour. She perked up a bit – it was a good day. She has early onset dementia: she doesn't always recognise me.' His eyes gleamed; Morwenna wasn't sure if tears shone there or if it was due to the harsh wind from the sea. 'I said she had a nurse – well, she's in a nursing home. I miss her. I was hoping the photos might, you know, make her smile, trigger a memory... but they probably won't.'

'Oh, I'm so sorry, Jack.' Morwenna pressed his arm inside the thick jacket. 'That's so tough.'

'Home's here now,' Jack mumbled. 'With Tam and Elowen.'

'And your mum's in Gloucestershire?' Morwenna asked gently.

'Guildford,' Jack replied, his expression distant.

'Oh, I thought you said Gloucestershire?'

'Ah, that's what I meant.' Jack muttered. He lifted the paintbrush. 'I'd better get on.'

Morwenna watched as he took off his jacket and began to paint the hull. There was a tattoo on his forearm. Morwenna frowned. 'I didn't know you had a tattoo.'

Jack looked up and smiled. 'Tam and I both got them.' He

shrugged, a little embarrassed. 'She got a heart and I got a key – for soulmates.'

'That's so sweet,' Morwenna replied, then she noticed Ruan approaching with Damien Woon, their heads close, talking. They stopped next to *The Pammy* and Damien nodded curtly. 'I hear you're all right now.' He addressed Morwenna.

'I am,' Morwenna agreed. She glanced at Damien, his shirt sleeves rolled up, a rose tattoo on one muscular forearm, the name *Claire* scrolled beneath. It must be the name of the wife who left him. He was watching her, eyes narrowed. 'So – I just wanted to...' Morwenna had an excuse ready. 'To apologise for being here the other day... and for falling into the water. I hope it didn't spoil your meeting with Pam Truscott?' She scrutinised his face, wondering if there were signs of guilt there, a blink, a twist of the mouth.

'Ruan said you were looking at boats.' Damien shifted position.

Morwenna nodded. 'For Tam's wedding. I wondered if they'd like to get married at sea. Silly idea. A whim, a senior moment.'

'I hear you have a few leads,' Damien muttered. 'But you haven't found the bloke who killed Pam's husband?'

'No, but I will,' Morwenna said quietly. She noted the word 'bloke' and how he looked away. 'Who do you think it was?'

'No idea. Someone with a grudge. Dangerous business, if you ask me.' Damien grunted. 'I hear the policewoman got hurt badly.'

'She's recovering,' Morwenna replied. 'She'll be fine.'

Damien dipped his head towards Jack. 'Good worker, your lad here. I got plenty he can do at the boatyard and he's very keen.' He wiped his mouth on his sleeve. 'I reckon your daughter has got herself a good 'un, Ruan.'

Ruan nodded agreement. 'I'll get Morwenna back home,

Damien, and leave you to it.' He smiled towards Jack. 'See you later, Jack. Maybe we can catch up down The Smugglers for a pint?'

'I'm working overtime tonight,' Jack said. 'And in between, I like to get back to Tam before Elowen goes to bed. I always read her a story.'

'I'll meet you for a swift half.' Damien sniffed. 'And I'll do what you asked, Ruan, keep my ear close to the ground. If I hear anything about Alex, I'll let you know.'

'Thanks, Damien.'

'Right.' Damien turned to go. 'I'll be seeing you. And take care of that maid of yours – it seems to me that she attracts trouble.'

Ruan placed an arm around Morwenna as he led her back to the car. 'You're shivering. Let's get you home.'

'I'm cold.' Morwenna conceded. 'I don't much like the boatyard. It's an eerie place.'

'After dark it gets creepy. The old boats creak a bit.'

'Damien has got Jack doing up Pam Truscott's boat.' Morwenna spoke her thoughts aloud. 'That must be an expensive job.'

'It is. It will put Damien right back on his feet.'

'So, Alex's money is paying for it all?'

'I'd imagine so. Alex wasn't too fond of boats though.'

They'd reached the van and Ruan opened the passenger door. Morwenna hesitated. 'But boats are Pam's passion. And her brother Barnaby's?'

'That's right,' Ruan agreed.

'I wonder if Barnaby has a tattoo?' She frowned. 'It seems like just about everyone else in the world does.'

* * *

Morwenna spent most of the next day sleeping, which was not what she intended. But on Wednesday morning, she felt chirpier and rode her bicycle down to the library, past Susan and Barb Grundy's pop-up shop. They raised their knitting needles in greeting and she waved back.

Louise was surprised to see her. When Morwenna arrived, she was crouching in the corner, scrubbing the carpet.

'Do we have mildew?' Morwenna asked, perplexed, sniffing the air.

'It's ectoplasm,' Louise answered matter-of-factly. 'This patch of it is still soggy. Lady Elizabeth hasn't long gone.'

'Only about a hundred and fifty years ago.' Morwenna grinned. 'And her ectoplasm smells like rising damp – or a dead fish.'

'Oh, don't.' Louise shuddered. Then she stood up and opened her arms. 'It's good to see you, though. I've been so worried since I heard you were attacked and nearly drowned. Let me give you a hug.'

'Definitely. And put the kettle on.' Morwenna clasped Louise in a tight squeeze. 'Then you can tell me all the gossip about the ghost.'

* * *

Morwenna reached the Proper Ansom Tearoom just in time for the lunchtime rush. Tamsin was serving soup from a huge urn to tables full of customers. She glanced up as Morwenna opened the door with a clang.

'I'm so glad to see you, Mum. Grandma's not helping today.' She glanced at Morwenna's head, the light pad and micropore tape over the wound. 'Are you sure you're up to this though? Can you manage?'

'Get on.' Morwenna grinned. 'I'll take over here. You go on out back.'

'I've got scones to make… and then some,' Tamsin muttered, then she disappeared into the kitchen.

Morwenna rushed around, placing fresh soup, collecting empties. She had become something of a local celebrity, everyone wanting to chatter about who might have assaulted her. One young woman with a toddler even asked when the next wild swimming was, saying that she wanted to come along just for the hell of it. Morwenna said she'd let her know.

At four o'clock, most of the customers had gone. Lamorna banged through the door with Elowen, who was clutching Oggy Two and berating Oggy One for misbehaving in the classroom that afternoon. 'He was a naughty dog. He bited Billy Crocker's English book and ruined his work and Miss Parker said it was me who ripped it up, but it wasn't me and I told her that her eyesight must be crap. She wasn't very pleased.'

'I bet she wasn't.' Lamorna groaned. 'Let me sit down, my lovely, I have to take the weight off my feet. I'm getting too old for this.'

'So Miss Parker told me I was a naughty girl for saying bad words and I said it was Oggy who said it not me, and he hearded it from Great Grandma but it wasn't rude because she always speaks as she finds…'

'Oh dear.' Lamorna sighed, then she beamed as Tamsin placed a mug of tea and a scone in front of her, juice and toast for Elowen. 'Ansom. That's just what I needed…'

'Thanks for fetching her from school, Grandma. Here, let's have a break…'

'Good idea.' Lamorna sipped from her mug. 'Oh, that's better.' She glanced across at Morwenna who was wiping a table clean. 'Come and join me, my bewty. You need a rest too.'

Tamsin brought more tea and toast. 'Yes, come on. Let's take five.'

'The nights are drawing in.' Morwenna slumped at the table; she was weary now and the thought of cycling back up the hill in twilight filled her with unease. She glanced at the tattoo on Tamsin's arm, touching it with light fingers. 'These are all the rage, Tam.'

'They are.' Tamsin sat down and reached for the mug of tea. 'A heart and a key, soulmates.'

'We'll need to be planning the wedding,' Lamorna said as she slurped.

'Jack's determined we'll have enough money for Christmas, though I think we should wait until summer. It's the only thing we argue about.' Tamsin said sadly.

'He's doing well at Woon's,' Lamorna encouraged. 'Plenty of work.'

'Oh, I hope so. The thing is, if the job at Woon's fizzles out, we'd have to go where the work is.'

'You're not going to move away, Tam?' Lamorna was shocked.

'Jack and I were talking the other night – there's not enough work in Cornwall.'

Morwenna shook her head. 'We'll manage, we're a family.'

'Do you think we should have sold to Alex Truscott?' Tamsin bit her lip.

'Not at all,' Morwenna said determinedly and Lamorna folded her arms.

'Over my dead body.'

'No, Great Grandma, it was Alex's dead body – somebody knifeded him in the back on the beach at Mummy's party,' Elowen said proudly and Lamorna was horrified. Elowen lifted Oggy Two, showing the purple face to Morwenna. 'Oggy Two says a naughty lady hit you when you were swimming and I couldn't sleep, Grandma. I had nightbears, but Oggy One kept me safe and said he'd look after me.'

Lamorna smoothed Elowen's dark hair. 'We'll keep you safe, my lovely. Don't you worry.'

Elowen gave a wide smile and Morwenna noticed one of her front teeth was coming loose. 'I don't want to miss my party on Friday after school. Did you know it's my birthday, Grandma?'

'Everyone knows you're six on Friday, Elowen.' Tamsin said proudly. 'And I've invited lots of classmates here after school for a celebration.'

'Even Billy Crocker's invited.' Elowen pouted. 'Mummy says I have to be nice to him but I said I'm not kissing him like she kisses Jack.'

Tamsin grinned to cover the sudden awkwardness. 'I'm baking a big cake—'

'A dog cake, just like Oggy Two.' Elowen interrupted. 'With purple icing, and my friends are coming here and we'll play games and chase round the tearoom.'

'It's fancy dress.' Tamsin smiled weakly and Morwenna thought she looked tired.

'Everybody is coming dressed as animals.' Elowen bounced in her seat. 'Mummy's making me an Oggy costume. I want to wear it for school on Friday but Miss Parker won't let me because that woman has no sense of fun. Great Grandma said that.'

'I did,' Lamorna admitted with a guilty shrug.

'Can you help out?' Tamsin turned to Morwenna. 'I've asked Dad, and if you're feeling well enough, I could do with a hand on Friday afternoon.'

'I'll be here.'

'Jack will too – he said he wouldn't miss it for the world.' Tamsin smiled. She ruffled Elowen's hair. 'Big birthday girl on Friday, aren't you, my sweetie?'

'Ah, Friday though...' Lamorna suddenly looked anxious. 'Friday the thirteenth. Unlucky day, that is.'

Elowen's face suddenly clouded. 'Can't I have my birthday party any more? Will I be unlucky if I have it on Friday?'

'Not at all,' Tamsin soothed. 'Great Grandma's being superstitious.'

'I might bring a bottle of wine along, just for the adults – for luck.' Lamorna said. 'It'll keep us all cheery.'

'Oggy likes wine, he just told me,' Elowen chirped. 'And I like it too. Can I have wine, Mummy? It *is* my birthday.'

'I don't think so.' Tamsin frowned. 'You can stick to lemonade.'

'We'll have the best six-year-old birthday party ever,' Morwenna said, leaning forward on her elbows. 'We'll have cake and games. You wait and see, Elowen. You'll be the happiest birthday girl in the world.' Her face was set, determined. 'This family deserves to have some fun.'

23

Morwenna found the next few days more difficult than she'd expected. The hospital doctor had told her she'd be tired, but nothing had prepared her for how sluggish her body would feel. It was hard to get up in the morning, and she was worn-out by half past seven in the evening. The time in between that was the worst, trying to stay alert. She felt lethargic as she rode her bicycle, even downhill; each turn on the pedal made the muscles in her legs burn. In the library, she found it difficult to concentrate. Simon Truscott came in to borrow a copy of *Cultivating Mushrooms in Britain*. Apparently, it was his latest money-making project. If she'd had more energy, Morwenna would have suggested he started his new hobby in the library corner – the ectoplasm deposited on the carpet was a perfect base for them to thrive. Louise confided in Morwenna that culinary mushrooms were probably not the type he was intending to grow; her evidence was that he was looking the worse for wear. Morwenna felt sorry for him: he was finding life difficult without his father.

Life in the tearoom was quiet. A few customers came in at lunchtimes and regulars popped in for tea and cake in the afternoon, but the takings were not matching the overheads. Morwenna did her best to chivvy the customers into staying on, despite her aching feet and the dull throb in her head. Tamsin's mood changed: she was immersed in her own thoughts most of the time. On Thursday afternoon, when the last customer slid through the door, clanging the bell behind them, Morwenna noticed her daughter poring over figures at the counter.

'Penny for them, Tam?'

'Oh...' Tamsin glanced up. 'Just working out a few sums.'

'How are we doing?' Morwenna asked cheerfully.

'So-so.' Tamsin was being non-committal. She checked numbers again, reaching for her mug without looking up.

Morwenna tried again. 'The soup's very popular.'

Tamsin looked up and her eyes glistened. 'It won't be enough, Mum.'

Morwenna moved closer. 'How can I help?'

'You can't. Jack's working all the shifts he can get at the boatyard. At least that's making a difference but...' She took a shuddering breath and Morwenna was reminded of her daughter at Elowen's age, plucky, a fighter. 'I've moved the wedding to the summer.'

'That's probably wise. Summer's nicer, warm weather, and you'll have more time to save up.'

Tamsin nodded vigorously. 'I thought that it made more sense. Jack thinks we should sell the tearoom.'

'The Muttons have had the tearoom for over thirty years! Mum started the business in the nineties.' Morwenna sighed.

'And it will end with me. I've failed, Mum.'

'No, you haven't, Tam. Business will turn round.'

'I don't think so...' Tamsin turned abruptly and was in Morwenna's arms, sobbing on her shoulder.

Morwenna tightened her grasp, pulling her close. Her jaw set determinedly. 'We'll find a way through this, my lovely.'

'I've got Elowen to think about.' She pulled away. 'Jack says it's probably not wise to sink all the money he's making at Woon's into a failing business. And I think he has a point but...'

'But?'

'It's our decision to make, selling, turning the place into a pizza takeaway – mine and yours and Grandma's, not his. I said that to Jack and we had a row.'

'You're right.' Morwenna saw herself in her daughter, she saw Lamorna, the Mutton grit, the stubborn determination.

'Jack said I didn't love him. Because I want to put the wedding back, he thought that I was pushing him away.'

'It's not like that, Tam.'

'He said I was turning my back on him like you turned away from Dad.'

'He's wrong.'

Tamsin wiped her eyes. 'I'm sure Dad still loves you, Mum.'

'We care for each other,' Morwenna said quickly. 'But this is about you and Jack. You need to talk things through.'

'At the moment we just argue.'

'Maybe it's just a phase – it'll make you stronger.'

'It didn't make you and Dad stronger – you split up.'

'Oh, Tam,' Morwenna sighed: Tamsin was right.

'And Grandma's had so many men friends, but she couldn't make it work with any of them.' Tamsin wiped her face with her fingers. 'Maybe it's the curse of the Mutton maids.' She forced a laugh. 'We're doomed to be alone.'

Morwenna shook her head and the wound twinged beneath the micropore tape. 'You need to talk to Jack.'

'He has no family of his own apart from his mum, and she's so unwell. That's why he clings to me and Elowen, and he loves you and Grandma. He says all the time how much he admires you both. And Dad. His mother told him to come here, you know, to make a new life for himself.'

'That's so sad,' Morwenna admitted. 'Look, Tam, It's Elowen's party tomorrow. If you like, I'll take her up to Harbour Cottages afterwards for a sleepover, a birthday night out with Grandma, so you and Jack can have some quality time.'

'Mum, that would be really good.' Tamsin hugged Morwenna again. 'That's just what we need.' She was suddenly anxious. 'Are you sure you're up to it, after what happened? I worry about you sometimes, all alone, up on the hill.'

'Your dad's just across the road.' Morwenna smiled and immediately regretted saying it. Having Ruan living so close was a blessing, they looked out for each other, but Morwenna didn't want to imply that she needed looking after, because she didn't. She immediately checked herself – Ruan had been the first person she'd called after she'd dialled 999 on the beach, her head bleeding, her body shaking with cold. She'd automatically thought of him. She sighed. 'I'm fine.'

'If you're sure.' Tamsin said. 'I'd better get on. Elowen's upstairs in the flat doing homework, copying from a book – Imelda Parker's got her drawing a parent in the L. S. Lowry style. I should start making her dinner. Jack's home at seven tonight and then I have Elowen's Oggy costume to finish and I'm the worst seamstress in the world.'

'You're not.' Morwenna grinned. 'I was awful at it, still am. I darned a sock for your dad once and it was so knobbly, he couldn't put his shoe on.' She remembered – those were happy times. 'I can't say I'm looking forward to pedalling up that hill in the darkness. I need to save up and buy myself an electric bike.'

'I wish I could buy one for you, Mum,' Tamsin said sadly,

hugging her again. 'Well, I'll see you tomorrow for the party. Elowen is six already.'

Morwenna thought that it seemed only moments since Tamsin was Elowen's age. She sighed. 'Time flies...'

'It does. I remember when the tearoom made a profit.' Tamsin pulled a face as she held up the sheet of paper she'd been working on, rough figures. For a moment, she looked as though she might crumble, then she forced a brave smile. 'We'll be all right, Mum – we're made of strong stuff.'

'We are,' Morwenna agreed heartily and stepped out into the night air, straddling her bicycle, pushing off into the road. The first turn of the pedal made her thighs ache. The second nearly killed her. It was going to be a long ride home.

* * *

It was past eight. The table lamp glowed dimly in the little sitting room of number four, Harbour Cottages, and a fire burned cosily in the grate. Morwenna sat on the squashy sofa, supported by cushions, her feet up. Her calves were cramping and it felt good to be surrounded by softness. She closed her eyes, thinking. The problem was that all the suspects had reasons why they might have killed Alex Truscott, but no individual stood out. She ought to meet Barnaby Stone, talk to Rosie Buvač and Milan. Something drew her back to Woon's boatyard. Then she thought again of her attacker – if only she could remember clearly what happened – there must be a clue about who had grabbed her from behind.

Morwenna's eyelids were growing heavy; she relaxed, surrounded by warmth, and dozed. For a moment, she was back in Half Moon Cottage, staring at the lovingly brushed paintings on the wall: naked Alex, the broad torso, naked Beverley in his arms, her signature, BEV O. She recalled Beverley painting the picture of the two lovers, her arm stretched towards the canvas, a small angel tattoo on her forearm. Another suspect with a tattoo. Even Rick Tremayne had one. Tattoos weren't the answer. She sat up, blinking herself awake. Someone was knocking at the front door.

Morwenna slid from the sofa and padded in thick socks through the hall, opening the door and peering through the crack. 'Ruan?'

'Can I come in?' He was holding a bottle of cognac. 'I thought you might like a nightcap.'

'Oh?'

'Tam phoned – she said you were looking tired.'

'Come on into the warm.' Morwenna led him to the sitting room. 'Tam's looking tired too. She and Jack have been arguing. The tearoom isn't doing well.'

'I know.' Ruan plonked himself on the sofa, watching Morwenna collect two glasses from the kitchen. 'I'm worried about her. She's lost her sparkle.' He poured brandy, passing a glass to Morwenna. 'And I'm worried about you, after everything. How are you feeling?'

'A bit better.' Morwenna sipped the fiery liquid. 'Thanks, Ruan. That's kind.' She sat down next to him. 'Thoughtful of you.'

'You have to take things steadily,' Ruan said quietly. 'It's Elowen's party tomorrow.'

'I'm bringing her back here for a sleepover, so that Tam and Jack can have quality time.'

'Tam told me. I'll help, shall I? I thought we could take her out in the van, maybe?'

'Ruan.' Morwenna met his eyes, her voice firm. 'I'm very grateful for your support after the note through the letterbox and the graffiti on the library wall and the incident on the beach with Jane Choy, but I'll be all right.'

'I'm not doubting that you're smart and feisty and tough and clever,' Ruan said. 'I just thought we could spend time with Elowen on her birthday.'

'When you put it like that,' Morwenna smiled. 'How can I say no?'

'We can forget about who killed Alex for a while, I'm sure.' Ruan brought the drink to his lips. Morwenna noted the word 'we' as she gazed at his face in the glow of the lamplight.

'You're right,' Morwenna agreed. 'I'll be glad when it's all over and we can get back to normal.'

'Me too. Who knows what normal will bring?' Ruan raised his glass. 'Whatever happens, it will be nice to relax again in Seal Bay. Here's to normal.'

'To normal,' Morwenna repeated. She closed her eyes. Right now, she was too tired to think about anything other than the sharp taste of brandy on her tongue, the basking warmth of the fire and the handsome man next to her with whom she felt completely at ease.

24

Morwenna was lying on the sofa, wrapped in a duvet. Her head felt fuzzy, although she'd only drunk two small brandies. She'd slept deeply; she still hadn't emerged from the liminal space of dreams, and was just beginning to realise where she was. She'd fallen asleep; Ruan must have covered her up, switched off the lamp and let himself out. She stretched an arm, fumbling for her phone where she'd placed it on the coffee table. It was past eight. He'd be out on the trawler already.

She eased herself upright. There was a message from Louise. Donald had volunteered to do her morning shift in the library so that she could spend more time helping Tamsin prepare for Elowen's party. Morwenna smiled; people in Seal Bay were so thoughtful. She texted back with thanks and she hoped they'd all be able to go swimming in the sea soon, probably not this Sunday, but the 22nd was a definite possibility. She'd have recovered by then.

Feeling decidedly chirpy, she took herself off for a hot shower, dressing warmly in a sloppy green cardigan with a mushroom border and bold flower-print leggings. She shrugged on a long yellow woollen coat that she'd bought twenty years ago, then added a scarf and mittens. Her bag was stuffed with party paraphernalia, a cat mask complete with fluffy ears and a pin-on tail, and Elowen's present, a vet's costume she'd bought online, including a thermometer, cloth bandage, toy syringe, and a stethoscope with sound effects. It might encourage Elowen towards a sparkling future career. Morwenna was ready for the day. It was all downhill to the Proper Ansom Tearoom. She wouldn't worry about the uphill journey home until later.

On her way to the tearoom, Morwenna called in at the pop-up knitting shop where Susan and Barb Grundy were knitting jumpers. Morwenna ordered a couple straight away for Christmas, matching stripey ones for Elowen and Tamsin. Barb noticed the mushroom design on her cardigan and immediately promised to create the most colourful jumper to go with her bright leggings. They delayed her for fifteen minutes, asking about the incident on the beach, whether she had a prime suspect and was it Pam Truscott, whom they were sure was the killer? Morwenna wished them a good day and turned her cycle towards the teashop.

There were no customers, just Tamsin standing on a chair, busily putting up balloons everywhere and a glittering sign with pink crowns and stars that read, *Now You're Six*. Morwenna called as she came in, 'I'm a bit early.'

Tamsin made a muffled reply: she was clenching drawing pins between her teeth. Morwenna said, 'It's party time!'

Tamsin clambered down, pins now in her palm. 'I'm shattered already, and we haven't started yet. It's gone ten – I've only had two customers and all they wanted was a pot of Cornish brew.'

'What's the soup of the day?'

'Mushroom.' Tamsin nodded towards her mother's cardigan. 'You're dressed perfectly for the job.'

'Right,' Morwenna rubbed her hands together. 'What shall I do first?'

'Let's sit down a minute and then we'll decide.' Tamsin plonked herself at a table and Morwenna moved to the hot water urn.

'Tea's up dreckly,' she answered, dropping teabags into mugs.

They sat at a table with a smart checked cloth and Morwenna said, 'How's it going, Tam?'

'Not bad. It was tough getting Elowen off to school this morning – she wanted to open all her presents, then she announced that it was Oggy's birthday too and I had to make sure he had presents... I told her that I had lots for him but they were all invisible. She wasn't impressed.'

Morwenna reached for her mug. 'That was quick thinking!'

'Mum, do you think this Oggy thing is a worry? Is it a sign Elowen is lonely?'

'You're her mum, Tam – what does your instinct say?'

Tamsin frowned. 'I used to think it was because I took up with Jack. Elowen had me to herself for the first five years of her life. I wondered if being with him meant that she invented a partner too.'

'Maybe she just wants a dog?'

'Perhaps. Do you think I should get her a pet?'

'It might be difficult while you're running the tearoom, and you're so busy with Elowen, especially now Jack's working long hours.'

'But a small dog might be all right. We could take it for a walk first thing, then out on the beach at night.'

'I don't know.' Morwenna was thinking about the dangers that lurked in the darkness. 'Maybe wait and see.' She brightened. 'Anyway, today's Elowen's birthday and we'll give her a great time.'

'I've been at it for hours. Elowen was up at six – she's lost a front tooth and she was checking if the tooth fairy had been. Jack put a pound coin under her pillow.' Tamsin closed her eyes. 'I have an Oggy Two cake the size of Cornwall, a fridge full of nibbles. And I'm still not done.'

'What do you need?'

'Sandwiches, drinks, I need to wrap the pass the parcel... I'm going to do face painting for the kids.'

The doorbell chimed. Morwenna and Tamsin looked up hopefully for a customer but Lamorna breezed in, all smiles. 'I got the bus and it was on time for once.'

Tamsin was on her feet, pouring tea. 'Have you come to help?'

'I have. I thought I'd make blancmange.'

Tamsin pulled a face. 'Oh, no, Grandma – the kids will just throw it about. It's disgusting stuff.'

'Do you remember the Angel Delight that we used to get in the sixties?' Morwenna sighed. 'It was lush, especially the butterscotch one.'

'I can't think of anything worse – the kids can have proper Cornish ice cream.' Tamsin grinned.

'Blancmange though...' Lamorna made a dreamy face. 'Made fresh from the packet with Cornish strawberries and the top of the milk.' She glanced at Tamsin. 'You youngsters don't know you're born. In the fifties we got food you could just whip up in a moment. It was glorious. We had instant mashed potatoes and then suddenly, everything was instant and in packets, trifle, curry and rice, lemon meringue.'

'Dream Topping... It was so sweet and fluffy!' Morwenna added enthusiastically.

'And now we try to cook our kids healthy food from scratch,' Tamsin insisted. 'I bake every day'

Lamorna winked. 'I've seen those burgers in your freezer.'

'They're Jack's; bad habits from his bedsit days,' Tamsin insisted with a laugh. Then the door chimed and an older couple in warm jackets walked in looking windswept.

'Hello.' The man raised a cheery hand. 'Is it too early for a cheese toastie? It's bitterly cold out there on the beach...'

'Coming up right away!' Tamsin was out of her seat. 'And the bread's home baked.'

'Oh, just what we need,' the woman in the anorak said. 'Proper Cornish home cooking.'

Customers began to trickle in, a steady stream of hungry people keeping Morwenna and Tamsin busy while Lamorna continued to talk about the good old days. Before they knew it, it was three o'clock, and Lamorna jumped up.

'Time for me to go and collect our little heller from school.' She glanced towards Tamsin. 'Birthday or not, she'll have got herself in hot water today with the teacher, that's for sure. What with Oggy the invisible dog. Did you ever hear the like?'

Tamsin's brow furrowed anxiously. 'Mum and I were talking about that earlier, Grandma. Do you reckon she's troubled?'

'I don't think so...' Lamorna folded her arms. 'She's not still fighting at school with Billy Crocker?'

'I think things are better now. She has nightmares sometimes, though.'

'There you are then, Tam. She's just a normal child. Don't you worry. Right...' Lamorna struggled into her coat. 'I'd better stand at the gate with all the other young mums and bring our little maid back for her party. Is everything ready?'

'We're nearly there,' Tamsin replied. 'The idea of all those kiddies running round screaming is giving me a headache before we start.'

'We should have asked Milan Buvač to come; he could have done his Captain Pugwash act and kept them quiet with a yarn or two,' Morwenna said.

'He might be at the school gates. If he is, I'll entice him back. Handsome man, good beard on him. I like a man with muscles...' Lamorna observed.

'I'll put a few pasties in the oven,' Tamsin suggested.

'I'll get the wine out as soon as I'm back,' Lamorna added. 'We adults need to stay sane somehow.' And with that she was gone.

Morwenna and Tamsin changed quickly into their fancy dress, both cats, Morwenna black with a long tail and Tamsin ginger with white whiskers, then they set to work putting out plates of sandwiches, buns, bowls of fruit and crudités, small pies, jugs of juice and water. In the centre of one table, Tamsin placed a huge cake shaped like a dog, covered with ragged purple icing and six candles.

Morwenna raised an eyebrow. 'Will that be safe there?'

'Or will Oggy eat it all?' Tamsin grinned.

The door was pushed open and Ruan strode in, his hair still damp, fresh from the shower. 'Am I on time?'

Tamsin rushed over and hugged him. 'Come in, Dad. The youngsters are due here any second.' Morwenna smiled at the close bond between them.

'What can I do to help, Tam?' he asked.

'Break up any fights. Make sure there's no punching or scratching or biting. Keep an eye on our Elowen and Billy Crocker. She's bound to fall out with him at some point.'

'Right, I have the easy job.' Ruan smiled at Morwenna, who

was laying out cups and saucers for the adults. 'Can't I help with the food?'

'Seriously, Dad – just watch the kids. It's a full-time job, keeping an eye on that lot.' Tamsin glanced towards the door. 'Have you got fancy dress?'

Ruan sat at one of the tables and pulled a pile of grey furry rags from his bag. 'Wolf... best I can do.'

'Jack's due any moment – he's got a fox costume. You and he can chat to the parents, while you're keeping an eye on the children.'

'Right you are,' Ruan said as the door flew open and three lively boys rushed in dressed as dinosaurs, followed by a tired-looking young woman in a long dress. She lifted a desperate hand towards Morwenna. 'I'm gasping for a cup...'

'Coming up.'

The three boys were already attacking sandwiches. Tamsin said, 'Can we wait until the others arrive, please? Elowen's not here yet...'

The door opened wide again and five children bundled in, dressed in wild animal garb, shrieking loudly. Two adults straggled after them, then another group of children scurried in, leaving the door open. One of the adults shouted, 'Born in a barn, were 'ee?' and a girl in a bee costume closed it instantly. Carole Taylor hurried in with a lively Britney, who was wearing a rabbit outfit, announcing that Maya Buvač wasn't coming because she was sick. The children continued to screech, then the door opened again and Billy Crocker bounded in dressed as a sheep with huge googly eyes. He pointed to Tamsin.

'Hey, Elowen ain't coming to the party now. The old woman who picks her up said she can't find her, so we may as well start without her.'

Tamsin turned abruptly. 'What?'

'She's disappeared.'

'What?' Tamsin said again and the room was suddenly quiet.

'Giss on, Billy!' Carole Taylor shook her head. 'Elowen wouldn't miss her own party.'

'It's true, I tell you – she ain't coming.'

Ruan was on his feet, then he crouched next to the boy. 'What's happened, Billy?'

'I was waiting ages because my mummy got stuck at work and came late to pick me up – and everyone else had gone off home to get ready for the party. The old lady with the yellow hair was still waiting by the gates, then I saw her talking to Miss Parker. Miss Parker said she'd have to go and check and the old lady was shouting "Where's Elowen gone?" Like I said, she ain't coming.'

'I didn't see anything,' one of the other mums frowned.

'Nor did I.' One of the dads agreed. 'Lamorna was waiting at the gates as usual, then I had to hurry back to get Fay changed for the party.' He indicated a small girl in a fairy costume.

'Mum will have sent me a message.' Morwenna checked her phone. 'Yes. She's on her way – she's just texted to ask if Elowen came back here by herself...'

'Then where is she? Where's my little girl?' Tamsin's voice was a whisper. The room was silent and Billy Crocker looked around himself to see if he'd done right or wrong.

'Come to think of it, Lamorna was still waiting when I left the school,' someone remarked. 'I never thought anything of it. Sometimes Miss Parker keeps the kiddies back after the bell...'

The door crashed open and Lamorna rushed into the room. She was breathless, flushed, a hand on her heart. She struggled to speak, her words muffled. Tamsin and Morwenna were at her side. Her face was ashen as she gasped, 'She's not here? Then where can she be?'

'What?' Tamsin was shaking. 'Where's Elowen, Gran?'

'Imelda Parker said she came out of class with the other kiddies as soon as the bell rang. And I was at the gate on time. But she was nowhere to be seen – I told Miss Parker she was so keen to get to her party, she might've rushed home by herself.'

'So where *is* she?' Tamsin jumped as her phone rang in her pocket. She tugged it out. 'It's the school…' She turned her back to take the call. Morwenna heard her say 'Oh… are you sure? Yes, I will – and get back to you…'

Ruan was at the door. 'I'll go back to check again. Maybe she's in one of the classrooms, maybe she's been delayed for some reason…' The door clanged behind him.

Lamorna could hardly speak, she was breathless. 'Where can she be? I don't understand—'

'I saw her.' Britney chimed. 'She was with a man.'

'What man?' Carole asked.

'A big man.'

'The school say there's no trace of her on the premises. They told me to call the police.' Tamsin clutched her phone, pressing buttons, fingers trembling. She spoke hurriedly. 'Jack… Elowen hasn't come home. Tell me she's with you…You haven't seen her? Oh, yes… soon as you can, please.' She glanced up. 'Jack's on his way from Woon's. He's just finished work. I thought he might have picked her up but she's not with him…'

'So where can she be?' Lamorna gasped.

Tamsin leaned on the counter for support. 'I don't know.'

Morwenna's phone was in her hand. 'I'm calling the police now.'

She gazed round the tearoom, taking in the staring eyes of children in animal fancy dress, no one moving. Parents stood with their mouths open, stunned.

'Hello, it's Morwenna Mutton.' She spoke breathlessly into

the mouthpiece. 'Can you send someone round to the tearoom on the seafront right away. Yes, now please. My six-year-old granddaughter has gone missing.'

25

The police arrived in minutes. The children were shepherded away quickly with doggy bags, many of the parents telephoning friends and relatives as they left, asking them to keep an eye open for Elowen. A tall man in uniform introduced himself as the CIM, a colleague of DI Tremayne, explaining that he managed critical incidents and would take charge. He reassured Tamsin that the police took missing children very seriously. They'd spoken to the head teacher at the school and this was deemed a critical incident: specialist teams would be involved. Morwenna listened intently; Tamsin was struggling to take it all in. A force support group – FSG – was already in action, and a dive team. The police forces in Devon, Somerset and beyond had been alerted – the CIM called this Mutual Aid. He asked for a recent photo of Elowen, selecting one Morwenna took at Pettarock, and DNA examples: clothing, a hairbrush. Rick's colleague reassured the family that a team of officers were searching Seal Bay and beyond, throughout Cornwall. Tamsin nodded weakly – everyone was doing their best.

Word of Elowen's disappearance travelled quickly across Seal

Bay. The photo of her, smiling, holding Oggy Two, was on the television six o'clock news programme. Ruan and a local search party scoured the town and the beaches into the night for any sight of the small child, but with no luck. By midnight they were back, drinking hot tea to warm freezing fingers, shaking their heads: they'd found no sign of the poor little maid.

Tamsin's face was creased with crying; Jack hadn't left her side all evening, constantly whispering heartening words, promising that Elowen would be found soon, safe and well. Tamsin clung to him, at times doing her best to believe him, at others dissolving into fresh tears, terrified at the thought of where her little girl might be.

At midnight, a police officer arrived with an update. He explained that he was a LPSM, Lost Person Search Manager, but they could call him PC Jim Hobbs. There was still nothing to report, so he encouraged Tamsin and Jack to try to get some sleep and the search would continue throughout the night. Drivers of all police cars had been made aware of Elowen's disappearance and were constantly vigilant. He offered soothing advice; Elowen might simply have wandered off. But Tamsin was distraught: Elowen had never strayed before and Jack repeated that Britney Taylor had seen Elowen leave the playground with 'a big man'. The officer said kindly that Britney might have made a mistake; no one else saw anyone at all. But the search was extensive and nothing had been ruled out.

It was gone two in the morning when Ruan took Morwenna and Lamorna home in his van, the bicycle in the back. A few lights twinkled across the bay, but it was mostly pitch dark. Everyone was thinking about Elowen. Morwenna and Ruan accompanied Lamorna inside her cottage, where she drank a whisky in two gulps and made Ruan promise he'd be round first thing on Saturday morning to bring her to the tearoom – she wouldn't sleep a wink all night. Then he drove to number four Harbour Cottages, depositing the bicycle in the hall. Hardly a word was spoken; they were both exhausted and numb. Ruan and Morwenna sat together on the sofa, shoulders touching, terrified that there might be a phone call or a knock at the door at any point confirming their worst fears.

After whispering quietly for a while about how they could best support Tamsin, they finally fell asleep, Morwenna's head against Ruan's shoulder. Morwenna slept badly, her mind full of thoughts that knocked together like rocks, the idea that Elowen might be alone outside, lost on the beach, or worse. She couldn't bear to think of it, but the image of a little girl slumped on the beach, the sea washing over her, continued to haunt her.

Her eyes opened in darkness. Someone was knocking. Morwenna switched on a lamp. The knock came again.

'Ruan?'

He made a muffled sound, then he was wide awake.

'There's someone at the door...'

Morwenna stood up, fully clothed and too warm, and surged forward. Ruan was at her shoulder. She opened the door to see Jane Choy outside, a bandage around her arm.

'Jane – what time is it?'

'Half six. I got out of hospital last night. I heard about Elowen.'

'Come in...'

Morwenna and Jane sat on the sofa together while Ruan bustled in the kitchen. Morwenna could hear water splashing into the kettle.

'How are you?'

'Well enough.' Jane shook her head. 'I'm not allowed back at work yet, obviously. And I can't go swimming. I can't exercise or lift or do much at all. I shouldn't have driven.'

'Should you be here?' Ruan handed her a mug.

'Not really,' Jane mumbled. 'But I can help. You and me, Morwenna, we're a team. I want to help find your granddaughter.'

Morwenna's eyes shone with gratitude. 'Thanks, Jane. Have you heard anything?'

'Not much. Jim Hobbs is the LPSM officer on the case. He's a good guy – he's liaising with Tamsin and her partner. He's with them now.'

'No news of Elowen?'

'No, but in some ways, no news is good news.' Jane's gaze was steady. 'Let's hope my colleagues pick her up soon and she's right as rain...'

Morwenna closed her eyes. She thought she might cry. 'Poor Elowen.'

'We have to stay strong,' Jane muttered. 'We have to put together everything we know and search for her. We'll start in Seal Bay.'

Morwenna nodded, taking a deep breath.

'Can I level with you both?' Jane asked. 'I mean, as a professional, this is my opinion.'

'Go ahead...' Ruan glanced to Morwenna who agreed with a sharp inclination of her head.

'There are three scenarios, unless she's genuinely just lost, in which case we'll find her soon; she'll be cold, hungry, someone will spot her or she'll simply come home. But I think the greatest likelihood is that someone has taken Elowen. There's nothing to be gained from anyone taking her other than to prove that they can, that they have control. Criminals like to demonstrate that they are in charge. If that's the case, they've made their point – they'll let her go soon and we'll find her safe and well in the next day or two.'

'The second scenario?' Ruan asked.

'Whoever has her will make a demand. They'll tell us what they want – Elowen is currency...'

'Right...' Morwenna caught her breath. 'You know I'll do anything to get Elowen back.'

'And the third possibility – we won't think about it at the moment.'

'It's unthinkable.' Ruan reached for Morwenna's hand.

'We have to find her.' Morwenna said determinedly 'How do we do it?'

'Carefully, so as not to arouse suspicion.' Jane leaned back on the sofa. It was clear that the visit was exhausting her. 'We'll make a plan, based on the suspects, and we'll check them out one by one and see what we can find out.'

'We can't assume anything,' Morwenna added. 'We can't let ourselves be led down the wrong path because we like someone or we think they are too nice to hurt Elowen. As far as I'm concerned, everyone in Seal Bay is a suspect.'

'We'll find her, or the police will. I'm quietly confident,' Jane said. 'They've drafted in an SIO to lead the incident team now.'

'What does that mean?'

'A superintendent who's overseeing the search: it's been escalated to the highest level. Jim Hobbs and the CIM who's an inspector in Truro will let me know any new evidence they have. I know Jim well and he promised me he'd fill me in on any developments. I can't go back to work yet, but I'm darned if I'm going to sit back while someone has kidnapped your child.'

'Thanks, Jane,' Morwenna murmured.

'I'm going home to do some research. I'll go through your list, dig around, talk to some colleagues beyond Cornwall and see if they have any information. If Elowen's out there, we'll find her if anyone can.'

'Good idea... Stay in touch.' Morwenna noticed how tired Jane looked. 'Ruan and I will check how Tam is and see if there have been any developments. Then I'm going to go to all the places Elowen might be and have a look around for myself. I'll see what I can find out. She has to be somewhere.' She took a deep breath. 'Tam must be going through hell.'

* * *

'I want to go back to everyone who was at the party, Ruan. Everyone. I want to search locations and ask more questions,' Morwenna said desperately as Ruan parked outside the tearoom behind Jack's white van and a police car. The door was open although the sign read *Closed*: it was almost eight o'clock. Tamsin looked like she hadn't slept. She could hardly stand; her legs faltered beneath her and her hand shook as she held the cup of tea Morwenna made for her. Jack stood with his arm around her, shaking his head. He looked stunned; clearly, he had no idea how to help. Morwenna led her daughter to a table, sitting her down, and Ruan and Jack joined them. PC Jim Hobbs sat opposite, talking quietly. 'Today we're going to knock on doors, ask members of the public if they've seen anything at all. The slightest clue might lead to us finding Elowen.'

'What can we do?' Jack asked, squeezing Tamsin's hand.

'You should go to work, Jack.' Tamsin said feebly.

'I'm staying with you.'

'We should try to carry on...' Tamsin sighed. 'We need the money.'

'I want to be here, in case there's any news.'

Tamsin gazed at him, her eyes dead as a fish's. 'I'll ring you if I hear...' Then she began to cry and Jack collected her in his arms, kissing the top of her head.

'If you really want me to, I'll go to the boatyard. But I'll text you every hour.'

'I'll message you if...' Tamsin was tired.

'Will there be more searches?' Ruan asked. 'I know everyone in Seal Bay wants to help.'

'Yes, we're organising that,' Jim Hobbs said.

'We have to do something,' Ruan replied.

'I'm closing the tearoom – I don't know what to do,' Tamsin murmured.

'Ruan will fetch Mum and she'll stay here with you,' Morwenna said. 'I'm going to get out and talk to a few people, see what I can find out.'

'I wouldn't do anything that would upset DI Tremayne,' Jim Hobbs said gently.

Tamsin's face was a mask of anger. 'I couldn't care less about Rick Tremayne. He's done nothing so far to help since Alex was stabbed. He better not come here with his excuses – there's someone out there with my daughter, and if my mum can find anything out, then she'll do it, and no one will stop her.'

'She's right,' Jack agreed, cradling Tamsin's hand.

'We'll do everything we can, Tam,' Ruan promised, his voice gentle. 'You have our word on that.'

Half an hour later, Jack left reluctantly for work. He was as fretful as Tamsin, nodding eagerly as she promised they'd keep in touch. She hoped that being at the boathouse might take his mind off the constant worry. Ruan drove to Tregenna Gardens, returning with Lamorna who looked, in her own words, washed out and hung to dry. She flopped at the table and clasped a mug of tea, staring into the murky liquid, too dispirited to listen to PC Jim Hobbs who was in touch with a search party. Ruan picked up the phone, calling on anyone who was available, friends, fishermen. He took Tamsin's hand tenderly. 'We're going out to look for Elowen now...'

'She's been out all night – in the cold and dark.' Tamsin's eyes brimmed. 'Oh, Dad, where is she?'

'We'll find her,' Ruan said encouragingly although Morwenna knew the expression on his face. He put a hand on Morwenna's shoulder as he was about to go. 'I'll keep in touch. Are you staying here for a while with Tam and your mum?'

'No, I'm going out to look for Elowen. I'll phone Jane first for an update.'

Ruan nodded. 'We'll search everywhere. I've got plenty of the lads coming to help. We'll find her if we can.'

'Thanks, Ruan.'

Ruan's voice was low. 'I rang Damien, left a message to ask for his help. He'll call me back.'

'Oh?'

He squeezed her arm. 'I'll be gone as long as it takes, but I'll keep in touch.'

Morwenna met his eyes. She found it hard to speak. They were both thinking the same thing: it was almost impossible to stay positive, to believe that Elowen would soon come skipping into the tearoom clutching Oggy Two, chattering happily. The recurring image playing in Morwenna's mind was of her granddaughter lying on the sand.

26

Another police car arrived outside the tearoom; a friendly-faced Family Liaison Officer, 'Just call me Fiona the FLO,' had arrived to support Tamsin, accompanied by a policeman who asked to search the flat upstairs. Lamorna had been initially furious – Elowen wasn't hiding under the bed, they should be out in Seal Bay with Ruan and the other fishermen, searching for her there – but she conceded that there might be a clue as to her whereabouts amongst Elowen's possessions, although she couldn't imagine what it might be. Morwenna rang Jane for a quick update, then she took the opportunity to leave. She clambered on her bicycle, her limbs aching with tiredness. She was determined to make two house calls, which she hoped would provide an extra piece of the jigsaw. Meanwhile, Jane was on the phone, talking to a colleague in Devon who was a specialist in missing children.

Morwenna gazed across Seal Bay. The wind blew salty air in from the ocean; it was a fresh morning, clouds buffeting along a turquoise sky. She narrowed her eyes and stared out into corrugated blue depths, listening to the rush of waves murmuring, surf swelling forward and lapping back again. It was difficult to push away the terrible thought: they'd never find Elowen if she was in the sea...

She took the road out of Seal Bay, navigating through bustling Saturday traffic. Morwenna couldn't help examining the passengers of each car, her eyes straining for the sight of a six-year-old girl.

Morwenna cycled beyond the Seal Bay sign up Pennance Hill, towards a row of little stone cottages. She slowed down, exhausted. The upstairs curtains were drawn. Beverley's car wasn't in the usual place, outside the gate. That was interesting: no car. Morwenna recalled the blue paint, the palette knives. She wondered if Elowen was inside the house. It was a distance from town – a child might be easily hidden from the public. Or perhaps Beverley had driven Elowen somewhere. She leaned the bicycle against the hedge and walked past dense foliage to the leaded light door of Half Moon Cottage. She knocked once and waited. There was no sound from inside, no music. She knocked again. After a few minutes, she tramped carefully through the overgrown front garden to the window and peered inside. She imagined Beverley in there, painting, Elowen at her side. The room was empty. Morwenna cupped a hand over her eyes and stared into the glass, surprised at what she saw. There were no paintings on the wall; every picture had been taken down and the easel wasn't there – all evidence of Alex was gone. Morwenna stepped back, looking up again at the bedrooms. If Beverley was asleep, why was her car missing? She made her way through a jungle of plants and grass back to the door and knocked again.

A ginger cat weaved through the hedge and scuttled into the undergrowth. She looked around in case there was a neighbour she could speak to and noticed a woman watching her levelly through the window of the adjoining cottage. Morwenna waved an arm, indicating that she'd like to speak. Seconds later, a door creaked open and a white-haired woman in a floral apron stood on the step. Morwenna said, 'Hello – I can't raise anyone...'

'Are you looking for the artist who lives at Half Moon?'

Morwenna was surprised that the neighbour didn't know her name and wondered why. 'Beverley, yes.'

'She's not at home.'

'Oh?'

'She's gone away. She went yesterday, late on.'

'Thanks.' Morwenna tried a smile. 'Do you know when she'll be back.'

'No idea. She gave me the milk from her fridge. She said it would only go off. And some cheese. I'm not fond of that smelly blue stuff, mind.'

'She's gone away, you say?'

'On holiday, she said'

'By herself?' Morwenna had to find out. 'Did she have a child with her?'

'No – it was a man she went off with. I've seen him here a couple of times, just recently. They were holding hands, kissing, all that silly stuff. I think she's got herself a proper fancy man.'

'Oh?' Morwenna took a step forward, interested. 'Do you know his name?'

'No, I don't. Are you the police? You don't look like the police in that yellow coat and bright leggings.'

'No, I'm a friend of Beverley's...'

'Then you should know where she's gone and who with.'

'She must have forgotten to tell me,' Morwenna tried.

'Then you'll have to ask her yourself when she comes back.' The woman turned to go. 'Have you seen Tipsy, my cat?'

'A ginger cat just ran through the hedge.'

The woman nodded wisely. 'Catching the sparrows, I reckon.' She took a step through her door into the cottage.

'Just a moment,' Morwenna called and the women poked her head back round the corner. 'What did he look like, this man?'

'Like any man...' The woman shrugged, as if it was hard to describe. 'Big, though. He was tall.'

'Right, thanks.' Morwenna returned to her bicycle: Britney Taylor had mentioned 'a big man' outside the school gates. So... Beverley Okoro had a new boyfriend. And her car was missing; they'd gone off together. Morwenna had hoped for some sign of Elowen, but there was nothing to go on yet. She peered inside the window again, but there were no indications of a child. She'd try her next suspect, quickly. She clambered back on her bicycle and set off back towards Seal Bay. She wasn't looking forward to this part of the journey.

The roads weren't so busy now, although Morwenna swallowed a lungful of diesel smoke from a chugging bus, and a wide lorry almost toppled her into the hedgerows. She was close enough to see that the sloes were ripe for picking. She cycled through town and began the ascent of Lister Hill. Today, her aching thighs wouldn't cope with the near-vertical gradient. She slid from the saddle on wobbly legs and pushed her bike up to number 42. She pressed the bell and Rosie opened the door almost immediately. 'Morwenna?' She looked taken aback.

'Hi Rosie. I just wondered if I could have a chat.'

Rosie leaned forward, blocking the door. 'I'm so sorry to hear Elowen's missing. Everyone is so worried. Has she come back home yet?'

'No.' Morwenna glanced at her phone: the last update from Ruan had been half an hour ago. There was no news.

'I'm very upset to hear that.' Rosie shifted her feet uncomfortably. 'What was it you wanted?'

'Can I come in?' Morwenna wanted to look around. Perhaps Maya might offer some information.

'Well...' Rosie seemed hesitant. Morwenna was surprised; last time she'd called round, Rosie had been warm and hospitable. Now she seemed decidedly unfriendly.

'I'm gasping for a cup of water...' Morwenna made an excuse, pointing towards the steep hill. She needed to get inside. 'It's a hard ride up here.'

Rosie frowned for a moment, then she stood back. 'Come into the kitchen. I'm busy, mind.'

Morwenna followed her through the neat hallway, the coats on hooks, wellingtons tidily arranged below. She glanced into the living room where Milan had been entertaining the children at Maya's party. The television was on and someone was slumped on the sofa beneath blankets watching cartoons, but she couldn't see who it was. It wasn't unusual for a child to watch television on a Saturday lunchtime. In the kitchen, Rosie filled a tumbler of water from a tap and handed it to her, watching, hands on hips, while Morwenna drank thirstily. Morwenna paused. 'So, how are Maya and the children?'

Rosie shook her head. 'Maya's not well. The others are all right, but I expect they'll catch the bug soon. Coughs and colds travel round all the kiddies...'

'Oh? I noticed Maya wasn't at the party...'

'She came down with a nasty virus. Milan picked her up from school yesterday, just before the others came out. She's tucked up watching *Old Jack's Boat*.'

'Ah... I hope she's better soon.' Morwenna frowned: Milan had been at the school. She thought again about Britney's words and gazed around the kitchen, searching for anything that might offer a clue.

Rosie glanced towards the door. 'Give her a day or two, she'll come bouncing back. But I don't want you catching it. That's why I didn't invite you in.'

Morwenna scrutinised Rosie's face, looking for signs of dishonesty. 'Right. Thanks. I hope Milan won't get it – or you, Rosie.'

'Milan is right as rain – he's out with all the other fishermen, looking for your little Elowen.' Rosie met her eyes. 'Do you think she took a wrong turn at the school gates? I mean, perhaps she was muddled and upset, a bit worried about her party, and she got herself lost...'

'I've never known Elowen to be worried about a party.'

'Someone told me she makes up imaginary friends,' Rosie said slowly.

'No, just a dog...' Morwenna stopped herself. She didn't need to make excuses for her granddaughter.

'I've always thought a big family is best. I'd have had more. Being an only child can be lonely.'

'Elowen's fine, Rosie – we're an extended family, she loves school now.' Morwenna finished the glass of water. 'I just came to ask if you've heard anything, any local chatter that might give us an idea about where she might be, maybe from the other parents...'

'No, I haven't.' Rosie folded her arms, her face suddenly closed and unfriendly. 'We had two policemen call here this morning, asking lots of questions. I didn't like the way one of them looked at me, as if he thought we were hiding something.'

'They're just trying to find Elowen.'

'Well, I'm afraid I can't help you. I would if I could.' Rosie's expression softened. 'I have enough going on here with my six kiddies, without the police bothering us. Every time they call here, I expect them to try to pin something on one of my boys or my husband.'

'Why would they do that?' Morwenna asked.

'Milan's an outsider. He came here from Bosnia over twenty-five years ago, and he's been living in Seal Bay ever since, but some people don't accept him.' She shook her head. 'I'm Seal Bay born and bred, yet there are people who say to me, "You're the maid that married that foreign bloke with the funny surname." It gets my goat, it really does.'

'That's ridiculous, no wonder you're annoyed – I'd be jumping.' Morwenna placed the glass on the table. 'Most people here are very welcoming though.'

'They are. Cornish people are lovely, but it only takes one or two to upset the applecart.'

Morwenna nodded. 'You seem the happiest of families though.'

'We are, although we have our ups and downs, like everyone does.' Rosie glanced at Morwenna meaningfully. 'But we stick it through thick and thin, Milan and me. Not everyone can.'

'You're right there,' Morwenna agreed sadly. 'Thanks for the water.'

'I hope you find your Elowen soon,' Rosie muttered quietly. 'There's been some nasty business in Seal Bay. They still haven't found the bloke who killed Alex Truscott. Or the one who attacked you and that policewoman.'

'No, not yet.' Morwenna turned as Rosie led the way to the door. 'Thanks for your help, Rosie.'

'Sorry I couldn't help more.' Rosie sighed. 'I'm a mother, and I can only imagine how you all feel. Your Tamsin must be worried sick. I hope you find the poor little thing soon.'

'Me too.' Morwenna was outside again, scrambling onto the bicycle. She had more visits to make, but she'd check on Tamsin first. It was all downhill from here.

* * *

When Morwenna reached the tearoom, a police car was parked outside; Jack's van was gone. She pushed the door open to be greeted with several silent figures, heads down over empty cups. She said quietly, 'No news?'

Fiona the Liaison Officer raised her eyes and pushed a hand through her short, fair hair. 'Not yet. We're working on it.'

Lamorna rested her chin on her hands as if her head was heavy with tiredness. 'The police didn't find anything upstairs. They took Elowen's toys, a few of her clothes, her portrait of a parent in the style of L. S. Lowry.'

Tamsin stood up, wiping a tear. 'Have you had anything to eat, Mum?'

'Don't worry, Tam, I'm all right.'

'I have to do something. I have to keep moving.' Tamsin's expression was taut. 'Or I won't cope.'

Morwenna watched Tamsin bustling at the counter. She met Lamorna's eyes and her mother offered an expression of pure pity; Tamsin had been strung out all morning. Morwenna reached for her phone and read a message.

Lamorna raised an eyebrow. 'Any news from Ruan?'

'They've done the beach as far as Pettarock Bay, the coastal path, the clifftops. They are moving to the woods next.' Morwenna shivered and Lamorna did the same as an image filled their thoughts. 'Jane's sent me a message...'

'What does she say?'

'I need to ring her. I won't be a moment – I'll be back dreckly, Tam.'

Morwenna stepped outside, gazing towards the beach. She wondered when she'd next be able to go for a swim in the sea. She desperately needed to clear her head. The sun sparkled, dancing gems on the waves. She pressed a button and heard a voice. 'Jane...?'

'Morwenna – how did you get on?'

'I came up with nothing really. Beverley is out of town and Rosie Buvač's youngest has a virus. Did you have any joy?'

'I'm sifting through lots of background stuff on your suspects.' Jane took a breath. 'A contact of mine has made a couple of discoveries. Apparently, Milan Buvač had a warning several years ago for hitting a man in a public house. It was recorded as a minor disturbance of the peace.'

'Right...' Morwenna thought about Rosie's words – she imagined Milan being goaded. Ruan had called him a gentle giant. 'Anything else?'

'One thing... Damien Woon's name came up. His ex-wife made an accusation before they split up. Sexual assault, apparently. The case was dismissed in the end but he's made a bit of a name for himself with his behaviour towards women. You and I know he can be brusque.'

'Just women?' Morwenna heard the tremor in her voice.

'Jim Hobbs said he spoke to a few women this morning who were eager to say that Woon can be a bit intimidating. Nothing we can really put a finger on, innuendo, trying to endear himself to single women – the usual sexist stuff not uncommon in a man of his age, sadly. Jim spoke to some of the fishermen, including your ex, Ruan, who all speak very highly of him, and they seem to put his behaviour down to too much drink and heartbreak. But I'm going to keep him on my radar nevertheless.'

'We're no nearer to finding Elowen, are we?'

'Not yet. But the first twenty-four hours are critical, Morwenna. We are all doing our best.'

'I know. Thanks, Jane. We'll talk soon.'

Morwenna pushed her phone in her pocket and trudged

back to the tearoom. Tamsin met her eyes questioningly. Morwenna shook her head: no news yet. She glanced up. The clock showed the time to be almost two. If the first twenty-four hours were critical, they didn't have much time left. Every additional hour Elowen was missing, the less chance they had of finding her alive.

27

The twenty-four-hour deadline came and went; time stretched like elastic. There was still no news. Jack trudged in after dark and suggested that Tamsin should get some rest. She was still sitting at the table, her head in her hands. It was decided that she'd move into Elowen's room for the time being – she wanted to smell Elowen's shampoo on the pillows, the scent of her small body on the sheet – and Jack promised that he'd keep an eye on everything while she slept. Morwenna wasn't sure Tamsin would get a moment's peace; her face was exhausted and her eyes swollen. She offered to stay, but Tamsin was adamant she'd be fine.

Ruan drove Lamorna home first, then paused outside Morwenna's cottage to unload the bicycle. He offered to come inside and Morwenna could see by the strained expression on his face that he needed company. She almost invited him in for a moment, then she shook her head. 'Come over first thing tomorrow, Ruan. I'm dead on my feet – I can hardly stand.'

'You'll be all right?'

'As right as I can be...'

Ruan offered a weak smile. 'Get some rest. I'll see you soon.'

Morwenna found it difficult to relax. Although she fell asleep quickly after a warm bath, she was wide awake two hours later, checking her phone for any messages about Elowen. After that, she stared into the darkness of the room, rolling over this way and that until four in the morning when her eyes finally closed again, and she drifted into a fitful sleep. Her dreams were invaded by terrible images of Elowen flailing in the sea, being sucked below.

Morwenna woke with a start. Someone was knocking at the door. She rushed downstairs in pyjamas and bed socks, pulling the door open. 'Ruan...' His expression told her that he was concerned. 'What's happened?'

'We need to go to the tearoom. The police have asked us to come straight away.'

'What is it? Have they got news of Elowen?'

Ruan shook his head. 'I've no idea. Tam rang. I came straight over.'

'Come in – wait there – I'll grab some clothes,' Morwenna called as she bolted upstairs, dragging herself into the same things she'd worn yesterday, strewn on the floor. She bounded downstairs again, her hair wild and unbrushed. 'Let's go.'

They arrived in the dark; it was just past seven. Tamsin and Jack were slumped over the table, their heads in their hands, tired and dejected. The Liaison Officer, Fiona, was sitting close to Tamsin and PC Jim Hobbs stood a little way off, his hands in his pockets, looking at his feet. Morwenna was surprised to see Pam Truscott, dressed casually, leaning against the counter, clutching an expensive handbag.

'What's happened?' Morwenna said straight away.

Tamsin lifted her head. 'They've been in touch.'

'Who has?' Morwenna stared from face to face. 'Have you found Elowen?'

'Mrs Truscott has been contacted...' Jim Hobbs began.

'A note was pushed through my door last night.' Pam Truscott said.

'Can I see it?' Morwenna held out her hand.

'Not at the moment. Forensics are looking at it.' Jim's voice was hushed. 'It's some sort of ransom demand.'

'Sort of? What does that mean?' Morwenna wanted answers.

Pam pushed a hand through her hair tiredly. 'It was on notepaper, written in capitals, no punctuation.'

Morwenna caught Ruan's eye as he reached for her hand.

Jim Hobbs took over. 'It seems Elowen is safe. But someone has taken her and will be in contact shortly. Apparently, they want money.'

'How much?' Ruan asked.

'Twenty thousand pounds. They'll be in touch about when and where. But they said specifically that my family has to pay it.' Pam sighed. 'Someone clearly has a vendetta against me.'

Morwenna turned to Jim Hobbs. 'What does this mean? What are the police doing?'

'The SIO has been informed and the specialist team has taken the new information on board. We're watching Mrs Truscott's house, looking at CCTV, ANPR, and we're constantly searching the Seal Bay area. We have alerts in all the towns and cities.'

Morwenna knitted her brows. 'So someone has Elowen and will give her back to us if the money's paid?' She leaned her head in her hands, puzzling. Who would be most likely to take the child for money and what did it have to do with Alex's death? She tried to make sense of it.

Tamsin gave a sob from deep in her throat. 'At least she's all right.' She twisted round to look at Pam Truscott. 'You can have anything you want, if you can get Elowen back to me.'

Pam lifted a hand. 'The money's not important. We need to get your daughter home safely and put the idiots who took her behind bars.' She frowned. 'I just don't understand why me. Why am I involved?'

'Maybe someone has a grudge?' Morwenna said. 'Or they know you have money? Elowen is just convenient bait.'

Jim Hobbs coughed. 'We have to tread carefully. The people who have taken Elowen said that the police should stay away or there would be consequences.'

'Then you have to stay away,' Ruan suggested quietly.

Morwenna shook her head. 'I can't make sense of it.'

'I just want Elowen back,' Tamsin wailed and Jack wrapped an arm round her.

'We're making progress. Mrs Truscott has offered to put up the money,' Jim Hobbs said. 'So we're just waiting for the next communication from the kidnappers...'

Tamsin closed her eyes. 'At least she's alive...' She made a deep sound: relief and terror. 'We have to get her back, please.'

'We will.' Jack gathered her in his arms.

'We have to ask you some proof of life questions... That's standard procedure,' Fiona said gently.

'Proof of life?' Tamsin was suddenly alarmed.

'Simple questions – for our records, and for when or if we talk to the kidnappers – about Elowen, her favourite things that only she and you and the family would know.' Fiona said quietly. 'You have your partner and your family for support. The FSG team are standing by. We'll get you through this, Tamsin.'

Morwenna was still frowning. 'It's odd though, bringing Pam into this. Why would they do that?'

'It must be the same people who killed my husband, the

same ones who attacked you on the beach, Morwenna, and burgled my home,' Pam said. 'They clearly want money. But once I've paid them, and we have Elowen safely home, what then? They are still out there and I don't feel safe. None of us is.'

'Right.' Morwenna agreed.

'We haven't discounted that it might be a team of people working together,' Jim Hobbs suggested.

'So, what's next?' Jack asked.

'We can't call off the search,' Ruan said. 'After all, Elowen's out there somewhere and we might still be able to find her.'

'I haven't finished looking yet.' Morwenna's voice was hushed.

'Sundays are quiet in Seal Bay,' Jim Hobbs murmured. 'We'll keep searching, see what forensics come up with.'

'I'll make a pot of tea,' Tamsin said. 'I have to keep busy.'

'I'll help you,' Fiona offered. She was on her feet already, collecting empty mugs.

Ruan stood up. 'I'm going home, I'll collect a few things, bring Lamorna down, then I'm going out to search. I can't be sitting around.'

'I'll come with you,' Morwenna said.

'I'm off to the boatyard for the morning – I can get some welding done.' Jack gazed at Tamsin sadly. 'Unless you need me here, love?'

'No, you go. I might try and get some more sleep. I spent most of the night sobbing into Elowen's pillow...'

'I heard you,' Jack said helplessly. 'I was wide awake, wanting to hug you, but you needed space.' He turned to Ruan. 'Do you want me to come with you and help with the search?'

'No, you go on to the boatyard,' Ruan muttered. 'Morwenna and I will drive around, give it some thought.'

'I'll only be a few hours.' Jack gazed anxiously towards Tamsin. 'You'll ring me if you hear anything?'

'Of course.' Tamsin nodded, but she was staring into space.

'I'll stay here with Tamsin.' Fiona took over, pouring tea. 'Perhaps we'll get an update from the kidnappers today and that will give us something to act upon.'

Morwenna leaned towards Ruan. 'I'm not hanging around. Come on, Ruan. We need to get out of here. I'm going to keep on looking.'

* * *

Two hours later, Morwenna and Ruan had driven around Seal Bay twice, checking playgrounds, back streets, staring into empty buildings. Then they left the town behind them and followed the coastal road, up high onto the cliffs. Ruan stopped the engine at a local beauty spot; an expanse of scrubby grassland, craggy rocks and a deep drop down to frothing waves crashing against the beach. They gazed out over the ocean, mottled indigo and turquoise, the sunlight glittering on the shifting surface. Ruan spoke first. 'Who do you think has got her?'

Morwenna sighed. 'She's alive, Ruan. We have to believe that.' She rubbed her fists across her face. 'We have to think about it logically. The chances are, someone's keeping her hidden in Seal Bay, or not far away.' A thought came to her. 'Can we drive to the school?'

'Of course. But it's Sunday – it will be all closed up.'

'That doesn't matter – I want to be at the place where she was last spotted. Then I can go through her last movements, work out who she might have seen, where she might have gone.'

'All right.' Ruan started the engine, reversed the van and set off towards Seal Bay. They weaved through Sunday traffic, mostly locals who wanted to enjoy the autumn sunshine, and came to a stop outside the railings of the primary school.

Morwenna knew it well. She closed her eyes, imagining all the children running out on a Friday afternoon, Lamorna waiting with the other mums and dads, chatting, looking around for the first glimpse of their child, the mayhem of children rushing, the joyous noise of squealing voices, the rumbling engines of passing cars. Then Lamorna, waiting alone, with no sign of Elowen.

'What are you thinking?' Ruan asked.

Morwenna made a muffled sound. 'It's somebody she knows, Ruan. Somebody she'd have left the school with willingly, and believed they were taking her home, back to the party. She'd have been excited. She knew her great grandmother would be here to meet her, so who would have persuaded her to go with them?'

'Maybe someone took her forcibly?' Ruan frowned.

'It's possible, but it would have been a risk with all those people around.'

'Maybe a stranger said, "Your mummy's waiting for you in my car," and she went with them.'

'Maybe, but it's more likely that she saw someone she trusted, and went off with them.'

'Who?'

'I'm thinking...' Morwenna rubbed her forehead and felt the micropore tape beneath her fingers. 'The same person who hit me, the same one who killed Alex. Maybe a parent of another child or – who else would she trust? A friend of yours or mine?'

'She knows some of the fishermen, she knows Damien, and she's a friend of Maya Buvač, so she knows Milan. She'd trust those adults...'

'The next question is – did she get into a car with someone or did she walk away with them? It has to be a local, Ruan – someone we know, who lives not too far from the school. That means she has to be in Seal Bay now, or not far away. So where would they hide her?'

'Anywhere – a house, a building, a shed.'

'Somewhere she couldn't escape or raise the alarm...' Morwenna shivered. The image of Elowen, bound and alone in a basement room, filled her mind. 'There are lots of old houses in Seal Bay, plenty on the outskirts. Think about Pam Truscott's place up on the cliff all by itself. It has grounds, outbuildings, it's surrounded by trees and hedges...'

'You don't think Pam Truscott has Elowen?'

'No, but Mirador is a big house with outbuildings. I want to check out several locations – where might she be hidden? There are plenty of houses where she wouldn't be heard. Not to mention garages, boatyards, churches, libraries – the school, even?'

Ruan agreed. 'It makes sense to look at where she might be being kept.'

'I can link locations with suspects...' Morwenna was thoughtful. 'I need to visit these places, see if anything jogs my memory. I need to sniff the kidnapper out. I'm almost sure two of the suspects aren't the person we're looking for, but I'll double-check. Oh, talking of sniffing...' She recalled the moment when she was attacked on the beach. 'The attacker's skin had a strange smell. If I could identify it, I'd know who it is for sure. What odours might linger on the skin, Ruan?'

'Fish?' Ruan suggested. 'Most fishermen shower every day. Most people do...'

'What else?' Morwenna spoke aloud, for her own benefit. 'It was an overpowering smell...'

'Petrol? A chemical? Paint thinners? Earth?' He tried again. 'Nail polish remover? Sweat?'

'I wonder if it was a man's smell? Britney Taylor said she saw

Elowen with a big man. Why would she say that unless it was true? Do you think she might be making it up, for attention?' Morwenna's mind was racing. 'Our little girl's not far away, Ruan. I know it.'

'It's good of Pam Truscott to offer to pay the ransom. At least we'll get Elowen back.' Ruan's face clouded. 'Unless it's some sort of trick.'

'We can't rule that out.' Morwenna met his eyes. 'And the amount, twenty thousand pounds. It's a manageable amount for someone like Pam to pay, but a big amount for someone with no money. Are we dealing with someone who needs cash instantly? Someone with a debt, who needs to pay someone back?'

'That could be half the people in Seal Bay...'

'You're right. There are so many time-rich, money-poor people, especially in the off-season.' She pressed her fingers together. 'We're narrowing it down. I've spoken to everyone who was on the beach that night and eliminated most of them. The tattoo clue isn't getting me anywhere. But I think if I find the right location, then I'll know who I'm looking for.'

The phone buzzed in her pocket. Morwenna tugged it out and held it to her ear. She mouthed to Ruan, 'It's Tam.' She listened a while, an excited voice rattling, then she said, 'Right, we're coming back now. Don't worry, we'll sort it all out. Yes, we're on our way now. See you in five minutes.'

Ruan placed a hand against her arm. 'What's happened?'

'Pam Truscott has had another message, same thing, capital letters on paper, no punctuation. The kidnapper wants to collect the money tomorrow night. Once the ransom's paid, then we'll get Elowen back. That's the deal.' Morwenna closed her eyes. 'This is our chance, Ruan.'

28

Back in the tearoom, a group of people huddled around a table; PC Jim Hobbs was standing behind Rick Tremayne who sprawled in his tired suit, creased at the elbows, holding forth about what was going to happen and what they had to do. Lamorna gripped Tamsin's hand tightly and Jack, who'd rushed back from the boatyard once he'd received the news, placed his hands on her shoulders. Morwenna and Ruan sat opposite, meeting each other's gaze meaningfully as Rick Tremayne continued in his monotone. Fiona the Family Liaison Officer was making tea.

'So, I've seen the note that was left by the perpetrators. We have to assume that we are dealing with the person or persons who have Elowen. I have spent some time talking to Mrs Truscott and her son Simon and we have agreed a plan of action. They will withdraw the money on Monday. PC Hobbs will go with them to the bank and accompany them home. It's been agreed that the money will be left in a small waterproof bag in the hedge outside the gate at Mirador by Pam Truscott at ten o'clock precisely on Monday night, and no one will step outside or visit the place until Tuesday morning. Instructions will be left at the same location as to where we can find the child.'

'We can't do that.' Lamorna was appalled. 'Why can't one of you policemen hide behind the hedge and jump out and get him when he collects the money? Bash his head, arrest him?'

'We have to assume we're dealing with an organised gang of professionals, Ms Mutton,' Rick Tremayne explained as if talking to a child. 'If we arrest one of them and the ransom isn't collected, the others will know, and we can't take risks. Of course, we've asked for proof of life, a video or something, but there's been no reply as yet.'

'Just pay them, please,' Tamsin closed her eyes. 'Let's get Elowen safely home.'

'What guarantee do we have that Elowen is safe?' Morwenna asked.

'We have the kidnapper's word. No other communication has been received. That's all we can go on.' Rick Tremayne rubbed his chin thoughtfully.

'But what if they are lying? What if it's someone else, a scammer or an opportunist, and they don't have Elowen at all?'

'Mum.' Tamsin gave a deep sigh. 'DI Tremayne has a point. We have to believe it's real, that they have her somewhere and she's safe and she'll come back to us.'

'Tam's right,' Jack echoed.

'But how are we ever going to catch them?' Morwenna said crossly. 'Whoever it is, we know they are dangerous. We have to find out who they are and bring them in.'

'ANPR surveillance will be in operation. We'll be able to identify any vehicles and then we'll move in quickly,' Jim Hobbs said calmly as Fiona placed mugs of steaming tea on the table. 'But leave that to us, eh?'

'We can worry about who took her afterwards,' Ruan said calmly. 'Let's get our little maid home.'

'Elowen might be able to identify the kidnapper.' Rick Tremayne added. 'Once she's safe, we'll ask her questions, show her pictures...'

'That's all the more reason why they might not let her go...' Morwenna began, then she saw the horrified look on Tamsin's face and closed her mouth.

Jim Hobbs shook his head. 'The team are looking through surveillance footage and CCTV. We know what we're doing.'

Ruan took her hands gently. 'Look, Morwenna, we have to believe that Elowen will come back. We'll concentrate on who's responsible once she's safely home.'

Morwenna shook her head. It didn't make any sense. Why would someone kidnap a child and then let her go, knowing they could be recognised afterwards? She wondered if Elowen was blindfolded, but she'd left school with someone she trusted, someone she knew. She gazed at Tamsin who was sipping tea, her face pinched and anxious. Their eyes met, and Tamsin looked away. Morwenna's heart was breaking: she was desperate to do something, anything to help. She'd go along with the plan for her daughter's sake, but she wasn't confident. Rick Tremayne was talking about police procedures again: he had allocated someone to deal with the press; he advised everyone to keep a low profile; to talk to no one about Elowen's situation; to avoid talking about the kidnapping to anyone. Lamorna retorted that she'd go where she bleddy well liked, it was a free country and then she burst into tears. As she sipped her tea, Morwenna texted Jane Choy. She needed a chat – they could pick each other's brains. More than anything, she wished she could go for a swim in the sea, where she'd be able to think clearly. But first, she had a house call to make. There was someone she needed to talk to.

* * *

Ruan dropped Morwenna off at home in Harbour Cottages, leaving her reluctantly, with the promise of catching up later. She immediately showered, changed her clothes, had a bite of lunch and clambered on her bicycle, setting off down the hill. The basin of the bay shone like a silver lamp, and the freedom of cycling through town gave her thoughts a chance to air. Then she turned up a hill and immediately wished she'd asked Ruan for a lift. She was sure her knee joints were creaking as the gradient increased. She stood hard on the pedals and made one slow revolution of a wheel after another, painfully climbing towards the clifftop, which seemed unfeasibly distant. She came to a standstill, tuckered out. Morwenna pushed the bike past the last few houses, listening to herself panting, and she laughed grimly – she sounded like a cow in labour. She pushed on, finally arriving at Mirador, standing by itself with the best view of the bay. She wheeled her bicycle closer and saw the exact spot where the ransom was to be left – there was a clear gap in the hedge. Someone knew the layout of this house well. She wanted to get inside and look for clues. She was sure something would lead her to the kidnapper.

There were three cars parked in the drive: an Audi, a Range Rover and a silver E-type Jaguar. Morwenna leaned against her bicycle, resting; she hadn't seen the E-type before. She approached the door, pressed the bell and heard it buzz. The door opened and a man stood watching her, a silver fox probably in his sixties, all T-shirt and muscles, twinkling eyes and smiling face. He was wearing cream shorts, despite the cool autumn weather. Morwenna shook her head as if she was dreaming. 'Hello. I was looking for Pam.'

'She's upstairs. Are you a friend?'

'I'm Morwenna Mutton... a friend of sorts...'

'Oh.' The man raised an eyebrow in recognition: he knew exactly who she was. 'Come in and wait – she's in the bath – I'll make you a coffee.' The man led the way into the large room with billowing cream curtains and two pink sofas. Morwenna's eyes moved to the photo of Pam on the wall, in a boat with huge white sails, smiling in a striped top. Then her gaze was tugged back to the handsome man who asked, 'How do you take your coffee?'

'Tea, please.' Morwenna struggled to find her voice. 'Strong, a dash of milk.'

'I'll be right back,' he promised. Morwenna watched him go, then she rushed to the mirror on the wall, smoothing her ruffled mane, gazing in despair at her wind-roughened cheeks. He'd smelled of something smoky, spicy cologne. She was sure she smelled of sweat after her gruelling ride. She shook her clothes in a vain attempt to dispel any aroma, rearranged her hair again, sat down on the pink sofa and crossed her legs in a semblance of sophistication. True to his word, the man came back with a tray, two fine china cups, one tea, one milky coffee. He sat next to her. 'I'm Barnaby Stone.'

'Morwenna,' she replied automatically, before realising she'd introduced herself already.

'You're related to the young girl that we're trying to help. I'm so sorry.'

'Thanks.' Morwenna took in his use of the word *we*; he knew all about Elowen. He was on her side, or pretending to be. She was immediately, gushingly grateful. 'Thank you so much – and

Pam – and Simon – for agreeing to put up the ransom. My family, Tamsin, we're all so...'

Barnaby put up a hand to stop her. 'It's really no problem. I'm intrigued why the kidnapper has asked us to pay, but I suppose they know we can. The main thing is that we get your little girl back.' He reached for the cup of coffee and Morwenna noticed his muscled arms, tanned, light hairs on the forearm. No tattoo, for the record. 'I'm assuming that's why you're here, to talk about the plans for tomorrow night.'

'Yes, I've just come from talking to the police. They are treating this as a critical incident.' Morwenna watched his face to see how he'd react; his expression remained unchanged. She wanted to look around the house and outbuildings for any clues. It had crossed her mind, after what Ruan had said, that Elowen could be locked in an attic or a garden shed. She wondered if she could find a way to explore. 'I wanted to thank Pam. She's been so kind. Especially after what happened to Alex. Shall I go upstairs? I mean – if she's finished her bath...'

'She needs to relax.' Barnaby sighed. 'My sister's been through a hard time, Simon too. Losing his father has affected him badly.'

'Of course,' Morwenna glanced towards the graduation photograph, Simon clutching a ribboned certificate, a small tattoo protruding from his gown. Alex was on one side, smiling proudly, Pam on the other, her hand on Simon's shoulder, an inked butterfly just above her wrist. Morwenna reached for her tea and sipped gratefully. 'As you say, the ransom is being collected tomorrow...'

'I think we're all organised at this end. The police have been very clear,' Barnaby said, his voice syrup smooth. 'Hopefully you'll get your little girl back, then they'll apprehend these rogues. We can get back to normal.'

'You don't live locally?' Morwenna asked.

'I live in London, in Islington. I'm a surgeon.' Barnaby turned his attention to the micropore on her brow. 'May I?'

Morwenna didn't move as he pulled the sticky tape away. She felt his breath against her face. 'The stitches are all dissolved bar one. You should rub cream into the scar, you know, something simple like calendula. Then keep the tape on for a few more weeks to support the healing.' He grinned. 'I'd have done a much neater job.'

'Oh.' Morwenna wasn't sure what to say. She wriggled in her seat, moving away. 'I was just hoping to pass on my thanks, but Pam's luxuriating in her bath, and Simon...?'

'Simon's outside in one of the barns with his mushrooms. He's making a go of growing them for culinary purposes. He has some fine oysters on the way, I believe.'

'I'd love to see them.' Morwenna said quickly. 'I'm quite a fungi-fan.' She knew she sounded ridiculous, but she wanted a chance to sneak around outside.

'He's probably up to his arms in grain spawn and composted manure. Smelly stuff.' Barnaby laughed. 'Maybe some other time. It would certainly be nice to catch up with you again, Morwenna, when all this awful business with the child is behind us...' Barnaby stood up to show her to the door. 'I see you came here on a bicycle. Very commendable. I love cycling and sailing – it keeps me fit, although the E-type is my preferred mode of transport at the moment, given the cold breeze from the north.'

'Indeed. I love my bike – I've cycled everywhere since I was a child. They say if you don't use it, you lose it, but all these hills in Seal Bay – it's getting harder.' Morwenna stood at the door. She was gabbling. 'Well, it's downhill now...' She held out her hand to shake his. 'It's been nice meeting you.'

He brought her hand to his lips gallantly. 'And you too. I look forward to our next meeting. And I hope your little girl is home soon. It must be such a worry for your family.'

'It is.' Morwenna straddled her cycle. 'Nice meeting you.' She'd just said that; she turned away awkwardly and rode off down the hill, doing her best to appear elegant, then the wheel hit a stone and she almost lost her balance, wobbling to one side. The bike picked up speed and she was descending the gradient, on her way home towards another steep hill that would lead to Seal Bay.

29

On Monday morning, Morwenna parked her bicycle in the corridor and strode into the library. Her heart thumped more than it should; it was difficult to pretend to be normal – she was riddled with so much anxiety about Elowen – but she was determined to show a brave face. The conversation she'd had last night on the phone with Jane Choy was still on her mind. Jane wasn't up for a swim yet, of course, but she understood Morwenna's need to spend time up to her neck in the icy ocean, clearing her head, thinking. Jane had a few leads of her own she wanted to pursue; she was working her way through Morwenna's list of suspects at home, propped up by cushions, phoning colleagues and searching the internet, determined to find any useful facts that might serve as clues to the identity of the kidnapper. They'd talk later: Morwenna would go to the tearoom this afternoon, then there was somewhere else she wanted to visit, another place where Elowen could be hidden. Afterwards, she'd spend time with Tamsin, then take herself off for a swim. She imagined her daughter would be more tense than ever today as the time for the ransom to be paid grew closer. Ruan had gone fishing early in the morning, but she'd meet him this evening.

Louise was leaning against the library counter looking perplexed, a sponge in one hand and a bottle of blue liquid cleaner in the other. Morwenna forced a grin. 'Do the shelves need a quick scrub?'

Louise shook her head, her eyes wide. 'No, I heard this eerie scratching in the corner when I came in, a kind of ghostly finger-nails against the carpet. I was terrified. Then there was a scrab-bling sound. I rushed over and there it was.'

'Termites?'

'More ectoplasm, soaking into the carpet.'

'Really? Show me.'

Louise led Morwenna to the library corner, beneath the shelves marked *Suspense and Horror.* She bent down, pointing to a damp patch on the grey carpet. 'Look – it's Lady Elizabeth.'

Morwenna sniffed the air. 'It smells of pee to me.'

'Pee?'

'Urine.' Morwenna tried not to smile. 'Maybe Lady Liz was taken short.'

'Pee?' Louise repeated. 'How can it be?'

Morwenna shrugged. 'An animal perhaps. Do mice pee in groups?'

Louise suddenly gasped and hugged her. 'Morwenna – I'm so sorry. I should have asked you about Tamsin and Elowen first – and you. How are you? Do you have any updates?'

'No, not really – the police have nothing concrete.' Morwenna remembered Rick Tremayne's instruction to say nothing about the case to anyone and Jane had advised the same thing. It made sense, however much she longed to confide in a friend. 'I'm just trying to keep things going for Tam.'

'Of course.' Louise nodded energetically. 'I'll put the kettle on.'

'That would be great.' Morwenna picked up a heap of books. 'I'll just shelve these…' She lifted a pile of returned books and was about to start filing them when she heard the scuttle of feet. Two figures bustled through the door, Susan and Barb Grundy rushing towards her, Barb clutching a long, knitted sweater in rainbow stripes. Susan's face was a picture of anxiety.

'Morwenna, we hoped you'd be here. We wondered if there was any news about little Elowen. We've heard nothing – we were so worried. How is Tam, and her boyfriend? How is Lamorna? And we're thinking of you. Barb said you'd need to keep warm after all that swimming, and the weather's turning proper chilly, so we made you this…'

* * *

Morwenna felt weary as she made her way to the tearoom. The sign on the door read *closed*, but she pushed it open and walked in, clutching her bag and the snuggly jumper the Grundy sisters had knitted. Tamsin was sitting alone at the table chewing a fingernail. Fiona the FLO was trying to get her to play cards. Morwenna called, 'I'm not stopping – just checking how you are.'

'So-so.' Tamsin sighed. 'Nervous. It's hard to believe that Elowen could be home soon.'

'We have to think positively,' Fiona said with a smile, pushing a hand through short hair. 'And we'll make a plan to keep you occupied for the rest of today.'

'What plan?' Morwenna asked.

'Fiona thinks it's important not to sit around and worry. We were talking to Jack about it at breakfast. He has the job at Woon's to keep him busy, although he's not sleeping well, neither of us is. I can hear him moving around the flat when I'm in Elowen's bed...' She paused, tears in her eyes. 'Oh, Mum, this is so horrible.'

Morwenna took her daughter's hand. 'How can I help?'

Fiona explained. 'Tamsin's grandmother is visiting soon and she'll be here all afternoon. When she leaves, we all agreed it would be a good idea for your daughter to stay at your house tonight.'

'Oh, of course.'

'Tamsin would benefit from the distraction of being with her parents and you should all be together. The weather forecast is for it to be a bit wild and windy tonight and Tamsin's exhausted, so having her mum around would be really helpful. I'll be here first thing tomorrow, Jack too. By then we'll know what's happening and the CIM team will take it from there.' Fiona looked pleased.

'Jack's been so sweet,' Tamsin said. 'I don't know how I'd have coped without you and Dad too, and...' A tear slid down her cheek. 'I'm not coping. All I can think is, what if Elowen doesn't—'

'Now, Tamsin,' Fiona said gently. 'We've talked about trying to deal with those thoughts. Take something of Elowen's with you, perhaps a favourite toy.'

'She took Oggy Two to school with her.' Fresh tears welled in Tamsin's eyes. 'Oh, Mum.'

'I think it's a great idea for you to stay with me tonight. Your dad can come round – we'll all be together.' Morwenna wrapped her arms around her daughter. 'Jack too...'

'He doesn't want to disturb my sleep. He can't rest. He's all over the place – he loves Elowen like his own child...' Tamsin pulled a knotted tissue from her sleeve and dabbed her eyes. 'Mum, she will be back tomorrow, won't she?'

'I hope so.' Morwenna sighed.

Tamsin picked up the playing cards, shuffled them and put them down again. 'I might have a lie down in her bed. The scent of her helps me believe she'll be back. I won't sleep, though. Every time I close my eyes, all I can see is Elowen, and I think – what if she doesn't...?'

'Make yourself a warm drink – play some soothing music,' Fiona said kindly. 'I'm here to talk, to pass the time.'

'Grandma said she'd be here soon; she's coming down on the bus. Then Dad'll give me a lift up to Harbour Cottages.' Tamsin scraped her chair back. 'I'll go upstairs for a bit and try to rest. I'm worn out.'

'I'll be here when you come down. And I'll be straight up if there's any news,' Fiona promised.

Morwenna watched as Tamsin dragged herself wearily to the door that led to the stairs. She said nothing for a while. Then she met Fiona's eyes. 'What do you think? Honestly?'

'About what?'

'Elowen.' Morwenna heard the tremor in her voice.

'Difficult to say.' Fiona shrugged sadly. 'It depends entirely on the kidnapper, and we know from what happened to you and Jane and Alex Truscott that they are violent. We can't rule anything out. As you said yesterday, if Elowen can identify them, then that doesn't improve her chances of being brought safely home.' She lowered her voice. 'I suggested this morning that Tamsin should see her doctor and ask for something to help her sleep. Jack agrees with me. She says she's not ready for medication, but she's exhausted.'

'I'll take her home tonight.' Morwenna was glad for the opportunity to look after her daughter. 'Then tomorrow...'

'We'll see what happens and support Tamsin through it,' Fiona said. 'I'm a Catholic. I was brought up as one, confirmed, white dress, everything. I believe it helps to have faith. I'll certainly be praying for Elowen.'

'Thanks,' Morwenna muttered. 'We're really grateful for everything you're doing.'

'It's a privilege.' Fiona said.

'I'm off on the bicycle.' Morwenna scraped back the chair. 'I have one more person I need to talk to...'

* * *

Morwenna cycled down a twisting road, past a few fishermen's cottages and accelerated through the gates of a boatyard. The sign said D. WOON, BOATS. She continued along the path towards a group of outbuildings. In the distance, little sailing boats with high masts were grouped together on the water. Jack was seated on a small stool, a welding mask on, spraying sparks onto a piece of metal. Morwenna stood at a distance and turned away. Jack saw her watching him and stopped work, pulling up his mask. He was alarmed. 'Morwenna, is Tam all right? Is there any news of Elowen?'

'No, I didn't want to worry you...'

She looked around. It was quiet in the boatyard, Jack's white van parked on gravel, outbuildings beyond, dipping boats, a row of masts. There was a large boat shed where all sorts of craft were repaired and rebuilt and next to it, Damien Woon's small business office. Morwenna nodded towards it. 'Is Damien around?'

'No. I haven't seen him for several days.' Jack put down the welder and came over. 'He's gone away.'

'Oh, do you know where?'

'Nope. He just left me his keys, asked me to look after the

place and do as much overtime as I could to get through the backlog of work. He said he needed a break.'

Morwenna felt her heart rate increase. 'Did he take anyone with him?'

'No idea.' Jack shrugged as if it was normal. 'Damien's a bit of a dark horse. I don't know much about him, except that his marriage broke up a few years back, and he's quite bitter about it.'

'Oh?'

'The way he talks about women sometimes – he can be disrespectful, you know what I mean? I think his ex stitched him up, took a lot of his money.'

'Jack, you don't think he's the type who'd take Elowen?'

'Damien? I wouldn't have thought so,' Jack murmured. 'I like him. He's a straight sort of person. But then, you never really know anyone completely, do you?'

Morwenna gazed around. There were outbuildings, dark unfriendly places. She wondered how she could take a closer look. 'How's your mum these days?'

Jack looked sad. 'Not good. She's getting worse. I phone the nursing home once a week but it's never good news.'

'I'm sorry to hear that. I never did send you the engagement photos...'

'You can still send them – after all this is over, eh?' Jack forced a smile. 'Tam's staying with you tonight, so she can get some rest.'

'That's right. Will you be okay by yourself, Jack?'

'I'll be fine.' He lifted his shoulders. 'I just keep thinking of Tam. It's so tough on her.'

'It is.'

'I hope they catch the person who took Elowen away.' Jack's face hardened and his tone was momentarily angry. 'Kidnapping a little girl for money. People like that are just parasites.'

'You're right.' Morwenna agreed. 'Hopefully, we'll get our little girl back safely.'

'I hope so.'

'You've no idea when Damien is back?'

'None at all – I'm sorry.' Jack raised the welding mask. 'I'd better get back to work. He's left me loads to do. I have a fuel pump to change before the evening's done.'

'Of course.'

'I'll see you soon, Morwenna. Take care of my Tam.'

'I will, Jack.' Morwenna took a look around the boatyard. Everything was silent, almost eerie with the tall masts and nodding boats, the disused outbuildings. She called, 'Don't work too hard.'

'Right!' Jack shouted as he sprayed an arc of sparks. Morwenna turned away. She moved towards one of the vast sheds and peered through a cracked window. Inside, it was full of junk, bits of boats. Cobwebs hung from the ceiling. There was no sign of a child. She looked back. Jack was still welding. Morwenna wondered where Damien had gone and what her next move should be. It was time for a swim in the sea. She had too many crashing thoughts and too many fears she needed to calm.

30

Morwenna stood alone on the beach in her wetsuit, shivering. It was past five; the sky was an artist's palette, dappled with pink and grey clouds melting into a silver sea. It would not be dark for a while. She would have her swim, then she'd go home, sit in front of the comforting warmth of the fire with Ruan and Tamsin and they'd all wait together. Morwenna wasn't looking forward to the agony of waiting, staring into leaping flames, the three of them enduring long silences, awkwardly avoiding the subject that was filling each of their minds. It was going to be difficult. There had to be something she could do. Briefly, she thought of returning to Damien Woon's boatyard and looking around again.

She wanted to talk to Jane too. She'd received a cryptic text saying they needed to catch up over the phone later – she might have some interesting news. A colleague was halfway through some online research. Morwenna hoped she'd made some interesting discoveries. She gazed at the rolling waves. Something in her held her back from the swim; it would be so easy to pull her clothes back on and go home instead. Ruan had arranged to pick her up at the sea wall at six, but she could text him that she'd be early, or start walking back instead. No, it was now or never.

Morwenna threw off the towel, covering her small bag of clothes, and made a run towards the sea. The sand was cold and squashy beneath her feet. She continued running, water around her ankles, calves, then she dived in with a splash. The thrill of the shock was immediate. Her breath stuck in her throat and she was gasping, icy claws pulling at her skin. She plunged down and came up spluttering, exhilarated. Her head was numb: she'd forgotten to put her swimming cap on. Stray strands of hair hung over her eyes, smooth as sealskin, and she pushed them back, blinking the salty drops away. The intense cold made her tremble as she gazed around; behind her the sea stretched to infinity, merging with sky. A wave rolled in and buffeted her face like a cold kiss. In front, the beach was clearly visible; Morwenna could just glimpse her bag on the sand, the sea wall, a jogger with a tiny puppy. Then beyond, shops, the tearoom, houses seemingly piled one behind the other, stretching up to the cliffs.

Morwenna rolled onto her back and gazed at a wide sky; the clouds were tinged purple. Her thoughts were never far from Elowen: where was she now? Was she hungry, cold, frightened? More to the point, where would Alex's killer hide her? Where would be the cleverest place to conceal a child so that no one would hear her screams? She gazed back towards the beach, to the place where Alex was killed, and his words rushed back to her, the wheeze of his voice: '...asked me to meet... by the seafront... quarter to ten...' Morwenna thought it through again. Who intended Alex harm? What was the motive? She cleared her mind and tried to remember what else he'd said. Morwenna dipped her head beneath the surface, holding her breath. His voice was there again, Alex, rasping. 'They were late... Parasite... I said I'd be here to talk about the money... then I felt something hit me.' She saw him again in the darkness, the knife in his back, dark blood on his jacket. She recalled the warning messages she had received: *BACK OFF BITCH*.

Morwenna held the thought as she remembered the moment on the beach, the attacker behind her and she imagined it again, the thick overpowering stench, and she knew at once what it was and where she'd smelled it before. Both thoughts crashed together followed by a third.

Instantly, it came to her: *Alex's killer had a strong motive, the means to kidnap Elowen and had engineered a perfect opportunity to collect the ransom.*

Morwenna lunged upwards, spluttering, catching her breath. She laughed out loud; a surging euphoria tingled from her head to her feet. It wasn't just the biting cold: she knew now, absolutely, who Alex's killer was. She was sure of it and the thought made her shake with intense shock. Lifting strong arms, she pushed towards shore. The truth was bright as dawn, everything had fallen into place. She needed to think what to do next – she needed a plan.

Standing on the beach again, she was quaking, but not just with cold. The clarity was blinding. The sharp smell she'd detected on the skin of her attacker – it was obvious now. Morwenna thought of the kidnapper's access to a trusting Elowen. And it would have been easy to burgle the Truscotts, to attack her on the beach, to leave the threatening messages – every time, the killer had the perfect alibi. And now, the kidnapper had every opportunity to collect the ransom.

There was a clear way to Elowen, to bring her back home: the fear of it shook Morwenna. Part of her wanted to go straight to Elowen's captor and demand that she be let go. Or she could go to Rick Tremayne and tell him to arrest the suspect, but he'd waste so much time questioning her evidence.

Morwenna tugged on her clothes, giddy, her teeth chattering. Her skin was numb, and Elowen filled her thoughts. She was annoyed with herself; she should have worked it out earlier. Looking back, the signs were there, but she was a novice at sleuthing. She was learning fast though: she'd go home and put her final plan into action; she'd make everything right. The night-time couldn't come fast enough now.

* * *

Two hours later a stew was bubbling in the oven. Ruan had lit the fire, sent Tamsin for a long soak in the bath while he and Morwenna stood in her sitting room, their voices low, discussing how best to support their daughter. Morwenna took the opportunity to tell him that she'd be going out at nine o'clock. She was positive she knew who had kidnapped Elowen but she had to make sure. Ruan wasn't comfortable with the idea at all.

'Shouldn't you get the police to deal with it?'

'Rick Tremayne? He'd rush in and ruin the whole thing; then where would Elowen be? Or, even more likely, he'd tell me I was talking rubbish.'

'What about the CIM and Jim Hobbs?'

'Maybe, but Jane has my back...'

'Then I'll come with you.'

'Can you stay here with Tam?' Morwenna met his eyes. 'I'm serious, Ruan. She mustn't know yet – she'll fret. I hate telling her lies, but she'll be worried all evening, worse than ever, if she knows anything. Keep it quiet, just for now?'

He sighed. 'There's no telling you... there never has been.'

'No.'

'Then how can I help?'

'Can you be on the end of the phone? I'll text you my every

move. Can you be ready to come out in the van at a moment's notice? And to call the police?'

'Of course. I can give Tam some sort of excuse – I have to pop round to see someone – Damien or...'

'Did you know he's gone away?'

'No, I didn't.'

'There's a tangled web...' Morwenna was thoughtful. 'Shall we eat? It's going to be a long night.'

Ruan put his mouth close to her ear. 'Tell me who you think it is.'

Morwenna hesitated. 'Well, I'm ninety percent sure.'

'Mum?' Tamsin wandered into the room in pyjamas. She sat down, hugging a cushion. Morwenna was reminded of when she was a child, how she'd hug toys the same way for comfort. Her voice was weak. 'Do you know, I'm a bit hungry. I forgot to eat today.'

'Your dad cooked dinner.' Morwenna smiled. 'Stew and rice. I'll dish up.' She moved to the kitchen and called, 'I have to pop out later. I want to check on Mum. It'll only be for an hour...'

'Mmm, right.' Tamsin wasn't listening and Morwenna was glad that she didn't have to tell her daughter more than a hint of a lie. Ruan arranged her on the sofa, a blanket on her knee, and Tamsin snuggled down. Morwenna brought two bowls of food, going back for a third. The three of them sat gazing into the crackling fire, their faces orange in the glow, the sound of spoons clanking against crockery.

The clock ticked slowly and conversation was a series of simple comments. By eight thirty, Tamsin was huddled on the sofa, her eyelids heavy, falling into a slumber. Ruan pointed to her, mouthing 'I think she'll sleep now.'

'Best thing, poor little maid,' Morwenna mouthed back from the kitchen and there was a sharp ache in her chest as she was reminded of herself and Ruan, not thirty years ago, creeping from the small bedroom, closing the door gently, their eyes meeting, trying not to wake their tiny baby. They'd been lovely times. She and Ruan stood in the kitchen now, looking at each other the same way, and Morwenna wondered how it had all gone wrong.

She said quietly, 'I'm going to text Jane. I need her to have my back too – she's my link to the police. I'll explain what I'm doing. I know I can rely on her if things go pear-shaped.'

Ruan took her hand. 'Promise me you won't do anything to put yourself at risk.'

'I won't.'

'I'm worried about you.'

'I'll be fine.'

'Tell me where you're going... what you're thinking of.'

'Ruan – I don't know yet – I think I know who has her and when they've collected the ransom, I'll be sure.'

'Can I drive you somewhere?'

'The bike will be quieter and I have good lights.'

Ruan shook his head. 'I'm not sure I should let you do this.'

'You know me.'

'That's the trouble.'

Morwenna grinned. 'I'm going to go up to my room, put on a black hoodie and leggings. No one will recognise me without all the colour.'

Ruan almost smiled. 'I'll make sure I'm on the end of the phone, every second.'

'I'll need you to be.' She winked. 'Imagine, Ruan, if I can get Elowen back. That's what it's all about. Imagine Tam's face...'

They both turned to gaze at their daughter, her face burnished in the orange firelight. Even in her sleep, her brow was puckered and she was making muffled, anxious noises. Morwenna frowned: Tamsin had a gold chain around her neck.

Morwenna had never seen her wearing it before, but it looked familiar. A diamond pendant caught in the light and glittered. Morwenna made the soft sound that all mothers make when they worry about their child. 'Look after her, Ruan...' she whispered.

'I want to look after you too,' Ruan replied, but Morwenna had already rushed upstairs.

* * *

Morwenna cycled down the hill into Seal Bay, her hood pulled over her hair. She'd stuffed her phone in her pocket – that was all she needed; she'd travel light and move quietly, her feet encased in trainers. She pedalled down to the seafront, pausing outside the Proper Ansom Tearoom. Her heart thumped in her throat already and her breath was scant. There was a light in the window of the flat upstairs, the silhouette of someone moving. She leaned her bike against the wall not far from Jack's white van to try the door. The surface smelled of paint – he had sprayed it to cover the signs on the sides. The back door was locked; she'd have to wait. It was dark everywhere; the sea beyond the wall was ink black, murmuring as the tide came in. No one was around; the only light came from the streetlamp across the road. Morwenna looked for somewhere safe to hide her bike; she didn't want it to be seen. There was a recess two doors away, where the dustbins belonging to the tearoom and two other neighbouring shops were kept. The bicycle would be safe there for a while and it was a quiet place where she could watch unseen. Morwenna wheeled her bike past the next shop, Celtic Knot Gifts, which had closed for the winter season, and into the alcove. She slid into the darkness, hoping she wouldn't be seen, and watched for any sign of movement.

Her breath came rapidly each time she checked her phone: 9.37 p.m.; 9.41 p.m.; 9.45 p.m. She waited. There was no one around: Seal Bay was deserted. She heard the clang of a doorbell and Jack emerged from the tearoom, wearing a black hoodie not dissimilar to her own. He was carrying a heavy rucksack, two big boxes – clothes perhaps, something soft. Morwenna watched him open the back of the van and load his things, then he disappeared back into the tearoom. She wondered whether to approach the van – the back doors were still open; there were other items in there, paint tins. There was something covering the numberplate – black gaffer tape. He intended to avoid the ANPR; he'd been there when Jim Hobbs had mentioned it. He'd had inside knowledge of police activity all the time.

Jack was back again, putting more boxes into the van, stacking them at the sides, closing the doors. Then he locked the tearoom door and moved quickly to the front, sliding inside.

Morwenna swallowed hard – she needed to make a decision now. She could follow him on the bike, but he'd be too fast. She'd lose him and, anyway, she'd be visible. She rushed forward to the van and squeezed the door handle at the back carefully. The engine rumbled and she wriggled inside with the boxes, the rucksack and the paint, curling low on the van floor, pulling the door behind her quietly as the van began to move away.

The road bumped beneath her and Morwenna swayed one way then the other as the van crashed forward. As it turned corners, she had to press a hand against the wall of the van to stop herself from cannoning forwards. She felt the gradient of a hill, heard the gears change. They were going towards Mirador; she was sure of it. She closed her eyes and tried to persuade her heart to stop pounding so violently. The rucksack toppled backwards and she heaved it upright to prevent it crashing on the floor. Then the engine slowed to a shudder and she heard the driver's door open. In seconds, Jack was back into the van, driving off sharply. He'd collected the ransom money – she was sure of it. Morwenna pushed herself into a seated position, using her legs and feet to balance upright. She reached out for the cardboard boxes, touching the contents. She felt the soft fabric of clothes, a hairbrush, the cool shell of a can of something – deodorant, perhaps, or paint. It was too dark to be sure what was in the back of the van. Then her fingers found something damp on the metal floor and she picked it up. At first, she thought it was a cloth that Jack used for cleaning paintbrushes, then she brought it closer to her face and saw the purple wool, the doggy features. It was Oggy Two.

31

They were cannoning downhill at speed and Morwenna thought her heart would burst, it was thumping so hard. She hoped Jack wasn't leaving Seal Bay. Climbing in the back of his van was a spur of the moment decision; she hadn't thought the consequences through, but it was her only route to Elowen. She felt the buzz of her phone in her hoodie pocket and checked the message. It was from Jane Choy. She caught her breath.

Update. Jack Greenwood has done two stretches in prison in gloucestershire for aggravated burglary. let me know where you are and be careful.

Of course, Gloucestershire. He said he'd taken courses there, painting, welding. Morwenna texted back quickly.

im hiding in the back of his van. i think he has collected the ransom money. ill keep in touch

The van slowed down, turned a corner and rumbled over

bumpy ground, perhaps gravel. Then it came to a stop and Morwenna heard Jack get out, slamming the driver's door. She waited a moment in the granular darkness, wondering if he'd come round the back, hoping that he wouldn't, not yet. Carefully, trying her best to make no sound, she eased open the rear door and wriggled out, shoving Oggy Two into her pocket. As she sidled round the van, she tried to work out where she was. Her face was cold; a breeze was coming in from the sea. The air held the overpowering smell of boat fuel. Behind her, sailing boats shifted, the wind whistling through wires in the rigging. Golden squiggles of light reflected on the water: she was in Woon's boatyard. Of course, Elowen was here. Morwenna had felt instinctively that the boatyard sheds were a place where a child might be hidden. Why hadn't she searched more carefully? She clung to the side of the van and edged steadily forward, watching Jack's shadow. He unlocked the door to an outbuilding, tugged it open and rushed inside. Morwenna held her breath, her body tense, quivering: fight or flight. In less than a minute he emerged on quiet feet, carrying something, another box, hurrying to the back of the van, heaving it inside with his other belongings.

Morwenna crouched down, hoping she wouldn't be seen, and texted three words to Ruan, and then to Jane.

Boatyard. Come now.

Jack went back into the building and Morwenna followed him, peering through the high window. He was mooching around inside, then he bent over, picking up another box. There was someone else in the room, a small figure sitting in the corner, her head down. It was Elowen. Morwenna almost called out. She stood on her toes to get a better view, wondering if Jack would come out with her, if he'd let her go. In the moment it took her to have the thought, he looked up and stared straight at her. Their eyes met in recognition. Morwenna turned to run but Jack was outside too quickly, facing her. She had no time to hide.

He was inches away. She could smell diesel on his skin. Despite her legs shaking, she tried to make her voice strong. 'Jack.'

'How the hell did you get here?' Jack had a hardness about his face that she'd never seen before. He loomed above her; she hadn't realised he was so tall. His eyes narrowed.

She took a breath and was dismayed by how terrified she sounded. 'I've come to take Elowen home.'

'You're having a laugh. You're going nowhere.'

Morwenna's mind raced. She'd try to reason with him. She took a step back. 'I don't understand why you're doing this? You and Tam... you're a couple.'

He rolled his eyes. 'She put the wedding back. If we'd married this Christmas, I could have had half the tearoom.'

Morwenna stared at him. 'Is that what this is all about?'

'No...' Jack frowned and she watched him clench his fists. 'It's Alex Truscott's fault.'

'Why Alex?' Morwenna was encouraging him to speak.

'I told him I'd get Tam to sell him the tearoom if he gave me a stake in the pizza takeaway. He laughed at me, called me dishonest. That was rich, coming from him. He said he'd tell Tam. I couldn't let him spoil things. So I had to get rid of him.'

'What did you do?

Jack shifted his feet, proud of himself, almost preening. 'After Lamorna yelled at him at the party, I told him that you'd all changed your minds and seen sense. He believed me that Tam was keen to sell – that she'd meet him on the beach to shake on the price. I fooled him. He was just thinking about all the money he'd make. I saw him by the water and I crept up behind him...'

'And stabbed him in the back.'

'He deserved it.' Jack's face twisted in an ugly grimace. 'That's not what I'm going to do to you though – and the kid. You'll get much worse than that.'

'You promised to let Elowen go.' Morwenna was breathing hard. 'You said once you had the ransom, she'd be free to go back to her mother—'

He interrupted her. 'I was going to leave her here for someone to find whenever. Or dump her in the middle of Plymouth. It wouldn't be my problem – I'd be miles away. The thing is, she knows who I am. I'd have had time to get up country, abroad. I have enough money. But now you've stuck your nose in, you'll both have to be shut up.'

'You burgled the Truscott's house...' Morwenna said quickly; she was playing for time.

''Course I did. It was easy – I had a ladder; I knew the layout because the Truscott woman got me to wallpaper her room. Snooty bitch. She had plenty of jewellery, money, so I took everything I could lay my hands on.' He was bragging now. 'I made it look like a threat – rolled the son's stuff under his bed covers and stuck a knife in it. They got what they deserved, all of them. I made them pay. I knew if I asked for twenty grand, they'd hand it over – that's nothing to people like that. They are stinking rich, just...'

'Parasites?' Morwenna said again. 'I remember before he died, Alex said his attacker used the word, then I heard you say it when I was here before.'

'Whatever.' He took a pace forward and Morwenna stepped back. 'Now I need you out of the way...'

'You gave Tam the necklace Alex gave Pam, the one with the diamond.'

'She'll have something to remember me by after I'm gone.'

He sneered spitefully. 'I cleared everything out of the tearoom, took my stuff, all the takings, whatever I can sell.'

Morwenna's lip curled. 'Don't you love her?'

'Don't be stupid.' Jack shrugged. 'She had a business. It was all right for a while. A roof over my head, hot food, a comfy bed...' He sniggered and Morwenna's fists clenched.

She took a breath. 'And what about Elowen? Don't you care about her?'

'I made a show of it but I'm not a family person. Never have been.'

'What about your mother?'

'She's in a nursing home in a nappy. She's nothing to do with me.'

'But you went up to see her overnight.'

'No, a mate of mine called – we went up to London and burgled a posh house. It paid well.' Jack shrugged. 'I don't care if I never see the old bag again.'

'Jack, she's your mother...'

'That means nothing.' Jack spat on the floor. 'I was born in Guildford. Then we lived in Greenwich when I was a kid, in a flat owned by some bloke just like Truscott. He was all mouth, smart suit, flash car, lots of money. My mother was so respectful to him. "Oh, don't put your feet on the walls, Jack, it's Mr Tomlinson's house." It made me angry...'

'Guildford, Greenwich.' Morwenna recalled how he'd mixed them up. It had helped give him away. 'I can see that life might have been difficult but that doesn't mean—'

'You don't see a thing, you and your stupid family, all happy together. Wonderful Cornwall, lovely people. It's a shithole.' Jack's voice was thick with spite. 'I should have sorted you properly on the beach. But I'll finish the job now.'

Morwenna had to keep him talking. 'Jack – you're a good person at heart…'

He laughed, an unpleasant leer. 'Don't talk crap.'

'Let Elowen go.'

'No way. I'm going to shove you in the barn with her. A bit of petrol, a spark of a flame and whoosh! There will be no evidence and everyone will think oh, a fire at the boatyard, old Woon keeps too much flammable stuff there…'

Jack's face shone with frenzy; his eyes were glazed. Morwenna could see he was gearing up for action.

'Where's Damien?' Morwenna said the first thing that came to her, playing for time.

'On holiday with some artist woman. He's an idiot.' He took a step forward. 'I need to get out of here.'

He lurched forward, grabbing at her, and Morwenna twisted away.

'Did you have a hard time in prison in Gloucestershire, Jack? How many times were you there?'

Jack clutched her shoulder, his grip like iron. 'Don't talk to me about prison.' He had her round the neck, heaving her towards the outbuilding. 'You're going in here, bitch. With the kid.'

Morwenna tried to wrestle herself free but he held her fast. His fingers were on her windpipe. She twisted and bit down, feeling the flesh of his hand, the bone of a thumb. He yelped and jerked back. Morwenna turned to run to the van, dodging behind it, and he rushed towards her as she whirled away. Then he had her by the hair and Morwenna felt her neck snap back, a searing pain over her scalp. She brought up her knee hard and it connected with his thigh. Jack swore, dragging her along bumpy ground towards the shed, lifting her as she struggled.

Morwenna screamed as loudly as she could. She felt the

crush of gravel beneath her face. Panting, she scrambled up but only made it to her knees. Jack kicked her back down, his foot catching her in the side, making her gasp, and she lay where she was. He hauled her to her feet and shook her. 'Stop struggling.'

Morwenna's vision blurred. Jack cursed as he tugged her along. Limp and dazed, she tried to stay conscious, her senses reeling. They were in the doorway and she found a final shred of strength, kicking out. Her foot connected with his shin, and he yelped. Morwenna seized the opportunity, hauled herself to her feet, ran towards the sailing boats and tripped, sprawling onto the rough ground.

The headlights of Ruan's van swerved around the corner, followed by a car, then another, blue flashing lights, the whoop of sirens. Morwenna scrambled onto a teetering boat, hugging the mast tightly, breathless; she was exhausted. Jack stood where he was, staring towards the headlamps. Ruan clambered from the van and behind him, PC Jim Hobbs and Rick Tremayne stood in the shadows.

The DI took over. 'Jack? It's DI Tremayne...'

Morwenna called over, pointing. 'Ruan! Elowen's in the building, over there!'

Ruan was already running, disappearing through the door. Jack still hadn't moved.

DI Tremayne advanced one pace. 'Jack Greenwood?'

'No way,' Jack whispered beneath his breath. 'I'm not going back to prison.'

Rick's voice was calm but commanding 'Jack Greenwood, you do not have to say anything, but it may harm your defence if you do not mention when questioned...'

Jack shouted something. It might have been an expletive taken away on the breeze, then he turned and started to run. PC Jim Hobbs sprinted after him, almost catching up with him at the quayside. Then Jack jumped. Morwenna watched from the sailing boat as he plummeted into the black water, sinking like a stone, and Jim Hobbs leaped in afterwards. There was some splashing and shouting, then silence, and Jim's voice floated on the night air. 'He's gone! I can't see him.'

Morwenna scrambled down from the boat just as Ruan emerged from the outbuilding, Elowen in his arms. She rushed over and flung herself at them both in one huge embrace. Ruan said quietly, 'He had her tied up in there. She's freezing.'

Elowen started to sob. 'Grandma, Jack is horrible. He sticked a big plaster tape on my mouth. Oggy wanted to bite him but he's got no teeth. One more of mine has gone too – look.'

'Is Oggy all right?' Morwenna asked, her own face wet with tears.

'He kept me safe. Can I see my mummy now?'

'You can. She'll be so happy to see you.' Ruan smiled. He gazed at Morwenna. 'Are you all right, love?'

'A few bruises… but I'll live.'

'Thank goodness,' he muttered into her ear and the three of them hugged again. Then another police car arrived. Jane Choy leaped from the passenger seat and rushed over. 'Morwenna.'

Morwenna threw herself into the embrace. 'Jane – thanks so much for everything you've done.'

Jane eased herself away; the wound in her back was still uncomfortable. She said, 'Where's Jack now?'

'I don't like him any more.' Elowen sniffled. 'He kept me locked up and gave me cold dinner, and I said I wanted my mummy and he said he didn't care.'

'I'll get her into the van.' Ruan hugged her closely. 'Come on my lovely, let's take you home.'

PC Jim Hobbs rushed over, his face wet, his clothes dripping. 'We've got back-up on the way. We'll search for Jack.'

'He can't swim. He told me...' Morwenna remembered.

'We'll find him.' Jim's face was concerned. 'Do you need an ambulance, Morwenna? Someone to check you over?'

She closed her eyes. 'I want my family to be together.'

'We'll need to take statements, interview all concerned...' Rick Tremayne said in his official voice.

'Later, eh boss?' Jane chirped. 'Let them have some family time. Tomorrow is soon enough.'

'Wait... Rick...' Morwenna remembered. 'Go and look in Jack's van – he's got the ransom money and the stuff he stole from the Truscotts and Tam's takings from the tearoom.'

Ruan was at Morwenna's side. 'Come on – Elowen's all strapped in, ready to go.'

'How's she coping?' Morwenna asked anxiously.

'She wants to see Tam. And her biggest worry at the moment is that she's lost Oggy Two.'

'No, she hasn't.' Morwenna pulled the purple-faced knitted dog from her pocket. 'Here he is. He'll need a bath though.'

'He's not the only one.' Ruan smiled, wrapping his arm around her. 'Let's go home – Tam's waiting.'

32

The door of number four Harbour Cottage flew wide open and Elowen ran full pelt, yelling 'Mummy!'

Tamsin was suddenly on her feet, her arms out, locking her child in a tight embrace, feeling the silky hair against her face as tears flowed. So many kisses, so many muffled words of love. Morwenna leaned against Ruan, who wrapped an arm around her. 'Are you sure you don't need to go to A & E?'

'I'll ring the GP tomorrow. Elowen might need a check over too.' Morwenna was aware that her side was beginning to ache and there was a dull throbbing behind her eyes.

'Shall I make hot chocolate?' Ruan asked.

'Please.' Morwenna hugged Tamsin and Elowen and sighed deeply.

'Oggy wants one.' Elowen clung to her mother's arms, the purple-faced dog squeezed in one hand. 'Oggy Two needs a bath.'

'Come here, my little one.' Tamsin hugged Elowen again. 'How are you feeling? Are you hurt anywhere? Did Jack—?'

'I don't like Jack any more.' Elowen made a face. 'He told me he would cutted off all my hair and leave me in Plymouth for the cops to find. I don't want to go to Plymouth. I don't want cops to find me.' Her face crumpled and she began to cry. 'I wanted my mummy.'

'I'm here, my angel. I'll always be here.' Tamsin swept her up and fell back onto the sofa with a sob. Morwenna was crying silent tears, her cheeks wet. In the kitchen, Ruan was clanking a saucepan and Morwenna thought she heard a gulp of emotion. She sank down next to Tamsin. 'How are you feeling?'

Tamsin snuffled. 'I've got my baby. I'm all right. How about you?'

'I'm all right too, now my baby has her baby back.'

Tamsin rested a head against Morwenna's shoulder. 'I can never thank you enough – or Dad.'

'It was all down to your mum.' Ruan carried mugs in on a tray. 'She was incredible.'

Morwenna closed her eyes and felt her legs turn to jelly. It had just occurred to her how close she had come to a completely different ending. She wouldn't mention Jack's words about setting fire to the outbuilding with her and Elowen inside, not ever. The image made her shudder; she didn't want Tamsin or Ruan to have to see it too.

'What happens now?' Tamsin whispered.

'Fiona will be round tomorrow, first thing, and Jim and the CIM – we have to talk to them about everything. And they will let us know – about Jack.' Morwenna was deliberately cryptic. She wouldn't mention in front of Elowen that he had flung himself into the sea.

'How are you feeling?' Ruan asked gently. 'You've been through a lot.'

'Bits of me ache. I'm tired.' Morwenna smiled. 'But I'm happy now.'

'Will you be able to sleep?'

'I think so.'

Ruan hesitated. 'What do you want me to do? Do you want me to stay?'

Morwenna shook her head: she was too tired to process thoughts. 'Are you going out fishing tomorrow?'

'I'll take the day off.' His face was lined with tiredness.

Morwenna glanced at the clock. 'It's midnight. You'd better go home.'

'Yes, I suppose I should.' Ruan sighed. 'I'll come back tomorrow morning.'

He walked towards the front door. Morwenna followed him, her body leaden, as if in a trance. Ruan stood on the step. He looked exhausted.

'Will you stay home tomorrow?' You won't try to go to the library?'

Morwenna shook her head. 'I'll go and see the doctor, talk to the police. Then I just want to be with Tam and Elowen... and sleep.'

'Can I come and see you? Cook dinner?'

'That would be nice.' Morwenna met his eyes and noticed the gleam. 'I'm glad you came to the boatyard when you did.'

'I was worried when I got your message.' Ruan glanced away for a moment. 'I just imagined, what if...'

'I know...' Morwenna shivered. 'I suppose I'd better go in.'

'Yes, you should. I'll see you tomorrow.'

'Thanks, Ruan... for everything.'

'Goodnight.' Ruan paused, so many words unsaid. He stepped into the shadows, on his way back to number nine.

Morwenna closed the door, locked it, and came into the warmth of the living room. Tamsin took up the whole sofa now, Elowen sprawled across her body, her eyes closed. She stroked her daughter's dark hair gently, her voice low. 'She's fast asleep, Mum. She's exhausted, poor little thing.'

'I'll get us a brandy,' Morwenna said mechanically. 'We both need one.'

Tamsin nodded. 'Do you know what she said just before she fell asleep?'

Morwenna handed a glass of amber liquid to Tamsin and sipped her own gratefully. 'Tell me.' She sank onto the rug by the fire, her body aching.

'She asked if she could have a birthday party – she missed the last one.'

Morwenna gazed into the glass, at the glowing light of the brandy reflected in the flames of the fire. 'We'll give her a party.'

'Mum, will she be all right after everything that happened?'

'She'll get lots of help. It'll take time for us all but – we'll bounce back.'

Tamsin closed her eyes and tears fell soundlessly. 'It's all my fault.'

Morwenna turned her head. 'No, Tam.'

'I trusted Jack and he turned out to be—'

'Don't say that.'

'He could have hurt her!'

'She's here now, safe and well.'

'He could have harmed Elowen. Mum, I was going to marry him. How could I have been so stupid?' She glanced at the ring on her finger, sliding it off, tossing it on the cushions. 'I'll never forgive myself for that.' Tamsin's face was fierce. 'I'll never trust another man, never again.'

'They're not all bad.' Morwenna thought of Ruan who'd arrived just in time. The thought of what might have happened made her shiver again. She gulped her brandy and her hand shook.

'No, I'll never trust anyone new – Elowen is everything, no one else matters now.' Tamsin made a snuffling sound. 'I'm hopeless. First Elowen's father, a holiday romance, a silly fling that ended badly, but at least I have my beautiful little girl. Then Jack – what was I thinking? You know I thought I loved him, that he'd be a good dad to Elowen. I was stupid.'

'He fooled a lot of people. Be kind to yourself, Tam.' She tried a joke. 'We Mutton maids don't have much luck with men.'

'You landed on your feet with Dad – you just don't know it,' Tamsin said, staring at her mother meaningfully.

Morwenna drained the glass. 'I'm so tired. I think I'll turn in.'

'I'll stay here, Mum.'

'The spare bed is all made up.'

'I just want to hold her all night. When she wakes, I'll be here for her. I'll always be here...'

'I'll get the duvet and cover you both then. You'll be fine.'

'We will.'

Morwenna moved to the stairs on aching feet. She wanted to lie down, to rest her throbbing head and wait for the replaying images to go away. She hoped she'd be able to sleep, but Jack's leering expression was still imprinted behind her eyes.

* * *

Tuesday and Wednesday passed in a daze of confusion. Morwenna didn't remember much about her visit to the GP. The doctor was very kind, but one sentence lingered in her mind, repeating like an echo. 'You need to take it easy nowadays; you're not getting any younger.' Morwenna thought it over: it was a phrase people often said, a nonsense, an obvious cliché. It annoyed her a little; she may be in her sixties but she wasn't done by a long way. Mutton women were strong – look at

Lamorna, in her early eighties, a bit of arthritis in her hip but nothing held back the indomitable spirit. Morwenna was made of the same stuff, Tamsin too.

Tamsin spent a long time in the doctor's surgery with Elowen. When she came out, Elowen was skipping, clutching Oggy Two, but Tamsin still looked tired and her eyes were red. Morwenna knew she'd do whatever it would take to support her daughter and her granddaughter. Ruan had been wonderful, cooking meals, making tea, chatting to Lamorna who'd been a constant presence at number four, bustling about and giving her opinion on men: most of them were a waste of skin and bone, especially Jack Greenwood.

PC Jim Hobbs visited the tearoom with the CIM, who was a uniformed inspector, and Fiona the Family Liaison Officer. Jack hadn't been found yet, but the police thought it was most likely that he'd been washed away by the tide. Tamsin and Elowen would have continued support. Everyone would try to make life as normal as possible. And on Friday, when Elowen returned from her first day back at school, she'd have the birthday party she'd missed a week ago.

Morwenna spent a few excruciating hours on Wednesday morning at the police station giving a statement. Thankfully Jane Choy, still recovering but in full uniform, sat beside her as DI Tremayne droned on, asking the same questions over again, reprimanding Morwenna for being foolhardy and taking police matters into her own hands. Jane reminded him pointedly that but for Morwenna, Jack would be long gone with the ransom and the items he'd stolen from Pam Truscott and Tamsin. And as for Elowen, goodness knows where she'd be, but Jane suspected she'd have been left at the boathouse until Damien Woon returned from his holiday. Morwenna couldn't help imagining her granddaughter alone and afraid with no food or water.

On Thursday afternoon, just three days after the incident, Morwenna rode steadily down to the beach. She leaned her bike against the sea wall and sat staring into the ocean. It was a cold day, the cloudy sky hanging low, full of the likelihood of rain. The wind took her hair, lifting it and covering her eyes. She sighed deeply: she'd puzzled out the clues, found the kidnapper and now Jack was gone. She expected to hear any day that his body had been found washed up on the shore. The thought left her numb; she had too many concerns for her family. There was no emotion left over for him, no pity, no feeling at all.

Elowen seemed chirpy and full of energy now, but she chattered to the invisible Oggy constantly about how she had been locked in a cold place in the boathouse by nasty Jack. Tamsin was suffering, her eyes fretful as if the thoughts behind them looped, a recurring nightmare of what might have happened. She held herself stiffly, constantly watchful, overcompensating with hugs for Elowen that she didn't want to end. Morwenna wondered if things would ever be the same.

Her body still ached where Jack's boot had caught her ribs. The doctor said that nothing was broken but she'd need to rest, and huge dark bruises blotched her skin and spread with no sign of fading. The moment before she fell asleep was the worst. She saw Jack's leering expression, she heard his tone, cold and dismissive, talking about Tamsin: 'It was all right for a while. A roof over my head, hot food, a comfy bed.' Morwenna cried angry, sad tears into the pillow before sleep took her.

Her eyes were watering now, but it was the salty sea breeze buffeting her face. Morwenna felt calmer staring at the rolling ocean; it had always been a constant throughout her life, the tide spreading across the shore and sliding away. She sighed; that was the natural way of things, rolling in and then out again.

Normality would return, slowly, eventually. They'd all be all right, her family.

Morwenna decided that she'd go back to work in the library tomorrow although it was probably too early, but she'd spend time with Louise, try to get some of the old rhythm back into her day. She'd cycle to the tearoom at lunchtime as usual, visit Tamsin in the afternoon and help out with Elowen's birthday party. It would be good to get back to normal. She'd enjoyed being a sleuth and she'd learned to trust her instincts, to be proactive, to employ guile. She didn't think she'd been particularly good at it, but Elowen was safe and alive, and she was pleased that she'd been instrumental in bringing her home.

She gazed at the ocean as if hypnotised, focusing on the dark blue line of the horizon where it met the pale cloudy sky.

More than anything right now, she longed to swim in the sea.

33

Louise and Donald were already in the library, returning books to the shelves, when Morwenna walked in. Louise was surprised to see her. 'When you said you'd be in this morning, I didn't think you meant it. You should be still at home, resting.'

'I'm back though.' Morwenna grinned. 'Ready for work.'

'How's the family?'

'Elowen's coming on in leaps and bounds. I'm surprised how resilient she is. On the outside it's as if nothing much happened to her. She seems to have bounced back, but we've been told it might take some time before she's processed everything.' Morwenna shrugged. 'Tam's the one with the nightmares. She can hardly bear the thought of Elowen being back at school today. She's very clingy, but that's natural.' Morwenna gave a short laugh. 'I'm clingy with them both.'

'We heard about your heroics, your impressive deduction,' Donald said. 'The whole of Seal Bay is in awe.'

'I'm still a novice.' Morwenna shook her head.

'We're coming to Elowen's birthday party later,' Louise added.

'The kiddies can play and we adults can have a well-earned rest. It's good to see you back.'

'Thanks.' Morwenna gazed around. 'How's Lizzie?'

'It's funny you should mention that.' Donald frowned. 'Both Louise and I heard an eerie scratching sound this morning.'

'It's bizarre,' Louise whispered. 'It seems to come from beneath the window over there.'

'Oh – you've shut the little top window,' Morwenna remarked.

'I closed it – it was getting draughty. It was fine leaving it open in the summer but...' Donald paused.

'Shhh.' Louise put a finger against her lips. 'There it is again...'

'It *is*... listen... the ghost of Lady Elizabeth... making herself known...' Donald echoed.

Morwenna listened. There was a repetitive scratching coming from behind the Social Science & Humanities shelves, the sound of nails digging into carpet pile.

'She might be angry,' Louise suggested.

'She's trying to tell us something,' Donald said anxiously. 'Maybe a message from beyond.'

'No, I don't think so.' Morwenna rushed forward and dived behind the line of shelves. When she stood up, she was holding a striped tabby cat, its fur pressed against her cheek. 'She's just telling us that she can't get out.'

'A cat?' Louise stated the obvious.

''You're not suggesting that Lady Elizabeth's ghost was a cat all the time?' Donald said disbelievingly.

'What about the ectoplasm?'

'Cat pee, I think, Louise. It explains the bad smell.' Morwenna was every inch the detective now. 'And it's no wonder she disturbed the piles of books, ate your cheese sandwich and turned off your laptop. She probably slept on it to keep warm.'

'Great sleuthing,' Louise exclaimed. 'You should take it up, Morwenna.'

Morwenna shook her head. 'Once is enough.'

Donald approached the cat as if it was from another world. 'Do you think it's a stray?'

Louise held out her arms for a cuddle and was surprised how light the animal was. 'She's not very big. Fur and skin and bones. She probably came in to shelter overnight and search for food.'

'What will we do with her?' Donald still looked as if he'd seen a ghost.

'I'll take her to the vets this morning if you two are all right here on your own for a while,' Louise announced. 'I'll see if she's chipped.'

'And what if she isn't?' Donald asked.

'She could become the library cat?' Morwenna joked. She held out her hands as Louise handed her back. 'You're a real cutie, aren't you? Listen to her purring.'

Louise stroked the cat's ears as the cat nestled in Morwenna's embrace. 'She's happy with you, Morwenna. She knows where she's well off.'

'She does.' Morwenna cuddled the cat.

Louise put out a finger and stroked the cat's chin. 'Let's see if she has an owner before we get too attached to her, though. She's such an affectionate little thing. Someone's bound to be missing her.'

Donald seemed to deflate with relief. 'Well, I'm glad she wasn't a ghost... but I still believe Lady Elizabeth haunts this library...'

* * *

At four o'clock the tearoom was full of excited children. The tables were mostly pushed back except for the ones holding the mermaid-topped cake with six candles and blue sea icing, sandwiches, sausage rolls, mini pizzas, cucumber and carrot sticks. The children were playing pass the parcel, Tamsin and Ruan doing their best to start and stop the music on an old CD player. Morwenna was seated between Jane Choy and Lamorna, dressed in purple leggings and the stripey pullover the Grundy sisters had knitted. Jane asked, 'How are you feeling now?'

'Not bad... stiff and achy in the mornings,' Morwenna admitted.

'Snap. It gets better with each day though.' Jane smiled. She pointed to two adults passing a parcel to the children, supervising the action, trying to sit on empty seats and falling off in an exaggerated slapstick roll, rewarded by the children's squeals of delight. 'I don't think Jim and Fiona have had such fun in their lives.'

'I didn't recognise Jim Hobbs out of uniform,' Lamorna called too loudly. 'He's handsome in ordinary clothes.'

'Rick Tremayne didn't come – Ruan invited him,' Morwenna said. 'Of course, he'd be welcome; half of Seal Bay is here.'

She pointed towards Susan and Barb Grundy, who were sorting out plates for the children's refreshments. Rosie Buvač and Carole Taylor had positioned themselves by the urn, making teas and coffees for the adults, dolloping scones with jam first, then cream.

The game stopped and Elowen rushed towards Morwenna. 'Grandma, Oggy said he wants some cake now. Can I get him some?'

Morwenna hugged her granddaughter. 'In a few minutes. It's story time now.' She glanced at Milan who was dressed as Captain Pugwash. He smelled of the sea, the same saltiness on his skin that Ruan had when he'd just returned from the boats. The children surrounded him and were staring up, round-eyed, as he prepared to start his story.

Elowen piped up, 'Britney and Billy have asked me to sit next to them, Maya too, but I'm going to sit right at the front because it's my new birthday. And Oggy will cuddle up on my knee because he's a good dog.'

'You're my sweetie.' Morwenna patted Elowen's cheek fondly as the small girl twirled round, rushing off to join the other children.

Milan Buvač began to recount his tale in his warm Cornish-European accent. 'Now, here's a story of how the pirate and the mermaid came to Seal Bay on a dolphin's back and found gold and treasure on the beach. Do you want to hear it, me hearties?'

'Yes please,' chorused fifteen saucer-eyed happy children, hands clasped.

Rosie and Carole brought refreshments for the grown-ups and Ruan and Tamsin came to sit down, glad to rest after the hectic games. Jim and Fiona joined them, and the adults listened for a while as Milan told tales of swashbuckling heroics. Lamorna closed her eyes as she sipped tea. 'I'll tellywot, I'm proper exhausted just watching all those games.' She patted Morwenna's knee affectionately. 'How are you, my bewty?'

Morwenna nodded. 'The same. Nice to sit down and rest a moment.'

Lamorna scrutinised her with a mother's searching eyes. 'You look tired.' She glanced towards Tamsin. 'You too, my lovely.'

'This is nice though – normality again.' Tamsin indicated the tearoom, the spread of party food, the entranced children captivated by the pirate. 'It does me good to see the children enjoying themselves. I think this party may be the first of many...'

'Tam and I were talking,' Ruan began. 'She could make a

proper job of organising kiddies' parties and themed events. She could branch out, use the space in the tearoom from time to time, bring a bit more business in.'

'Dad's idea.' Tamsin looked at her father with affection. 'Lots of people are keen to help, Carole and Rosie. Milan will do the entertainment. We thought it might be a useful sideline for us all in the off season.'

'Great!' Lamorna clapped her hands. 'I told you things would work out.' She leaned closely to Morwenna and lowered her voice. 'I told you that emmet was no good as well, but you didn't listen. I never trusted him – he was shifty.'

'You were right,' Morwenna said. 'I should listen to you more often.'

'And what about Ruan?' Lamorna gave her daughter a meaningful look. 'He's one of the good ones...'

Morwenna met Ruan's eyes. 'Thanks... for everything.'

His gaze was level. 'We're family.'

The doorbell chimed and Louise and her husband Steve came in. Louise carried a box under her arm and, as Morwenna reached her for a hug, she realised that the box was purring.

'Is this the cat?' Morwenna asked.

'No chip, unloved, unwanted, unregistered. A stray. The vet thinks she could be about two years old, she's still young.'

Steve, broad-shouldered and smiling, took the box from his wife and plonked it in Morwenna's arms. His voice was a Cornish burr. 'We can't have her. I'm not fond of cats – they make me sneeze. She's all yours.'

'Of course, she can come home with me...' Morwenna began.

The story time finished and Elowen was on her feet, rushing to her grandmother's side. 'What have you got in that box?'

Morwenna lifted out the striped tabby cat. She held her in

her arms, feeling the soothing vibration of the purr. Elowen was delighted. 'Is she your new cat, Grandma?'

'She is.'

'Can she be a friend for Oggy and Oggy Two?'

'Of course.'

'What's her name?'

'I don't know. You decide.'

'I've decided already.' Elowen reached a hand to stroke the thick fur. 'She's called Brenda.'

'Why Brenda?' Morwenna smiled.

'Because she does a big purr that says her name. Brrr-brrr-brrr- Brenda.'

'Then Brenda she is,' Morwenna agreed. 'Shall we settle her in her box with the cushion and give her some cat biscuits?'

'Dreckly,' Elowen replied. 'It's time for my cake. I'm starving.'

'Off you go then,' Morwenna said as Elowen rushed off to join her friends. She placed Brenda gently back in the box and gave her to Lamorna, who petted the cat's velvet ears. The children were lined up at the table under Susan's orders as she checked they had clean hands, while Barb served up each guest with an individual plate of food. The room quietened as the children sat in groups to eat. Morwenna took a breath; Jane and Lamorna were deep in conversation – she could hear Lamorna's loud cackle, so it was almost certainly about men. Jim and Fiona were eating scones; Jim had a button of cream on his nose. Tamsin was talking to Carole, both of them sipping tea, their eyes seldom straying from the children. Morwenna thought about going home: she was so tired. Then Ruan was at her shoulder. 'There's someone to see you outside.' He indicated Tamsin. 'You too, my lovely.'

Morwenna frowned. 'Can't they come in here? It's chilly outside.'

'They'd rather talk privately.' Ruan led the way to the door.

Pam Truscott stood on the pavement, leaning against a bicycle. The Range Rover was parked opposite, against the sea wall, on yellow lines. Simon waved from the passenger seat. The wind ruffled Pam's hair as she gazed from Morwenna to Tamsin. 'I came to say thanks – and to see how you were. I know you have a children's party going on, so I don't want to intrude.'

'You'd be very welcome.' Morwenna reached out an arm and squeezed Pam's shoulder. 'How are you?'

'Things are slowly getting back to normal. I'll get out sailing as much as I can; it always helps.' Pam turned to Tamsin. 'I'm so glad your little girl is all right. Your mother was incredible.'

Ruan was behind Morwenna, a gentle hand against her back. 'She is.'

'What's next? What will you do?' Morwenna asked.

'I like Seal Bay and I love our house. I want to stay here, Simon too now. We'll take our time to decide – we might go away for a while. It'll be difficult without Alex. I know he wasn't perfect but we both loved him in our own way. The community is very supportive, and that helps. My brother works in London, but he visits a lot.'

'I know.' Morwenna recalled the handsome silver fox she'd met at Mirador.

'In fact, Barnaby and I talked on the phone last night and we decided to buy you this...' Pam stood back so that Morwenna could see the bicycle. 'It's electric. It might help with all those hills.'

'It certainly will.' Morwenna was thrilled. 'You shouldn't have!'

'By way of thanks. You've helped incredibly, Morwenna. Nothing can bring Alex back, but you've allowed him to rest, so to speak. So, Simon and I can start to grieve and heal. It was such an ordeal.' Pam shivered.

'It was...' Morwenna couldn't agree more.

Pam forced a smile. 'And Barnaby says he'd like to take you out to dinner next time he's down in Cornwall.'

'Oh... right.' Morwenna didn't know what else to say.

'So, Simon and I wanted to offer you our heartfelt thanks. And we hope you'll stay in touch, come up to Mirador for coffee sometime... And of course, we'll be frequent visitors at the tearoom. I know Simon loves to curl up in the window with a book.'

'That's good,' Morwenna said.

'Oh – sorry – I think this is belongs to you.' Tamsin unclasped the necklace with the diamond pendant and handed it to Pam.

'It was a present from Alex.' Pam gazed at the necklace in her palm. 'Where did you get it?'

'I think it was stolen from your house...' Tamsin smiled awkwardly. 'Please – it's yours.'

'Thank you.' Pam pushed the bicycle forward. 'Well, Morwenna – do enjoy the electric bike.'

'I will. And thank you again. You've no idea what a difference it will make.'

'I'm so pleased, and Barnaby will be delighted. We'll catch up soon. I must be off home. I've parked on double lines...'

Morwenna grinned. She watched as Pam walked away elegantly on heels. From her heart, she wished her all the best.

'I didn't know you knew Barnaby?' Ruan asked from behind her shoulder.

'I met him up at Mirador while I was sleuthing. I can't help it if he's an admirer.' Morwenna waved a hand as if it didn't matter. She pointed the new bicycle towards the door. 'Come on – we'd better get back inside or there'll be no cake left. I've been looking forward to a bit of blue icing.'

She waltzed back into the tearoom, pushing her new cycle. Tamsin met her father's eyes. 'Well, Mum's mojo is definitely on its way back, Dad.' She winked. 'She doesn't hang around...'

34

Sunday morning was the beginning of a wet Cornish day, rain teeming as Morwenna's bare feet sank into damp sand. She wrapped her arms around herself in the wetsuit, her skin shivering beneath, her hair pushed into a bright swimming cap. She stared into the sea. Louise tapped her arm.

'Penny for them?'

'I'm feeling the cold.' Morwenna smiled. 'Brenda's at home in her basket in the warm, by the fire. I was just wishing I was curled up with her.' She smiled. 'I often feel like that before a swim. Storm before the calm.'

'Isn't that just like life? We worry about things and then they turn out all right.' Louise shrugged. 'We should go in.'

'Is it just us two today?'

'Susan, Barb and Donald all send their excuses.' Louise raised an eyebrow. 'We're the only tough ones.'

'Jane will come with us next time. The wound on her back is getting better. She's looking forward to joining us every week.'

'We should become a proper group,' Louise said. 'I might

advertise us on the library notice board. I thought about calling us SWANs.'

'Why swans – apart from the obvious?'

'Seal Bay Wild Aquatic Natation…' Louise suggested. 'It's not perfect but then – who is?'

Morwenna agreed. 'Come on – I'll race you in.'

Louise surged ahead and Morwenna padded a few feet behind, pressing a flat palm hard against her side. It was still bruised and sore, but swimming would help her recovery. She rushed in, the warm rain falling on her shoulders and face, feeling the ocean's cold clutch and shivering, up to her neck in lapping waves. Diving deep, Morwenna held her breath, Louise's squeals in her ears, then she was beneath the water. She stayed there for a moment, then she was surfacing again, gasping for air, feeling it shudder in her chest as she rolled onto her back, her eyes closed against the falling rain. She let the sea lift her in its arms.

Then the euphoria came and along with it the clarity of thought. Here she was swimming in the sea in the pelting rain: Morwenna Mutton; a grandmother, a mother, a daughter. A sleuth, maybe. A survivor, definitely. She'd taken on the world, fought for her family, for those she loved, and come out triumphant on the other side.

Twisting, turning, splashing her arms, keeping herself afloat; that's what she had learned to do, and she was learning all the time. Each day was a blessing.

And Ruan? Morwenna had no idea. She cared for him, yes, of course she did, but she wouldn't repeat the same mistakes. What would be would be. They couldn't live apart but they couldn't live together. Morwenna laughed out loud – all the clichés in the world applied to her and Ruan.

She blinked salt water from her eyes. Louise was swimming

back to the shore, already too cold. Morwenna struck out to sea. The smooth round head of a seal appeared, another one by its side, staring towards her. They frolicked and splashed for a moment, dipping beneath the waves, their bodies silky in the sunlight, and then they were gone. Morwenna wondered if she should swim out towards them.

Or she could turn round and swim back to dry land, the comfort of a fire and a warm room. The choice was hers. It would always be hers.

ACKNOWLEDGMENTS

When Boldwood Books offered me the chance of writing a cosy (cozy) crime series, my third genre, a new journey began. I couldn't believe my luck or how much fun it was going to be. Now I have so many people to thank from the bottom of my heart.

Kiran, my agent, who said, 'Why not write a Cornish sleuth?' remains an inspiration. She is a great professional whom I admire beyond words.

Sarah, my editor, who I trust absolutely. She is one of life's stars.

Everyone at Boldwood Books, the dream team, singly and combined.

The writers of cosy crime at Boldwood and beyond, all the writers whose books I read avidly as research and pleasure. I'm learning so much!

Friends, family, fellow writers, bloggers, reviewers, without whose support I would be invisible. Not forgetting the wonderful Solitary Writers and my fabulous neighbours. Each day I realise that you are blessings for whom I am grateful.

Tony and Kim, two diamonds. Liam, Maddie and Cait, precious jewels. Big G, who is golden. I have the whole bracelet.

And huge thanks to my police consultants, James and Nina, and Kitty, the wild swimmer. Their knowledge and kindness have been invaluable.

To the people of Cornwall, who always inspire warm, wonderful characters.

And to you, the reader, I give my deepest thanks. A story without readers is a world without sunshine.

Sending warmest wishes, always. x

MORE FROM JUDY LEIGH

We hope you enjoyed reading ***Foul Play at Seal Bay***. If you did, please leave a review.

If you'd like to gift a copy, this book is also available as an ebook, hardback, large print, digital audio download and audiobook CD.

Sign up to Judy Leigh's mailing list for news, competitions and updates on future books:

http://bit.ly/JudyLeighNewsletter

Explore more fun, uplifting reads from Judy Leigh:

Sign up to Judy Leigh's mailing list for news, competitions and updates on future books.

https://bit.ly/judyleighnews

Explore more fun, uplifting reads from Judy Leigh.

ABOUT THE AUTHOR

Judy Leigh is the bestselling author of *A Grand Old Time* and *Five French Hens* and the doyenne of the 'it's never too late' genre of women's fiction. She has lived all over the UK from Liverpool to Cornwall, but currently resides in Somerset.

Visit Judy's website: https://judyleigh.com

Follow Judy on social media:

facebook.com/judyleighuk
twitter.com/judyleighwriter
instagram.com/judyrleigh
bookbub.com/authors/judy-leigh

Printed in the USA
CPSIA information can be obtained
at www.ICGtesting.com
LVHW030221021123
762861LV00026B/311